WIFE TRIES SOMETHING NEW

A Hotwife Adventure

Alex Lee

Copyright © 2023 Alex Lee

This book is copyright © 2023 Alex Lee. All rights reserved.
No part of this book may be reproduced or modified in any form, including photocopying, recording, or by any information storage and retrieval system, without written permission from the copyright holder.
This book is a work of fiction. Any resemblance to persons, living or dead, is entirely coincidental.

CONTENTS

Title Page
Copyright
1. New friends   1
Ella   2
Gerhard   5
Mikkel   13
Agnete   17
Johan   25
2. Games   37
Poolside photos   38
Confessions   50
At the pool bar   56
Pool volleyball   64
3. Temptations   80
Paulo   81
Surprises   94
Saving the dessert   115
4. Running away   124
To the beach   125
Joao   134
Sea turtle   144

5. The island tour	157
Sharks and razors	158
The knickers incident	167
Overcoming fears	172
It's a maybe	181
Photos and souvenirs	189
A journey of thoughts	199
6. Music night	207
At the lobby bar	208
Indecision	222
The test	232
Remorse and forgiveness	244
About The Author	255
Books In This Series	257
Books By This Author	259

1. NEW FRIENDS

ELLA

It was Monday afternoon when Ella and I arrived at our hotel. We were on a seven-day holiday in Cape Verde to celebrate the tenth anniversary of our honeymoon.

Ella's mum had come from Croatia to London to look after the kids so Ella and I could be on our own. No kids around to worry about. That was our idea. We wanted to have drinks, bathe in the sunshine whenever we wanted, and have sex, a lot of sex! We wanted to feel like we were on a honeymoon again. And we had chosen to do so in one of the best beach hotels in Santa Maria!

We left our luggage at the reception in the main building, and while waiting for our room to get ready, we went for a stroll outside on the hotel grounds. The outdoor area was like a piece of paradise. It consisted of gardens with lush vegetation and fields of neatly trimmed grass crisscrossed by lanes surrounded by palm trees and sidewalks leading to amenities like cafés, outdoor bars, and two-storey block buildings where the guest rooms were located. We found the main outside pool and joined the queue at the poolside bar for lunch. We waited about a minute before we realised they were not serving food. I asked a man in his late sixties or early seventies, who was in the queue in front of Ella and me, where we could have late lunch.

"Oh! You need to walk down the stairs," the guy said in a German accent and pointed at the stairs to our left leading out of the pool area. "If you turn right when you reach the foot of the stairs, a hundred yards further down, there is a restaurant—Mandalay or something—forgot its name. They serve food in the afternoon. It's in the hotel complex, next to the gate to the aqua park."

I noticed that the old man was checking Ella out while giving us instructions on how to get to the restaurant.

You wished, old man! I said to myself.

The guy was old, yet I felt flattered that he was ogling my wife.

I put my hand on the small of Ella's back. The sun had warmed the exposed skin below her cami crop top, and I liked feeling her warmth on my palm. As we walked away, I deliberately slid my hand underneath the waistband of Ella's denim shorts, just a little, but enough to feel the soft flesh of her bum.

She did not stop me.

I hope you watch this, old man! I thought to myself.

I couldn't help but look over my shoulder.

Yes, he was watching us. He smiled and waved at me. I smiled back and looked forward.

"This way, hon!" I said and nodded to the steps to our left as if Ella had not listened to the old man's instructions. At the same time, my hand slid further down and squeezed her ass. Ella had put on a Y-back G-string, which meant her ass cheeks were bare under her shorts, and I loved the feel of her soft flesh. I knew the old man was watching us, and my cock hardened. I liked being watched while I felt Ella up, and it turned me on knowing someone envied me for having such a beautiful wife. I enjoyed showing her off to this total stranger, and I was full of pride and lust. This feeling was not something new.

In fact, I had always liked showing off Ella. She had just turned 29, yet she looked like she was in her early twenties. At five feet five inches tall, with a firm butt and slender legs, a flat stomach, and B-size round-shaped breasts, she always attracted attention. Looking at her toned, hourglass-shaped body, people could not tell she had given birth to two children.

It was not only her body that impressed people. My wife was blessed with smooth white skin without freckles and a pretty face with deep blue eyes complemented by eyebrows with soft angles and shallow arches. Her high cheekbones, straight nose, narrow jawline, and full lips made her face look perfect. She wore her wavy blonde hair shoulder-length, emphasising her long neck. When she spoke, her slight Croatian accent made her sound exotic and combined with her tender voice and soft smile, her charm was irresistible. Ella knew she was sexy and pretty and knew I liked to show her off, but she never flirted or tried to deliberately attract men's attention. Ella played along with me when I showed her off, but that was all. She would never cross a boundary or in any way suggest she would do anything beyond being friendly and polite. Thus, although Ella turned men's heads, she had never cheated on me or made me feel insecure or jealous, so I enjoyed making other men envy me for having her as my wife.

Ella and I found the restaurant, had lunch and spent the rest of the afternoon walking around the hotel grounds, having drinks at the bars in the hotel compound, and enjoying the tropical garden they had turned the place into. We had an early dinner followed by more drinks at the bar, went to the show that the hotel organised every evening in the auditorium next to the main restaurant, had another drink and went to our room to have sex. Well, it turned out we had drunk too much, and since we were knackered, having woken up at 3 am London time to catch the flight to Sal, we postponed sex to the next morning.

GERHARD

The next morning, we did not have sex because we wanted to be at the pool early to get sunbeds and rushed for breakfast. Then we went straight to the reception desk to check when our holiday briefing was. It was scheduled for 11 o'clock.

Ella looked at her watch. "We've got time to pop in the pool. But we'd better hurry up if we want to have a lounger. It's a quarter past nine already!"

We went to our room to put on swimsuits. Ella put on her string bikini and looked stunning in them. The black fabric helped emphasise the smoothness of her white skin, and the delicate strings accentuated the low hip-to-waist ratio of her body. Ella ought to turn heads, and I looked forward to relishing the feeling of being envied for having such a beautiful wife.

We realised we were awfully late when we got to the outdoor swimming pool. There was not a single sunbed that did not have someone on it or a towel spread on it. We looked around. Nope! All sunbeds were occupied.

"I guess we can leave our bag there," I said to Ella and pointed at a spot on the ground behind a bush where someone had left their beach bag.

"Yes," Ella agreed with me. "Let's pop into the pool and return to our room."

"Hey! Hello!" we heard someone shouting.

"Hey! Over here!" we heard again and looked in the direction from where the voice was coming.

It was the old guy who had helped us with directions to the restaurant the previous day. He was sitting on a sunbed. There were some drinks on the plastic table beside him.

"I have two sun loungers for you!" he said and pointed at the two sunbeds on the other side of his table that had towels spread on them.

Ella and I looked at each other.

"Why not?" my wife murmured and walked to the old man.

I followed her with our beach bag.

"Aren't they someone else's?" I asked as we stood in front of our new friend.

"Nah!" the old man said and put the book he was reading on the table. He stood up, took the towels from the two loungers, folded them, and put them on the ground. He sat down on his sunbed and nodded at the empty sun loungers. "Come on! Put your towels down, or someone else will snatch your sunbeds!"

Ella and I put our towels on the two loungers and sat down next to each other on the one closer to the good Samaritan.

"Gerhard!" the old man said and stretched his hand to Ella for a handshake.

"Ella," my wife responded and shook his hand, smiling politely.

"Nick!" I introduced myself and also shook Gerhard's hand. "Thank you for the sunbeds!" I added.

"No problem!" Gerhard waved his hand. "I wake up early; that's what happens to you when you turn seventy. You can't sleep when others sleep!" He chuckled. "He-he! But the silver lining in the cloud is that I am first at breakfast and first at the pool!" He leaned towards Ella and me and whispered, "I know it's a bit mean, but I always take three sunbeds. This way, I can choose who can keep me company. And today, I chose you!"

"Thank you!" Ella smiled with a charming smile.

"No worries!" Gerhard smiled back at her. "So, where are you from?"

We told Gerhard we came from London, but Ella was originally from Croatia, and I was from Greece. We also told him we had come to celebrate our tenth wedding anniversary.

"We left the kids back in London with the idea of reliving our honeymoon," I said.

"Well, good idea leaving the kids at home!" Gerhard said. Then he smiled and added, "However, reliving your honeymoon? Mmm, not so much. You see! You shouldn't just relive your honeymoon because reliving it would mean making it as good as the first one. While after ten years of marriage, you can and should make it better than what it was ten years ago."

"I see," I said out of politeness despite thinking the old man was talking nonsense.

Ella tilted her head to the side and, smiling at Gerhard, spoke out what I had thought when she said, "How can we make it better if we are ten years older?"

Gerhard leaned toward Ella and me and whispered, "It's very easy. After ten years together, you know each other's bodies much better, what you like in bed, and what you don't. You have way more experience with each other now than ten years ago. You trust each other much more than back then. You are ready to spice things up! Take your sex life up to the next level on this holiday, and you will have a better honeymoon than ten years ago, regardless of how great the first one was!"

"Right!" I said, beginning to doubt Ella and I had made the right choice in taking up Gerhard's offer of using his loungers.

He seemed to have read my mind because he said, "Sorry! I didn't mean to be patronising, but professional deformation, you know!"

"What's your profession?" Ella asked.

"I am a sex psychologist!" Gerhard replied. "Was. I don't practise anymore. But I used to do couples therapy. I've helped so many couples. Saving their relationships. Spicing up their marriages. I was good at it. Maybe because I and Monika—my wife—applied my advice to our own life." Gerhard looked at the pool and held his gaze on a couple standing next to the swim-up bar. "I miss my wife. She passed away two years ago."

"I am sorry!" I said.

"Sorry!" Ella chimed in.

Gerhard sighed. "It's OK. We had a great life together. We had lots of fun after we took the plunge into the world of sex for pleasure, as I call it; we were about your age when we did it. That's why when I see a young couple like you, I see myself and Monika of that time. I remember the day when, after a lot of deliberation and trepidation, we decided to make our marriage even greater and our sex beyond fantastic! We never regretted our choice; we only wished we had made it earlier!" Gerhard looked at Ella and me and chuckled. "He-he! Now I come to places like this one on my own and observe couples and analyse them. I watch people's behaviour and look for signs. Just by looking at a man's face, I can tell if he's still into his wife or looking to stray. Or, by observing how a woman interacts, I can tell whether she's flirting with her man or someone else sitting next to her. I catch the signals she sends to the guy she wants consciously or subconsciously." Gerhard paused and looked at me, then at Ella.

"Am I boring you?" he asked us.

Ella smiled politely. "No! Actually, I find it interesting."

I thought he was bat-crap crazy but still chimed in, "Me too!"

There was silence, and I felt obliged for some reason to break it, so I asked Gerhard, "What can you say about my wife's signals?"

"Nick!" Ella squalled and slapped me lightly on the knee.

Gerhard laughed. "Ha-ha!" He leaned towards Ella and me and said quietly, "Ella is sending a lot of signals!"

Ella blushed.

Gerhard continued, "But that's great, Ella! That's what your man needs! That's why I said you two are ready to take this honeymoon to the next level!" He turned to look at the swim-up bar and nodded in its direction. "Look! Do you see the couple that is laughing? I've been watching them since this morning."

Ella and I looked at the swim-up bar. There was a couple in their mid-twenties who were chatting and laughing.

Gerhard explained, "They often touch hands and keep eye contact a lot, even when it is too much. They are newlywed. There's a lot of passion. I can tell by the way they kiss! Here they go; they kiss again." Gerhard paused and watched the couple kiss. When they broke the kiss, he said, "Do you see how she smiles? The glint in her eyes? She sends signals."

"She is playing with her hair," I said. "That's a sign she's flirting."

"She is," Gerhard agreed with me. "But with whom?"

I shrugged my shoulders. "With her husband, I guess."

A smile flittered across Gerhard's face before he said, "But not only with him. Look at the guy sitting next to her husband! Watch how he's laughing and looking at her. You see? She's flirting with her husband but also sending signals to his friend there. Her husband's friend is falling for her, and she likes it. She likes being desired, which makes her send more signals to her hubby and his friend. I bet the three of them will end up in bed together, if not tonight, tomorrow."

"No way!" I said. "The husband—"

"The husband suspects. No. He knows that his friend is into his wife," Gerhard said.

"So, there will be a fight!" Ella interjected.

Gerhard shook his head. "No! The husband doesn't know it yet, but subconsciously he wants this guy to sleep with his wife. The hubby's friend, here, look, now he's tapping the wife's hand playfully. Look at the way the hubby looks at his friend! Watch how the husband laughs when he sees his friend touch his wife? The hubby feels challenged and flattered at the same time. And look now! The hubby takes his wife's hand, and they kiss."

Indeed, the husband and wife leaned toward each other and kissed.

"And look at her!" Gerhard continued to whisper. "Did you notice? Look! She did it again. She is kissing her husband, yet she glances at his friend. Only for a brief second, but she does. And her husband's friend catches her glance. He knows she's interested in him. She's saying, 'Look at me! I'm kissing my husband. I love him very much! But I would have gladly done the same with you if you and I had been a couple!' And the hubby's friend receives the signal and knows there is a possibility. The hubby has also caught her glances and keeps kissing her passionately, with zeal. He enjoys the kiss a lot more because he notices the signals flowing between his wife and his friend. The husband is in fighter mode. I am sure he is rock hard because he's enamoured by his wife, but even more so because his friend is into her! It's called sperm competition!"

We watched the couple pull away from each other as the wife giggled when their friend said something.

"Yep! I am certain! These three will have a fantastic threesome soon!" Gerhard said, not taking his eyes off the couple and their friend. Then the old man sighed and added, "I see in them so much of Monika, myself, and Manfred when we first met!"

Ella and I looked at Gerhard. *Is he saying what we think he is saying?*

He looked at us and smiled. "Yes, we were swingers! Or rather, Monika was a hotwife. I used to share her. We started doing it when we were about your age! I wished we had started much sooner. I was advising other couples on how to spice up their sex lives, but it took me a while to jump into the lifestyle myself!"

There was an uncomfortable silence.

Gerhard smiled at Ella and me again. "Sorry! I am not your therapist, nor do I think you need my therapy. I am just an old man who misses his wife, her boyfriends, and the fun they brought to our relationship. And I was by no means suggesting the lifestyle to the two of you. Sorry if I made you feel uncomfortable!"

"No, it's OK!" I said.

"Yeah, it's OK," Ella said too. "You didn't make us feel uncomfortable." She looked at me. "Right, honey?"

"No, not at all," I replied. "It's always good to hear these things from a specialist with practice."

"Ha-ha!" Gerhard laughed. "You could say that! I am a specialist who was practising his own advice!" He paused for a second, then added, "Just to be clear! Wife-sharing and swinging were not the only pieces of advice I gave couples. There are many other ways to spice up a relationship." Gerhard took his book, opened it, and prepared to lie on his lounger, but then closed the book and looked at the swim-up bar. "Do you see that other guy at the far end of the bar, sitting on his own, watching those three flirt? The blond guy that is drinking from his beer?"

Ella and I nodded yes.

"Do you know why he looks so miserable?" Gerhard asked but then answered his own question. "Because he's not part of the game those three are playing. However, that woman's signals have taken hold of him too! You see. Sometimes, there are unintended recipients of a woman's signals." Gerhard placed his book on the table. "Come on! Let's have a drink with him and try to cheer him up!"

Ella and I looked at each other, unsure. *Should we take up Gerhard's offer? To go for a drink with two strangers—one whom we have just met and the other we have never met? It doesn't feel right. Yet, wouldn't it be too rude to decline Gerhard's invitation?*

"I guess you came for the pool and the drinks," Gerhard said when he saw we hesitated. "The swim-up pool bar gives you both."

"Mmm, now that you say it," I said. "You're right. Let's go and have a drink."

Ella smiled in agreement with me.

Gerhard leaned toward us and whispered, "Plus, I feel bad for the guy. He and his friend turned up earlier and asked for the sunbeds, and I sent them away. They thought I was a prick. Let's keep the guy company for a few minutes as a gesture of my apology."

Gerhard stood up and headed for the swim-up bar. Ella and I followed him.

MIKKEL

We walked down the stairs into the pool, and the guy Gerhard wanted us to cheer up shifted his gaze from the woman with her two admirers to Ella. The newlyweds and their friend also sized up my wife's body. The foxy girl smiled friendly at Ella before turning her attention back to her hubby and his friend.

Gerhard leaned his mouth to Ella's ear and whispered, "She doesn't like you. She sees a competitor in you!"

Ella smiled and whispered back, "I know!"

"Yeah, of course, you know," Gerhard murmured and turned to me. "Nick, women have a much better sense of these things than men."

I nodded in agreement with him.

We took seats at the bar next to the lonely man.

A bartender, a handsome young man, turned up.

"What would you like?" he asked us.

"Gin and tonic, please," Ella chirruped.

"A beer for me," Gerhard said.

"A beer for me, too," I added.

The sad man sitting next to us was no longer staring at the foxy girl. He was not taking his eyes off Ella. He was not sad anymore and smiled at my wife and me.

He looked at Gerhard and said, "So, these are your friends you kept the sunbeds for."

"Yeah," Gerhard replied. "Where's your buddy?"

"At the aqua park!" the man said and stretched his hand to Ella. "Mikkel, by the way!"

"Ella," my wife introduced herself and shook his hand.

I smiled politely at the guy. "I'm Nick."

"And I'm Gerhard," Gerhard said.

"You're German, right?" Mikkel asked.

Gerhard nodded. "Yes."

Mikkel turned his attention back to Ella and me. "And where are you from?"

We started the usual chit-chat. Ella and I explained we lived in London, but Ella was from Croatia, and I was from Greece originally and had come for our tenth wedding anniversary to Cape Verde. Mikkel also told us about himself. He was from Denmark. He had been looking forward to his holiday in Cape Verde but had ended up heartbroken. His girlfriend had cheated on him shortly after his arrival, and he had broken up with her. He was getting over the breakup by keeping himself drunk. We moved on from the touchy subject and chatted about the resort and Cape Verde for a while. However, when Gerhard mentioned that the island was a perfect place for having fun, the conversation unexpectedly came back to Mikkel's breakup.

"Fun?!" Mikkel exclaimed. "It cost me dearly the last time I tried to have fun on this island." He shook his head from side to side and said in a lamenting voice, "I knew that doing it would destroy my relationship. I knew it."

Gerhard drank up his beer. "Well, why did you do it then?"

Mikkel finished his drink, too and put the glass on the counter. He stared at Gerhard with a rather hostile look before saying, "Because someone talked me into it, didn't he? That someone ruined my relationship!"

Gerhard said quietly, "I am sorry to hear you feel that way."

Mikkel looked away and sighed before looking back at Gerhard. "When I saw the lust in her eyes"—Mikkel choked back tears—"I felt. . . . It changed my perspective!"

It seemed that the poor guy had caught his girlfriend in the act with another man, and both Ella and I looked at him with compassion.

Gerhard tried to comfort him. "I know exactly what you mean. But I've said it many times: having fun is a learning curve, and it might be hard in the beginning, but most couples learn to have fun and still have a healthy relationship. I had all the fun a man could have while I was married. And I stayed married to the same woman for almost fifty years."

Mikkel stared at Gerhard, struggling to understand what Gerhard meant. However, I knew where the old man was coming from and said, "Gerhard and his wife were swingers."

Ella pinched my thigh under the water. She was right. I shouldn't have told Mikkel that Gerhard and his wife had been swingers. I was risking an angry rebuke from Gerhard.

However, contrary to Ella's and my expectations, neither Gerhard nor Mikkel reacted badly in any way.

Gerhard simply said, "The best marriage arrangement if you ask me."

Mikkel shook his head. "Maybe for you, Gerhard. Not for me! I don't want to be in such a marriage. I don't want to be cucked. I want to be a bull!"

Gerhard chuckled. "He-he! That can be easily arranged." He tapped Mikkel's shoulder. "Have faith, play along, and things will turn around for you! I'll find you a couple to play with. A couple who wants to have fun and still have a healthy relationship."

The frown on Mikkel's face gave way to a smile. "I'll hold you to your word, Gerhard!"

Gerhard seemed to have achieved his goal. He had succeeded in cheering Mikkel up, but not for long because Mikkel frowned again when his eyes fell on the newlywed and their friend. The woman was giggling again, looking lustfully at their friend, while her hubby was holding her hand, shaking his head, and smiling.

Mikkel sighed a deep sigh. "Gerhard, how many couples are out there having fun and a healthy relationship, as you say?"

"He-he!" Gerhard chuckled quietly, tracing Mikkel's gaze. "Them too, Mikkel, them too! They know how to have fun."

Mikkel looked at Gerhard, and they smiled at each other.

"Can we have another round of the same, please?" Mikkel asked the bartender, who had noticed our glasses were empty and turned up.

"My bladder can't hold more than one beer, I am afraid," Gerhard said and got off his stool. "Nick and Ella are looking for fun. I'll leave the three of you to get to know each other." He headed for the pool steps.

Ella and I looked at each other. *Did Gerhard try to set us up with Mikkel?*

We looked at Mikkel. He had turned his gaze to us. The three of us blushed.

Mikkel felt obliged to break the awkward silence. "How do you like the island so far?"

It was going to be rude if Ella and I left Mikkel alone, so we stayed behind and had another round of drinks with him. We had a small talk about Cape Verde and Sal again before Ella and I excused ourselves, saying we had to see our holiday rep.

When we got out of the pool, Gerhard had gone. We dried ourselves and rushed for our room to change before attending our holiday welcome meeting.

AGNETE

We watched the presentation by our holiday rep—a pretty young woman—and stayed behind for the Q&A session. We spent ten minutes chatting with her but didn't book any trips. The tour we liked the most was a day long, and Ella was not keen to spend a day on a coach.

The rep moved on to talk to the next couple in the queue, and Ella slapped me playfully on the butt.

"She could be your daughter, you know?" Ella whispered in my ear in Croatian.

She knew a little Greek, and I knew a little Croatian, so sometimes we talked in our local languages when we didn't want others to understand what we were talking about.

"Are you jealous?" I asked Ella in English after we had walked away a few steps, and our holiday rep could not overhear us.

Ella giggled. "Hi-hi! Should I be?"

"Nah! Her tits are too flat," I said quietly.

Indeed, the girl was very tall, with a beautiful face, long blonde hair, and slender legs. She had perfect body proportions, except for her boobs. They were A-cup size at best. I don't like huge breasts, but still, they have to be B- or C-size to pass my quality check. D- and above are too big, on the other hand.

"Really?" Ella said. "You didn't like her?"

I shrugged my shoulders. "No. I didn't. I mean, not particularly."

"Then why did you ask her so many questions? 'What's it like to work as a rep?' 'How often do you go back home?' 'Do you find time to travel around the island?' What was all that about, Nick?"

"It was just chit-chat. I was interested to find out what life abroad feels like for these youngsters."

"Is that so? Huh! How lucky for you that she seemed more than willing to tell you."

We headed for lunch in the main restaurant.

"Agnete was her name, wasn't it?" Ella said as we walked down the aisle to the restaurant entrance. "She loves meeting new people, she's only 19, she's from Copenhagen, she loves travelling, did not enjoy the zipline, but she likes sunbathing—I bet she goes topless because she does not have much to show anyway—she enjoys having drinks with her colleagues after work, and the only thing she doesn't like in her job was that it cost her her boyfriend."

"Well, she didn't say it exactly like that," I said. "She said they grew apart in the months they were away from each other and ended up breaking up."

"Exactly! She implied her job cost her her boyfriend," Ella said. She stopped walking, as did I. She looked at me. A mischievous smile flickered across her face before she added, "I saw the glint in your eyes when she said she broke up with her boyfriend."

"No, Ella! There's no such thing!"

"Oh, yes! There is! I bet it crossed your mind."

Ella knew me perfectly well and had seen through me. When the girl had said she had broken up with her boyfriend, the thought of taking her out for a drink to comfort her and fuck her afterwards had crossed my mind.

Nonetheless, I played innocent by asking, "Crossed my mind what?"

"To ask her for a drink," Ella clarified, still smiling at me.

"Ask her for a drink? Why would I do that?"

"To fuck her afterwards!"

"Ella, you know I love you, and you are way more beautiful than her!"

"Oh, I know that!" Ella said with confidence. "But thank you! I like hearing you say it!"

I put my hand on the small of her back and rubbed it. "Ella, you are the most beautiful woman on this island. Half of the men were gawking at you during the presentation. Even more than half. And I can't blame them. You've got a flawless body, and you know how to dress. Honestly, you look stunning in your dress. Its light fabric flows down your body so graciously, accentuating your perfect figure and curves."

"Thank you. I hope my nipples don't bulge out!" Ella quickly pulled on the front of her dress and looked down at her bust.

Her nipples protruded slightly through the white fabric of her light summer dress, which she had put on in a hurry without a bra.

"Oh, shit!" Ella squealed. "I'll put on a bra!"

I wrapped my arm around her waist. "But I like you without a bra!"

"Apparently, not only you!" Ella said, and we resumed walking.

"So you admit you noticed those looks," I said. "And did you see that guy that was waiting for us to finish talking with Agnete? How he stared at your legs?"

"Nick, I always notice when men look at me. But I never fantasise about doing anything. Unlike you. Dreaming of an affair with someone like that Danish foxy, Agnete!"

"You never fantasise?"

"Never!"

"Nah!" I waved my hand. "I don't believe you! Admit you fantasise! At least sometimes?"

"I admit nothing." Ella elbowed me in the ribs playfully. "But you must admit you wanted to have drinks with that girl!"

"Well, maybe."

"And you fantasised about having sex with her!"

"Only if you were with me."

Ella stopped walking. I stopped walking, too and looked at her. She looked confused.

"Why not?!" I shrugged my shoulders. "Two pretty women! The perfect threesome!"

Ella shook her head in fake disappointment.

I chuckled. "He-he! Spice it up a little, Ella!"

"You do worry me, you know," Ella said sternly but a second later smiled.

"Two female bodies, intertwined in—"

"Stop it! It's disgusting!"

"No. It's not! It's awesome! Every man's ultimate dream. Being with two girls at the same time!"

"Your dirty dream, Nick!" Ella slapped me playfully on the butt. "Not every man's! Yours! Only misguided men like you can dream of sleeping with two women."

I continued to wind Ella up. "Not misguided men like me, but capable men like me can have two girls all night long."

"Really? You'll fuck another woman and me all night long?"

"Why not? You're multi-orgasmic!"

"But you're not!" Ella tapped me on the shoulder, smiling. "You're not! You know these fantasies are the most irrational possible. One man! Think about it! Satisfying two women at the same time! How's that gonna work?"

"Well, why does the man have to do all the work? One woman can go down on the other!"

"Eww! Disgusting! I'm not a lesbian! I'd never go down on that girl. Agnete! Or let her come anywhere near me!"

"OK! What if I am fucking her while I am giving you head?"

"OK! What about, instead of Agnete, we do the threesome with the handsome waiter who served our drinks at the pool bar? He'll be fucking me while I'm giving you head?"

"So you fantasise!"

Ella put on a serious face. "No! I don't! But you see how it feels now?"

We resumed walking, but after five or six steps, I said, "Actually, I think Mikkel will be a better choice for an MFM threesome than the waiter!"

Ella stopped walking again, looked at me and, shaking her head, said, "I think you're too horny, and your brain has mushed. Right after lunch, we are going back to our room, and we are going to have sex! As a matter of urgency, before you have completely lost your mind!"

We resumed walking, reached the restaurant's entrance and got inside.

We had lunch and decided to return to our hotel room to take our swimming gear and beach towels and visit the aqua park. When we came back to the hotel room, the moment I closed the door behind us, I grabbed Ella by the waist and turned her to face me.

She put her hands on my shoulders and looked me in the eyes.

"What?" she asked me, and a flirtatious smile spread across her face.

"I want to fuck you," I said and planted my lips on hers.

She crossed her arms around my neck and opened her mouth to let my tongue in. The way she kissed—deep tongue, urgency in her lips, her hot breath—told me how aroused she was.

My hands slipped to her ass, and I squeezed it. She moaned into my mouth. She was horny as hell.

I hiked her light summer dress up to her waist, baring her bum and upper thighs. Keeping my right hand on her butt, I moved my left hand to her stomach. A second later, I slipped my hand between her legs, squeezed her inner thigh, and ran my hand up to her pussy. I grasped her labia through her panties.

Ella moaned. And I knew it. She wanted to be fucked badly. She let go of my neck and slipped her hand into the front pocket of my Bermuda shorts, where she knew I had tucked a condom in before going to the meeting with our holiday rep. Ella took the condom out.

We broke the kiss to take a breath and looked into each other's eyes. We saw lust. Raw lust and passion. We smiled and resumed kissing.

Ella pulled my shorts down, along with my briefs, down to my mid-thighs. My rock-hard cock sprang out.

She broke the kiss and hastily unwrapped the condom. She ran her hand over my cock shaft and then rolled the condom onto my cock. Ella put her hands on my chest and leaned her back against the wall, pushing her pelvis forward and pressing her crotch against mine.

"I want to fuck you as if Mikkel is fucking you!" I said.

I was not sure if the second part of my sentence made sense. *As if Mikkel is fucking you?!?* I had no clue how Mikkel fucked, or what fucking as Mikkel would mean. But it had just come to my mind, and I had blurted it out.

Nonetheless, regardless of whether what I had said made sense, Ella seemed to like my dirty talk and breathed out a moan. I looked at her face. Her pupils were dilated, her breathing heavy, and her lips engorged.

Encouraged, I repeated, "I want to fuck you as if Mikkel is fucking you!"

"Then fuck me!" Ella said and playfully pushed me in the chest and, at the same time, spread her legs apart.

I hooked my fingers under her lace-trim thong, and my knuckles brushed her pussy lips. Her pussy was wet! Really wet if her labia majora was wet!

I needed no more invitations. No more clues. I pulled her panties to one side with one hand, grabbed my cock with the other, bent my knees slightly to lower my pelvis, and pointed my cockhead at her pussy.

Ella grabbed my ass cheeks and drew my crotch forward while grinding her pussy against my cock. The moment I felt the familiar feeling of her spread apart warm inner pussy lips, I thrust into her vagina.

My cockhead slid in, and Ella gasped.

She was not only wet but loose.

Ella let go of my butt and crossed her arms around my neck. I grabbed her ass and pulled her up. She wrapped her legs around my waist and pushed her shoulders back against the wall, impaling her pussy all the way to the base of my cock.

Ella gasped again when she felt my entire length inside her.

I squeezed her ass cheeks and began thrusting in and out of her pussy.

I fucked her for no longer than two minutes and cummed, at the same time as she cried, "Oh, my God!" and shuddered in orgasm.

I kept thrusting for another minute or so until her orgasm subsided, and then I stopped.

With my help, Ella pulled her crotch up, releasing my still erect cock from her pussy.

I let go of her ass, and she stood on her feet. I removed the condom and tied it off.

Ella slapped me playfully on the butt and smiled.

"Do you like how Mikkel fucks?" I asked her as I tossed the used condom into the trash basket.

"Hi-hi!" She giggled. "I don't know how Mikkel fucks. But I liked how my husband fucked me." She adjusted her thong and straightened her dress. She smiled. "Happy?"

I chucked. "He-he! More than happy!"

We kissed again. Then I pulled my briefs and shorts up, grabbed the beach bag with our swimsuits and towels, and we headed for the aqua park.

JOHAN

We had no problem finding free sun loungers in the aqua park. It was nowhere as busy as the swimming pool at our hotel. Perhaps because the water park was in another hotel's compound, only a hundred meters away from our hotel grounds, and many guests of our hotel were unaware they had a free pass for the water slides. Ella and I changed into our swimsuits and went on each of the six different water slides at least twice. After that, we had a drink at the bar and talked about which of the slides was the hardest and which one was our favourite. We decided to have one final ride on the water slide each of us liked the most. I went for the red one because it gave an excellent lift-off in the middle of the ride, while my wife went for the blue slide since she felt it was the fastest and liked to slide fast. I went first. I splashed in the pool, stood up and watched Ella go into her slide. It seemed that at that point, the lifeguard at the top of the slides coordinating who should go when had a brief lapse of concentration, and a bloke went into Ella's water slide straight after her. Ella landed in the pool, got up and took a step to one side but not enough to move out of the way of the guy sliding behind her, and he knocked her down when he landed in the water. The bloke quickly stood up on his feet and pulled Ella up.

"I'm so sorry," said the offender of the water slide rules.

Ella steadied herself on her feet and wiped the water off her face and her eyes. I sighed relief: she was fine. The whistles of the lifeguard at the poolside were a clear sign of how bad the whole incident could have been.

The remorseful guy put his hand on Ella's shoulder, looking at her face with concern and asked her, "Did I hurt you?"

"No, I'm OK," Ella said and smiled at him politely.

The guy, who was probably mid-to-late twenties, smiled at her too. He stepped beside her and moved his hand to the small of her back.

"I'm so sorry," he apologised again. "I was going to offer to buy you a drink as an apology, but I guess it makes no sense." He raised his hand, showing that he had the all-inclusive wristband like us.

The lifeguard approached Ella's 'new friend' and, pointing at the bar, said sternly, "You can chat with her over there! Not here in the pool, please!"

"OK, let's have a drink!" the scolded man said to Ella, keeping his hand on the small of her back. He nudged her towards the steps out of the pool leading to the bar.

Ella and her new acquaintance walked out of the pool, and I followed them.

Ella took a seat at the bar just as I caught up with them.

"This is my husband: Nick," she introduced me.

"Hi, I'm Johan," Ella's newly found friend said as he looked at me, a little taken aback, perhaps disappointed that my wife was married and her husband was around, but still smiled. "Sorry for knocking your wife off her feet."

I smiled too. "It's OK if she says it's OK."

Johan turned to Ella. "And what's your name, if I may ask?"

"Ella," my wife introduced herself, smiling politely.

"Ella! What a beautiful name!" Johan said.

"Thank you!" Ella chirruped.

"A name that befits your beauty," Johan said, shamelessly giving my wife a stilted compliment and making her blush.

Ella looked at me as if to ask me: *What's going on here, Nick? Is he hitting on me?*

My subtle smile conveyed my answer: *You're damn right, darling.*

He's definitely hitting on you!

I thought to myself: *She is a catch for sure, but still?!* I felt slightly irritated that this man showed no respect and tried to flirt with Ella in front of me, but at the same time, my ego was flattered. Also, my cock had hardened. I was turned on by the thought of my wife being seduced by someone else.

I must admit I was confused by my mixed emotions. However, I kept my cool and smiled. "Yes, Johan, I thought the same when I first met Ella, and she told me her name. We ended up sleeping together!"

The last sentence slipped out of my mouth. Inadvertently, I implied causality between liking my wife's name and sleeping with her.

Ella abruptly turned to look at me, her eyes going big: *What's up with you, Nick?!?*

Johan laughed. "Ha-ha! I'm sure the name is not the only thing to do with it, but it certainly helps, I guess!"

Ella looked at Johan, and blushing profusely, she smiled appreciatively.

The bartender turned up.

"I'll have vodka with tonic," Ella said, eager to change the subject.

"I'll have the same," I added.

"OK, may we have three vodkas with tonic, please?" Johan summarised our order.

"Where are you from, Johan?" I asked him after the bartender walked away.

"From Denmark," Johan replied.

"There seem to be many Danish tourists in the hotel," Ella interjected.

"Yeah," I chimed in. "You are the third Dane we have met today!"

"Well, some major Danish tour operators have contracts with

this hotel," Johan said. "They are keen to fill in their quotas after they struggled during the pandemic and offer juicy discounts. That's how my friend and I got attracted to come to Cape Verde. It was not a good idea, though."

"You mean?" I asked.

"Coming together," Johan clarified. "His idea for a holiday is different than mine. He doesn't like what I like."

"Like what?" Ella asked and smiled somewhat coquettishly.

Johan smiled too. "Like: he doesn't like the water slides. He stayed behind in the pool"—Johan nodded in the direction of our hotel—"he prefers to drink himself into oblivion."

Our drinks arrived, and we started to chit-chat. Ella and I told Johan why we were in Cape Verde and also talked about our family. He asked about how our kids did at school. Then he spoke about how naughty he had been at school and even naughtier at uni, dating three women at the same time. Unusual confession, but nonetheless, the hilarious way he told us about his adventures made Ella and me laugh. We learned he was single but not in a rush to marry because he was only 29.

I was tempted to tell him that 29 was not too young to marry—I had married much younger—but decided not to share my views on the matter and risk coming across as rude.

We finished our drinks, and it turned out Johan was going back to the hotel, like us. So we took our stuff from the sunbeds, and without changing, the three of us left the water park.

We were walking inside our hotel compound and passing by the stairs leading to the hotel's main pool when we saw Mikkel standing at the top of the stairs. He waved at us to wait for him.

"This is my friend," Johan said. "Let me introduce you to him."

I smiled. "We've already met him."

"Oh, have you?" Johan asked, surprised.

"This morning, at the pool bar," Ella clarified.

"He-he!" Johan chuckled. "Of course, at the pool bar! Where else? He doesn't leave it, does he?" He nodded at his friend, who was wobbling down the stairs, visibly drunk.

When Mikkel reached us, Johan said to him, "I understand you've already met Ella and Nick."

"Yeah!" Mikkel responded in a drunken voice and turned to Ella and me. "Are you coming from the aqua park?"

"Yes," Ella said. "Have you been there?"

"Nah!" Mikkel waved his hand. "I am more of a 'bar' guy."

"Yeah, we can see that," Johan interjected jokingly.

Mikkel said something to Johan in Danish, sounding somewhat hostile.

Johan responded in Danish, and by the tone of his voice, it looked like he was trying to pacify his friend.

Mikkel seemed unwilling to calm down and raised his voice at Johan, speaking in Danish again.

Johan shook his head disapprovingly, then turned to Ella and me and said, "Mikkel had a little too much to drink. I'll take him to our room. See you around!" He put his hand on Mikkel's shoulder and nudged him to turn around in an attempt to lead him away from us.

Mikkel seemed to have none of that. He pushed Johan away and said to Ella and me in English, "I'm not drunk. Let's carry on with our conversation from this morning. Come! Let's have a drink!" He nodded in the direction of the pool.

"No, thank you," Ella said politely, then added, "Maybe later."

"Later?" Mikkel smiled a drunken smile. "OK! What about after the show tonight? You're coming to the show, aren't you?"

Ella and I looked at each other.

I shrugged my shoulders. "Why not?"

Ella looked at Mikkel and smiled. "Yeah, let's have drinks at the show!"

"See you tonight!" Mikkel mumbled. "I'll be there, waiting for you!"

Ella and I smiled politely and were about to walk away, happy that we had helped Johan calm down his drunken friend when Johan made a mistake.

He winked at us and said, "Don't count on that!"

"Don't count on what?!" Mikkel snapped at Johan.

Johan put his hand on Mikkel's shoulder. "Let's go, Mikkel!"

Mikkel pushed Johan's hand away, turned to Ella and me, and said, raising his voice, "He's constantly patronising me! He thinks he can do that just because he fucked my girlfriend."

Johan smiled and blushed, embarrassed. "Don't listen to Mikkel! He's had too many shots."

"No! Listen to me! Nick!" Mikkel shouted. "Nick, be careful! He's destroying relationships. You and your wife are next!"

Johan shook his head. "Don't listen to him! He's drunk and doesn't know what he's talking about."

"Don't know what I'm talking about?" Mikkel glared at Johan, then looked at Ella and me. "He fucked my fiancée in a gangbang!"

"Shh! Lower your voice, Mikkel!" Johan shushed his friend and turned to Ella and me. "It's not what happened."

"It is exactly what happened!" Mikkel shouted. "Three days ago!"

"Right," I said. "We'd better get going!"

"He wants to fuck your wife, Nick!" Mikkel blurted out.

Ella and I were stunned.

"Don't mind him! He's drunk!" Johan said, blushing profusely.

Mikkel waved his finger at me. "I am telling you! The old man will talk you and your wife into having a gangbang! And this one here"—Mikkel pointed at Johan—"will jump straight into it and fuck your wife!"

"Shut up!" Johan scolded his friend.

Ella raised her hands in the air. "Look! Obviously, the two of you have some emotional drama going on. Nick and I are sorry for your troubles, and we shall leave you to sort things out between the two of you."

Mikkel waved his hand frustratingly at Ella, turned around and walked away. Ella, Johan, and I watched him climb up the stairs back to the pool, mumbling something under his nose and teetering from side to side.

Johan looked around apprehensively, concerned the squabble with his drunken friend might have attracted unnecessary attention.

Once he had assured himself that no one had paid attention to the little incident, he stepped closer to Ella and me and said quietly, "I'm sorry you had to hear that. But that's not what happened! I had always liked his fiancée but had never done anything about it until the other day when the three of us got drunk, and well, one thing led to another, and we had a threesome. The next morning Mikkel had regrets, became difficult, made a scene, and, well, they broke up. But no one talked anyone into anything. Someone suggested a joint hen and bachelor party, and we all went for it, and it happened." Johan sighed. "In hindsight, we shouldn't have done it. Honestly, I regret doing it. Mikkel is my friend; the last thing I want to do is hurt him. I didn't expect him to take it so badly, but he did. And worse: instead of moving on, unfortunately, now he sees the same scenario unfolding with every pretty woman we meet. Yesterday he accused me of hitting on the receptionist for interjecting in his conversation with her. I hope you understand."

Ella stared at Johan for a while before saying, "Yes, I understand. Don't worry." She smiled politely.

"Yeah, don't worry! These things happen," I chimed in and then quickly corrected myself, "I mean, not the threesomes...."

Ella looked at me, and I blushed.

Holding her gaze, I began mumbling, "I, I, I mean, threesomes happen. We are not against them." I paused before exclaiming, "Oh, God! I'm digging myself a hole, am I not?"

Ella nodded, eyebrows raised. "Yes, you are!"

"Let me start again!" I said. "I mean, misunderstandings happen, and Ella and I understand. Not the threesomes. I mean, threesomes happen. But, what I mean is. . . . Right!" I paused and took a deep breath. "What I mean is: we understand that threesomes happen. And we understand that misunderstandings happen."

Now I finally looked back at Johan. A faint smile flickered at the corners of his mouth. I turned my gaze back at Ella. She shook her head from side to side, suppressing a smile.

"I sound like an idiot, don't I?" I murmured, and the only thing I managed to do was to smile stupidly.

There was an uncomfortable silence between us for a few seconds.

Johan broke it. "Right! I suspect you aren't keen to have drinks with Mikkel and me after what was said."

"Nah! It's nothing!" I waved off his concern. "We can have drinks!"

"Yeah," Ella concurred with me. Like me, she was trying to be polite and, at the same time, move on from the subject of threesomes and misunderstandings.

"Oh, that's great!" Johan's face spread into a happy smile. "So, shall we meet at the theatre bar after dinner?"

"Yeah, why not?" I said. "Only for drinks, right?"

I paused. I had said something stupid again.

Ella looked at me, shaking her head.

Johan burst into laughter. "Ha-ha! Yes, only for drinks! Not for a threesome."

Ella turned to look at him, and despite blushing profusely, she giggled. "Hi-hi! Yes, Johan, let me clarify this on behalf of my husband, who seems to have had too many runs on the water slides, and his brain must have mushed up. We'll catch up over a drink only and nothing else!"

Johan smiled somewhat playfully at her, put his hand on her shoulder and rubbed it gently as he said, "See you tonight, Ella!"

Then he turned around to head for the stairs to the pool, apparently having decided to check up on his drunken friend, but took only one step and stopped. Johan turned around again to look at us. A broad mischievous grin spread across his face.

After a few moments, staring at Ella and smiling, he said, "A threesome is on the table if there are any takers!"

Ella's eyes went big.

"Although, technically," I said, "it would be a foursome, wouldn't it?" I giggled. "Hi-hi! A foursome!"

The reason I had decided to go along with Johan's joke was not only that I saw joking as a way of defusing the potentially tense situation we could have found ourselves in if his joke had been taken seriously. But also because I had found the thought of doing something kinky with my wife and the two Danes arousing. My cock was rock hard, and a tingling sensation was building up in my groin, imagining Ella having sex with Johan and Mikkel. And I couldn't resist playing with the idea, although briefly, of course.

Johan chuckled. "He-he! Yeah. Ella, Mikkel, you, me. Yeah, you're right. It makes us four! It would be a foursome."

Ella's jaw now dropped. Literally. She couldn't believe we were serious, and that was when Johan burst into laughter. I joined him.

"Oh! You're awful! Both of you!" Ella squealed and slapped me playfully on the shoulder. She raised her hand at Johan but did not hit him. Instead, she put her hand on her stomach and burst into laughter too. "Ha-ha! Yes, I vote yes for a foursome at the bar! Drinking! The four of us will be having drinks only! Ha-ha."

Johan's face turned serious. "Yeah, drinking only. See you after dinner, Ella! Nick!"

He turned around, and this time he walked up the stairs without stopping or looking back. Ella and I resumed walking towards our block.

We had walked about thirty yards when Ella poked me in the ribs. "What was all that about, Nick?"

"About what?" I asked, pretending I did not know what she was talking about.

"What was all that with the threesomes?"

"Oh, that? Well, apparently, they had a threesome with that girl, Mikkel's fiancée, or whatever she was and—"

"No! Not their threesome! You know what I'm talking about! You! What you said!"

I slapped myself on the forehead. "Oh, that?! Oh, yeah! I was just messing around, hon!"

"Well, don't!" Ella said sternly, but then a mischievous smile curved her lips. She slapped me on the butt and added, "Or I might believe you!"

I stopped walking and looked at Ella. She stopped walking, too and turned to look at me.

"Really? Might you believe me?" I asked her.

She stared at me for a while, then smiled. "No."

We resumed walking, but a few seconds later, I said, "But if you believed me and did it, you'd make my day!"

I don't know how I gathered the courage to say something like that, but I said it. I guess the erection in my trunks was speaking.

Ella stopped walking and grabbed my wrist. I stopped walking, too and put a sheepish grin on my face as we stared at each other.

Ella held her gaze on me for some time before saying, "You are not serious, are you?"

I shrugged my shoulders. "Why? What if I was? Would you do it?"

"Do what?" Ella giggled. "Hi-hi!" She let go of my hand and tickled me in the stomach. "Do what, Nick?"

"A threesome!" I squeaked, laughing, and squirmed backwards.

"I thought you were talking about a foursome!" Ella giggled again. "Hi-hi! A foursome, not a threesome!"

"Yeah, a foursome. Would you do it?" I slapped her on the butt.

Ella stepped back, and her face turned serious. She gave me a long look before asking me, "Would you want me to do it?"

I shrugged my shoulders again. "Well, I find it arousing."

Ella raised her finger and pointed it at me. "Be careful what you wish for!" Her eyes turned playful again, and she giggled. "Hi-hi!" A second later, the smile disappeared from her face. She pressed her finger against my chest and said, stressing her words, "Don't! Even! Joke! About! These! Things! Nicholas!"

Ella turned around and resumed walking.

I stared at her bum. Her thigh muscles moved graciously, and her butt cheeks peeked out of her bikini bottom. I ogled her backside, thinking about how sexy she was. At the same time, I was trying to figure out if her comments meant she had taken the conversation about threesomes and foursomes as innocent banter or if a tiny part of her considered them a possibility.

Ella stopped walking, turned around and shouted to me, "Nick, are you coming or not?"

I ran to her, wrapped my arm around her waist and said, "Let's go have sex, shall we?"

Ella giggled. "Yes, we shall!"

Five minutes later, we were in our hotel room.

This time I decided to fuck Ella in the shower. It wasn't very comfy, but we were too horny to be put off by some minor inconveniences like tight spaces or slippery floors.

I made Ella face the wall and lean against it. She stretched her arms up, put her hands against the wall and spread her legs. I placed my hands on top of hers and ground my crotch against her butt for a while, enjoying the feeling of her ass cheeks squishing against my thighs. Then I lowered my pelvis and slowly began moving it up until my hard cock found her pussy hole, and I penetrated her from behind with a single powerful thrust. It wasn't easy to thrust while my knees were partially bent, so I couldn't move too much. The good thing was that not only I was very turned on, but so was Ella and within less than a minute of her pussy being subjected to my cock, she began orgasming. Moaning and shuddering, she ground her pussy against my cock, pushing her ass against my crotch. That pushed me over the edge, and I hastily pulled my cock out of her pussy because I had not put on a condom. I turned my pelvis away from her and shot my load in the shower, pressing my chest against Ella's back and squeezing her tits from behind.

Ten minutes later, we had finished showering and were lying in bed naked, watching TV. I found the movie Ella had picked boring and soon drifted off.

Ella woke me up at 7:30 for dinner. We put our clothes on and headed for the restaurant.

2. GAMES

POOLSIDE PHOTOS

We did not see Johan or Mikkel in the restaurant, but we saw Gerhard at the cheese bar with Agnete.

"What is she doing here?" I whispered to Ella from across the table.

"Don't know!" Ella replied. "Do the holiday reps stay overnight in the hotel?"

"Apparently, this one does."

We watched Gerhard and Agnete talk for a while. Agnete seemed upset about something, and Gerhard often put his hand on her shoulder and rubbed it comfortingly. When he saw us, he waved at us hello but did not come to talk to us. Instead, he said something to Agnete, who looked at us and nodded with a brief smile, and then the two of them went away, continuing their conversation.

Ella dropped her sandal on the floor, reached her foot under the table and put it on my knee.

"I think Gerhard is doing what you wanted to do," she whispered with a playful smile.

"What do you mean?" I asked.

"Comforting Agnete over the loss of her boyfriend."

"Ha-ha! She needs something more than his lectures!"

"You never know! He might be able to offer her that too!"

Ella's foot slid between my legs. She rubbed my cock with her toes.

"Ha-ha! As if!" I laughed again. I felt my cock grow in my pants and squeezed my legs, trapping her foot. "What about me comforting you?"

"Hi-hi!" Ella giggled and pulled her foot out of my grip. "After dinner!"

Even though Ella and I had fucked a couple of hours earlier, we were still in the mood to talk about sex. During the whole dinner, we giggled and joked about hypothetical threesomes with one waiter or another, commenting on their masculine physiques or fantasising about how they would react if we invited them to fool around with us. Ella was in such a promiscuous mood that she didn't mind when I gave the elevator eyes to a waitress—a tall young black woman. Ella even joked that she would make an exception for the waitress and take part in an MFF threesome with her.

We chuckled quietly, enjoying the dirty talk. The waitress caught us talking about her, and we both froze when she turned to stare at us. To our surprise, she only smiled. Both Ella and I giggled with our hands over our mouths. The waitress carried on doing her job, ignoring us, probably thinking: *Another western couple drinking themselves silly!*

After dinner, Ella and I went to the concert hall for the live performance organised by the hotel. The concert had not started, but we knew the hall would get full quickly once people had finished dining. Hence, we decided to take seats while we could and wait ten minutes or so for the concert to start.

Mikkel and Johan were already at the bar, and when they saw us, they came to say hello. Mikkel had sobered up and behaved himself. In fact, he was rather quiet and even reserved. Johan, on the contrary, had become even more talkative and brazen.

Mikkel sat next to me. Johan did not sit down. He squatted in front of Ella, put his hands on her knees and said jokingly, "Have you thought about my proposal?"

Ella knew what he was joking about but pretended she did not and giggled. "Hi-hi! Johan, what proposal are you talking about?"

Johan looked around and, when he saw that our conversation

had attracted attention from the people in the row behind us, decided not to use the words 'threesome' or 'foursome'. Instead, he said quietly, "The game proposal for three or four players that I said was still on the table."

"Oh, that one?" Ella said. "Nick and I have been talking about it during dinner."

The way she spoke gave the impression she was serious. And in a way, she was. Because we had joked about threesomes.

"Oh, that's..., um, yeah, that's...," Johan mumbled, taken aback by my wife's unexpected answer.

Ella took him out of his misery by bursting into laughter. "Ha-ha! With the waiters! With the waiters, Johan, not with you!"

Johan was even more confused, so I clarified, "We joked about having a 'dinner game'"—I made a sign with my fingers—"with the different waiters passing by while we ate."

He blinked a few times, totally confused. "With the waiters?"

"Ha-ha!" I laughed, shaking my head in amusement. "Johan, Johan! We were fooling around. That's what it was."

"He-he!" Johan chuckled, finally realising Ella and I had been pulling his leg. He rubbed Ella's knees, and his hands slid up her thighs. "You got me, Ella! For a moment, I thought you considered it indeed."

"As I said, I did, but not with you!" Ella said and stuck her tongue out at Johan.

Ella was very much in a playful mood. I liked her when she was mischievous. Whenever she was being naughty, something in her smile made me like her even more. And then there was that playful, suggestive sparkle in her eyes that turned me on.

"Oh, that's a shame!" Johan said, faking disappointment, and his hands slipped further up my wife's thighs, on the insides, coming dangerously close to her pussy.

Ella grabbed his hands and pushed them away from her legs.

Johan sat in the chair next to her. "If you change your mind, Ella, I—"

"OK! Now stop it!" Ella cut him off and slapped him on the leg.

She smiled, but, nonetheless, Johan decided that, at this point, he was pushing his luck too far and changed the subject of the conversation by asking if we had booked any tours. Ella said we had not, and he invited us to join him and Mikkel on a turtle-watching tour they had booked with a local guy for Thursday night. Ella liked turtles but declined his invitation, explaining we had decided not to go on tours. And when I added, under Ella's scornful look, that the reason was that we wanted to stay in the hotel as much as we could so that we had more sex, the two Danes laughed. The conversation was about to take another dangerous turn towards discussing Ella's and my sexual life when a guy from the bar waved at Mikkel and Johan to join him. The two Danes invited us to have drinks with them; however, Ella and I declined.

Johan and Mikkel went to the bar while Ella and I stayed in our seats. The concert started, and we watched it for about ten minutes before one of the professional dancers going between the rows of the audience and urging people to stand up and dance came to us and talked us into getting on the dance floor. At first, Ella and I were a little anxious, but after the first song, we got into the swing of it, and not before long, we were moving our bodies in rhythm with the music, smiling at each other and enjoying ourselves. We were not concerned about what others thought of our dance technique and danced freely, pulling out moves we didn't know we had. We danced for ourselves and the joy of it. Especially Ella! Swaying her hips and shaking her ass, she showed off her body and looked seductively sexy!

Mikkel and Johan were talking to their friend at the bar and drinking, but they both kept looking at us. And while Mikkel only smiled friendly, occasionally waving at us, Johan was shamelessly checking my wife out. He wasn't even trying to hide his lustful looks. And when he saw I caught him, he grinned at me and gave me a thumbs-up. And what did I do? I also smiled at him and gave him a thumbs-up. I did so because I liked him checking Ella out. I was proud of my wife and was excited at the thought that another man had the hots for her.

I lowered my face to Ella's ear and whispered, "Johan's checking you out, honey!"

"I know, right?" she said and stopped dancing. She looked at Johan and smiled coquettishly.

"You like it, don't you?"

"Like what?"

"Giving him hope you'll change your mind."

Smiling coyly, Ella asked, "Change my mind?"

I nodded, smiling too. "Yeah! Change your mind."

"About what?"

"About the threesomes and the foursomes!"

"Ha-ha!" Ella laughed. "I like teasing! And you?"

"What about me?" I asked.

"Do you like me teasing him?"

"Yeah, it's fun watching him getting hooked on you! Tease him!"

"Ha-ha!" Ella laughed again. "You want us to play a little game with him, don't you?"

I nodded. "Yes!"

She slapped me playfully on the butt and resumed dancing, swaying her hips even more seductively.

I looked at Johan and again gave him a thumbs-up.

Taking my gesture as approval, even encouragement, Johan doubled down on checking Ella out. He watched her move her body in sync with the music for another five minutes until he got up from his stool and joined us on the dance floor. Mikkel stayed behind to chat with his friend at the bar, getting himself drunk again.

Johan positioned himself in such a way that he danced close to Ella. He flirted with her subtly but overtly enough to make her aware he was interested in her. He lowered his face to her ear and told her jokes, to which she laughed. He wrapped his arms around her waist as if trying to dance with her one-on-one, pulling her into him and pressing his thighs against hers as they swayed together in rhythm. From time to time, he moved behind her, placing his hands on her hips, and the two danced in sync. Ella was giggling and not pulling away. She didn't mind Johan. I didn't mind him either. It seemed that both Ella and I had gotten ourselves into some weird horny state of mind and were letting our promiscuous sides take over us, going along with Johan's advances.

I was taking in the sight of my wife and this stranger dancing tight to each other, and I had a hard-on. It would have been embarrassing if people had noticed the tent in my shorts, so I tried to tamp down my excitement by telling myself: *He's flirting and checking her out, but so what? It's not up to him, is it? He's just being played! Ella is responding, but she's not flirting for real; she's playing along so we can joke and have fun. Gerhard put these ideas in my head! With his swingers stories and all that! Nothing will happen between Ella and Johan; the three of us are just having a little fun on the dance floor.*

The live music ended, and they announced that the Karaoke session of the night was about to begin.

"Are you going to stay for the Karaoke?" Johan asked us.

"It's not our thing," Ella replied on hers and my behalf, trying to catch her breath and wiping a few beads of sweat off her forehead.

"Neither is mine," Johan said and brushed sweat from his face, too.

Ella was standing in front of him, staring him in the eyes and smiling. Johan was holding her gaze and smiling too. Ella's face was red because she was tired after dancing for over forty minutes, but perhaps there was another reason: arousal. For quite some time, Johan had been touching her arms, breathing in her ears, brushing his cheek against hers, placing his hands on her hips and thighs and pressing his masculine body against hers. There was no way she would not have been aroused after that.

Ella blew away a strand of hair that had fallen across her mouth and looked at me. "What shall we do, honey?"

Before I could answer her question, Johan put his hand on her waist and said, "Let's go for a walk."

Ella looked back at Johan. "For a walk?!"

"Yeah!" He smiled at her and brushed away another strand of hair from her cheek. "Let's go to the pool!"

"Hi-hi!" Ella giggled. "To do what? To swim?"

Johan chuckled. "He-he! No! To take some photos! It's beautiful out there in the evening. I took some pictures yesterday evening. I'll show you! The colours of the night sky are magnificent. There is dust in the air blown from the Sahara desert, and the sky looks fantastic. Look!"

He took out his mobile phone and showed us a selfie of him and Mikkel with the night sky in the background.

"It's beautiful!" Ella said as she looked at the photo.

Johan tucked his phone back into his pocket. "Come! Let's take some photos at the pool. It's quieter there, and the palm trees with the night sky make a wonderful background for pictures!"

"OK!" Ella hooked her hand under my arm. "Let's go!"

"Let's go!" I agreed with her, and we headed for the pool.

As we walked down the walkway meandering through the garden, Johan talked about how the desert dust scatters the blue light making the sky appear redder. He was walking on Ella's other side, talking enthusiastically and occasionally putting his hand on the small of her back for a second or two before removing it. I pretended I did not notice his wandering hand, but of course, I noticed it. Even if I could not see what he was doing out of the corner of my eye, the trembling of Ella's body each time she felt his touch betrayed his actions. Johan kept gauging Ella's and my reaction to his advances until halfway through our walk when he gained enough confidence and wrapped his arm around her waist. Ella let him be. I did not stop him either.

Thus, my wife walked sandwiched between Johan and me, asking him various questions about the desert as if he was a geography expert, glancing at him seductively and smiling flirtatiously. She was flirting with the young Dane, and I didn't mind it. In fact, I enjoyed it. My only concern was that someone could notice the tent in my shorts. Fortunately, the garden was not very well-lit and was not the most popular place at night. We met only one couple who were too preoccupied with themselves to notice anyone else.

Johan had the pleasure of keeping his arm around Ella's waist until we reached the pool, where he took his phone out and pulled Ella closer to him, saying, "Let's have a photo with the moon in the background!"

Ella smiled politely as Johan leaned his head towards hers and took a selfie of himself with her.

"Can I have a look?" she asked.

"Sure!" Johan showed her his phone's screen. "Can you see the sky's colour?"

"Oh, it's beautiful!" Ella gushed. "Orange-red colours on a dark-blue background! Beautiful! Isn't it, Nick?"

I looked at the photo, and just as I said, "Yes, it is," we heard someone's voice behind us, saying, "Oh! There you are!"

We turned around and saw Mikkel, having just climbed up the stairs to the pool area. He was drunk again, swaying as he walked up to us.

Johan showed him the photo on his phone. "Look at Ella's and my photo! It's beautiful, isn't it?"

Mikkel had a quick look at the photo before mumbling, "Yes, she is beautiful! And sexy like hell!"

Ella blushed upon hearing Mikkel's blunt compliment but pretended it was all right and said, "Thank you, Mikkel."

I pulled my phone out. "Johan, would you take a photo of me with my wife, please?" I stretched my hand with the phone to Johan.

Johan finally let go of Ella. He tucked his phone into his pocket, took my phone, stepped a few steps backwards and squatted, taking aim with the camera at us.

He took a photo of Ella and me with my arm around her. He gave me back the phone, and Ella and I looked at the picture. We both liked it.

I put my phone back into my pocket, and just as I thought we had done taking photos, Mikkel pulled out his phone. "Nick, would you take a photo of me with your wife?"

"Umm, yeah...," I said hesitantly and looked at Ella. She smiled shyly and nodded affirmatively, so I added more confidently, "Sure!"

I took Mikkel's phone and stepped back from Ella and him.

I expected Mikkel would stand next to her and, at most, put his arm around her waist as Johan had done, but the drunk man stood behind her and hugged her, wrapping his arms around her waist from behind and hooking his chin over her shoulder.

With his hands on her exposed stomach, below her cami crop top, he pulled her closer to him and pressed his crotch against her ass. Ella trembled and blushed profusely but still smiled. She was showing understanding for Mikkel in his drunken state.

I squatted to take a shot of the two of them with the moon in the background.

Mikkel mumbled something unrecognisable for Ella and me. However, Johan seemed to have understood what Mikkel had said and scolded him in Danish, judging by the sound of his voice.

"No!" Mikkel responded in English, raising his voice. "I want to piss her off! I'll show her the photo and—"

"You don't have to do that!" Johan said in English, too, shaking his head from side to side.

"I have to!" Mikkel shouted. "I have to show her I have moved on. What better way than sending her a photo of me with a woman like Ella? I want her to feel jealous!"

Ella was flattered that Mikkel wanted to show off with her and continued to smile. However, her smile froze when she felt Mikkel's hands slide up under her crop top. He cupped her breasts!

Ella's face flushed crimson red, but she did not push Mikkel's hands away from her tits. She stood still with her chest moving up and down rapidly, making Mikkel's knuckles bulge under the fabric of her top.

I couldn't take my eyes off her chest and Mikkel's hands kneading her boobs, and I felt my cock stiffen rock hard. Mikkel smiled at me as he continued to squeeze my wife's breasts, gently, slowly massaging them.

My cock was about to burst out of my shorts, and I couldn't take it anymore, so I quickly pressed the camera button on the phone.

I stood up and walked up to Mikkel and Ella, holding my hand in front of my crotch. I did not want anyone to see the tent in my shorts. I did not want to reveal to the two Danes or my wife how aroused I had become watching another man feel her up.

"Here you go!" I murmured and stretched my hand with the phone to Mikkel.

Ella was standing still and staring at me.

"Thank you, Ella!" Mikkel said and pulled his hands out from under her tank top. He stepped on her side, put one hand on the small of her back, brushed her hair aside with his other hand, and kissed the side of her exposed neck.

Ella's body trembled as she felt Mikkel's warm lips touch her soft skin, and her mouth opened as if she was trying to say: *What did we get ourselves into, Nick?*

I swallowed nervously but smiled, still holding my hand in the air with Mikkel's phone.

"Thank you!" Mikkel whispered into her ear as his mouth moved away from her neck.

As if in a trance, not taking her eyes off my face, Ella murmured, "You're welcome, Mikkel!"

Mikkel finally let go of her and took his phone from me, saying, "Thank you, Nick!" He tucked the phone into his pocket.

Ella snapped out of her trance-like state and took a step back. Her face was still flushed out of embarrassment but also arousal. She pulled her top down, making sure her breasts were covered and said, "Nick, let's go!"

"Yeah, thank you, guys! It's time to call it a night," I said and reached my hand to Ella's.

She grabbed my hand tight, and we were about to head to the stairs out of the pool area when Johan stepped in front of her.

"You're all right, Ella?" he asked her with concern in his voice and put his hand on her shoulder.

She pushed his hand off her. "Yeah, I'm all right. Good night!"

She hooked her hand under my arm and urged me again, "Nick, let's go!"

This time Ella turned around and pulled me to follow her.

"Good night!" I managed to say to the guys, and we walked briskly to the stairs.

We literally ran down the stairs. We turned right and took the walkway leading to our block building.

We walked fast, with long steps, without looking back, as if trying to run away from a crime scene.

CONFESSIONS

We did not speak, just walked with haste, almost ran.

I was thinking to myself: *God, what a sight she was! Standing and staring at me with Mikkel's hands on her boobs! Blushing and unable to move, shocked and, at the same time, excited.* My hard cock was poking in my shorts. It was uncomfortable to walk. Especially that fast. I looked at Ella. She was looking ahead of her. She was rushing.

Probably she's reflecting that she allowed too much tonight! Flirting with Johan at first and then letting Mikkel feel her boobs.

I was horny but also worried. I was concerned that Ella was distraught by what she had let Johan, and especially Mikkel, do to her. And in turn, I was worried she might blame me.

She might blame me that I didn't stop her from doing it. Stop her? I actually encouraged her to do it! I started to panic. *Fuck me! Of course, she'll blame me! Fuck!* My excitement got replaced by dread. Yet my cock stayed hard as ever. *Whatever!* I told myself. *It can't be helped. I'll just have to face the music. Yep, the moment we get in our room, she'll give me hell!*

We reached our room, and I opened the door.

I took a deep breath. *Here we go!*

We entered the room, and I shut the door behind us.

Ella turned around to face me and wrapped her arms around my neck. Our eyes met, and I read lust in hers. Nothing but lust!

I had misread my wife so much!

She wanted us to have sex! Now!

I grabbed her by the waist and pulled her towards me. We kissed passionately for a while, breaking the kiss for a second or two only to catch our breaths before resuming kissing.

Finally, after two minutes of incessant kissing, Ella let go of my neck, grabbed the waistband of my shorts, and pulled them down. I pulled down my briefs myself, letting my hard cock spring out. Then I pulled Ella's top up. She raised her arms, and I pulled her cami over her head, baring her tits. I threw the tank top onto the chair next to us, grabbed her shorts and pulled them down to her knees. A second later, her thong was at her knees too. I put my hands on her shoulders and nudged her to lie on her back on the bed.

She kicked her sandals off and lay on her back. She lifted her legs up, and I completely took off her shorts and thong.

I took a condom out of my pocket, unwrapped it and rolled it over my cock. Then I peeled off my t-shirt, kicked my shoes off, stepped out of my shorts and briefs and climbed on the bed.

"What do you think of Mikkel and Johan?" I asked Ella as I looked at her horny face.

"What am I supposed to think about them?" Ella asked me back, a little irritated by my question.

She bent her knees and spread her legs with her feet flat on the bed. I knecled between her legs and reached my hand between her thighs. I felt her pussy. She was wet. Ella reached down between my legs and grabbed my cock.

"Did you like them?" I said.

"Fuck me!" she whispered, ignoring my question.

I ran my hand over her neatly shaved labia up to her clit and onto her landing strip, teasingly scratched her pubic hair and then dragged my fingers down to her vaginal entrance, parting her pussy lips.

Ella moaned.

"So, what do you think about Mikkel and Johan?" I asked as I drew my fingers up between her pussy lips, along the length of her wet slit.

"Urgh!" she moaned as the excitement in her groin grew. "They are brazen," she finally said.

"But you like them, don't you?"

"Nick!" Ella put her hand on my stomach. "I know what you're on about. It bothers you; it bothers me too. We wanted to mess around a little, tease them a bit, laugh, and that's fine, but it went out of hand in the heat of the moment. It went too far, and God knows what they're thinking about me now. I am ashamed, and so are you. I know! And I worry they've taken something that was just a game too seriously."

"Yeah, it was just a game, but I was thinking maybe—"

"Are you gonna fuck me or not?"

Ella removed her hand from my abdomen. I lay on top of her, and we kissed.

After we broke the kiss, Ella looked at me and, saying, "Fuck me!" she opened her legs further apart.

Propped on my left hand, I used my right hand to guide my cock to the entrance of her pussy. My cockhead touched her pussy lips, and Ella trembled.

I moved my cock up and down her slit, opening up her pussy lips and whispered, "I know it was just a game, but if it weren't. If we turned it into something else. Whom would you like more?"

Ella put her hand on my chest and stared at me. "You are not serious, are you?"

"Not serious about what?" I asked.

Ella whispered, "Like . . . you aren't implying that you want me to have. . . ."

She did not finish her sentence but gasped because, at that moment, I pushed my cock between her inner pussy lips and penetrated her in one thrust.

I thrust again, and she groaned, "Urgh!"

Ella wrapped her legs around my waist, locked her arms around my neck, and I started fucking her with long slow thrusts.

She closed her eyes and began moaning.

"What I meant was whether you find one of them more attractive than the other," I said and switched to thrusting hard and fast.

"Oh, fuck!" Ella squealed and opened her eyes. "Fuck me harder! Harder!"

She grabbed my hair and pulled it.

I was quickly coming to the point of no return. Now I was thrusting frantically.

"So?" I asked.

"Ahh!" Ella moaned and then said, breaking the words as I was shaking her body with my thrusts, "I think they are both attractive.... Ahh! Oh, my God! Oh! Oh!"

Ella was reaching orgasm.

I felt my cock twitching.

"Urgh!" she groaned and squeezed her thighs around my waist. "I like Johan more."

I increased the speed of my thrusts. "But Mikkel seems pushier. He felt your boobs!"

Ella squeaked, "Fuck! Oh, fuck!"

"Urgh!" I grunted. "Which of the two you'd enjoy more?"

"I won't have sex with them, Nick!" Ella shouted, followed by a high-pitched "Oh!"

My cock began throbbing. "Why not?"

"Oh! Fuck!" Ella cried before adding, "'Cos, I'm your wife!"

I began slamming my cock deep into her.

"Oh! Fuck!" she squealed, let go of my hair and crossed her arms around my neck.

I kept thrusting, and she kept moaning, "Oh-oh-oh!"

"Ah! Ella, you're amazing!" I shouted, thrusting in her pussy like there was no tomorrow. I asked through huffs and puffs, "So you won't let them fuck you?"

"Ugh!" came from her mouth before she muttered, "Do you want me to?"

"I don't know!" I wailed.

My cock began throbbing uncontrollably as I started to ejaculate.

I rasped, "Maybe!" A second later, I shouted, "Argh!" overwhelmed by the feeling of semen gushing through my urethra. "Would you do it, Ella?"

Ella did not answer my question. Instead, she closed her eyes, savouring the pleasure spreading from her groin throughout her entire body, and a couple of seconds later, she shuddered in orgasm.

Once our orgasms subsided, I pulled my cock out of her pussy and lay beside her.

"This was great, hon!" I said, panting.

"Yeah! It was, wasn't it?" Ella rubbed her tits before she turned her head to look at me and smiled.

"We're having great sex, aren't we?" I sat up. "As good as when we were newlywed. Maybe even better!"

"Yep! Better!" Ella got off the bed. "Isn't that what we said we wanted when we booked this holiday?"

I took off the condom and tied it up. "What about taking it to the next level?"

Ella watched me get off the bed, not answering my question, so I clarified, "I mean, the Gerhard and Monika's way. What would you say?"

She held her gaze on me for a few moments before she sighed and said, "Be careful what you wish for, Nick! Be careful!"

Ella headed for the shower, but stopped in front of the bathroom, turned around and asked me, "You're not being serious, are you?"

I smiled sheepishly. "I might be!"

"Do you know what that would mean?"

"I know one thing, Ella. I want us to have fun!"

"You do realise that it's one thing to fantasise and another to do it!"

"I do." I nodded. "But you have no idea how much what Gerhard said got stuck in my head and how horny the idea makes me!"

Ella raised her eyebrows and pointed at her chest. "I have no idea?"

I shook my head. "No, you have no idea, honey."

Ella gave me a long look and then said, "Why do you think I've been so turned on since this morning, Nick?"

She caught me by surprise.

I stared at her, trying to comprehend what she had just said. *Did she just admit she also found the idea arousing?*

As if Ella read my question, she said quietly, "But I know very well that it is one thing getting aroused by talking and fantasising about it and a very different thing if we actually did it!"

She went into the bathroom, and I followed her.

We took a shower together, kissing and fondling.

We did not talk about Mikkel, Johan, Gerhard, or Monika for the rest of the evening.

AT THE POOL BAR

The next morning, Ella and I woke up on time and were much better organised than the previous day. We went to breakfast early, changed into swimming gear and were amongst the first to get to the pool. Of course, almost all of the loungers already had towels on them because most of the guests were waking up at ridiculously early hours to run to the pool and reserve loungers by placing towels on them before going to breakfast.

Fortunately for us, Gerhard was already there and had 'reserved' two sunbeds for us next to his own.

"Hello, my friends!" he greeted us.

We said hello, and Ella bent over to lay her towel on the sun lounger closer to Gerhard's. Gerhard raised himself up on his elbows and turned his head to look at her backside. Her firm ass cheeks poked out of the edges of her bikini bottom. They were so round and white. And the sight between her legs! One could see so clearly the outlines of her pussy from behind.

I caught Gerhard's gaze on my wife's ass, and he winked at me. He wasn't hiding that he was ogling her butt.

"How was your evening?" he asked Ella after she sat down on the lounger, facing him.

"We went to the concert," she said.

"And we danced," I added and tossed my towel on the other sunbed.

"I saw you!" Gerhard said. "I was sitting with a friend at the bar at the far end of the hall. Unfortunately, I'm too old to dance; otherwise, I would have loved to join you and your new friend on the dance floor. The three of you looked great! Nick was dancing like a real pro, and Ella, swaying from side to side in sync with the young fellow, so intimate and sensual! You looked great! Loved it!"

Ella blushed, hearing Gerhard imply she and Johan had been dancing too close to each other.

"The young fellow's name is Johan," I said and sat beside Ella on her lounger, facing Gerhard. "We met him in the aqua park. It turned out he's a friend of Mikkel."

Gerhard sat up on the edge of his sunbed. "I know they're friends. They asked for my sun loungers yesterday, remember? I just didn't know his name." He leaned towards Ella and me and said quietly, "He's got a feminine face. Initially, I thought he was gay."

"He's definitely not," I said as I shook my head, smiling. "Trust me!"

Gerhard chuckled quietly and looked at Ella while talking to me. "Oh, now I know, Nick. I watched how this Johan bloke was hitting on your lovely wife last night! He didn't look gay to me!"

Ella's eyes went big.

"Sorry!" Gerhard said. "Did I overstep with my comment? I'm sometimes overzealous in my role as an analyst. Sorry! Let's go have a drink! They just opened the pool bar."

The three of us got up and slowly walked down the pool steps. The water was still cold. The pool was unheated, and it was barely eight o'clock in the morning. The good thing was we were the only people at the bar and were served straight away.

Gerhard sipped from his vodka and said, "While we are alone, let me tell you a little bit about the lifestyle Monika and I had and how we came about it."

Gerhard went on to tell us that he had always been keen to share Monika, but she had been hesitant initially. However, when he had a cancer scare, she decided to help him live out his dream, and they went to a swinger's club. Their plan had been to proceed slowly, perhaps by starting with Monika kissing another guy, see how it goes, then doing a soft swap and maybe eventually a full swap. Nothing was set in stone, though. They had agreed to pull out at any moment if one of them felt even slightly uncomfortable. Thus, at the club, Monika got spooked, and they went home without doing anything. A week later, they visited the same club, and this time Monika seemed determined to at least kiss another man, but then Gerhard got scared, and they went back home again without doing anything. For two months, they went to the sex club every week and, each time, backed off. Then they had a long conversation, and to Gerhard's surprise, Monika admitted that after she had watched others make out and fuck, she had warmed up a lot to the idea of doing it, but she was concerned about his reaction afterwards. Gerhard assured her he was still keen to go ahead with it and that he would be OK. Thus, they decided to try one last time, and if they couldn't do it, they would give up. They went to the same club again, and as before, once there, they had second thoughts and were about to leave without doing anything when a guy called Manfred walked up to their table.

The bartender noticed we had finished our drinks, came to us and asked if we wanted a refill. Gerhard ordered a second round of vodka, and after our drinks arrived, he continued his tale.

"So," he said, "Manfred took a seat at our table, and we introduced ourselves. Then he said, 'I've been watching you two come and go without swapping.'

"And I said, 'Well, we are not into swapping. I only want to share my wife. But we've never done it before, and we kinda want to do it, but each time we come here, we chicken out.'

"'I see.' Manfred smiled. 'May I give you some advice?'

"Both Monika and I nodded yes.

"Manfred said, 'Most people recommend starting it slowly, just a kiss, then a soft swap, then a full swap. I think otherwise. I believe that going straight on with a full swap is the best way.

Going slow is like going on the beach and walking slowly into the water. Going slowly means you have time to overthink and talk yourself out of doing it. You keep telling yourself how cold the water is and not only missing out on the excitement of getting into the sea but getting scared to the point of turning back and getting out. That's why I think the best way is to just jump into the deep. Just dive in! It's easier and safer. I can help you dive straight into the deep. Shall we?'

"'Now?' I asked.

"And he went: 'Yeah, now! Remember: don't overthink it and dive straight into the deep!'"

Gerhard paused and ordered a third round of drinks since our glasses were empty. We were so engrossed in his tale that we were not noticing how quickly we were drinking.

As soon as the drinks arrived, he continued his story by saying, "So, Monika said, 'The thing is, Manfred, each time a man approaches me, I am thinking that he is not my husband, and I become too self-conscious and back off.'

"And I chimed in, 'Same here! Each time it is about to happen, I get butterflies in my stomach. I get scared and start to doubt if I can let it happen. I get worried if I will be able to cope with jealousy. We come back home, and I regret not letting Monika do it. The next time we come here, it happens again.'

"Manfred said, 'Make it ambiguous!'

"And I went: 'What do you mean?'

"He smiled. 'Make it so that you are not sure if it is happening or not.'

"Both Monika and I raised our eyebrows.

"'I don't get what you mean,' I said.

"'There is a game for this,' Manfred explained, taking a deck of cards out of his pocket. He pulled three clubs and put them on the table. Then he added a spade and shuffled the four cards. He took another three clubs, added a spade, and shuffled the second deck of four cards."

Gerhard paused because two blokes came to the bar, but after they ordered and sat at the other end, he continued with his story. "So, where was I? Oh, yeah! So Manfred said, 'We'll ask Klaus, a friend of mine, over there'—he nodded at a bloke who waved at us—'to help run the game for us. You and Monika will be blindfolded. Monika, you'll draw a card from this deck'—he placed one of the two decks of four cards in front of my wife and turned to me—'and you'll draw a card from this deck.' He placed the second deck in front of me and continued to explain, 'You won't know which card you have drawn. Klaus will put the card each of you has drawn into your pocket.

"'We have several private rooms in the club. Klaus will take you to separate rooms. You'll both take your clothes off but won't take your blindfolds off or take the cards out of your pockets. OK? But Klaus will know what cards you have drawn.

"'The rule is this: If Monika has drawn a club, she won't be fucked. If she has drawn a spade, she will be. So, if Monika has drawn a club, she will be left alone in the room, and nothing will happen. She won't know if she is about to be fucked or not. This will allow her to live through the motions.

"'Gerhard, you also won't be told what she has drawn and will wait in your room for a while. You won't know if someone is fucking her or if you will be taken to fuck her. Thus: if Monika has drawn clubs, it doesn't matter what you have drawn. Nothing will happen. The two of you will be just living through the motions.

"'However, if she's drawn a spade, then what you've drawn matters. If you have drawn a spade, too, Klaus will take me to her, and I will fuck your wife while you're waiting in your room without knowing it. Monika won't know who's fucking her because I won't talk. If you have drawn a club, you will be taken to your wife, and you will fuck her. You won't talk either!

Remember! This is an important rule: neither you nor I will talk! So, she won't know who's fucking her. You both won't talk or look at the cards in your pockets until you are back home. Only then you'll take them out and find out what has happened.'"

Gerhard paused and waved at the barman for a fourth round of drinks.

The guy brought the drinks, and Gerhard continued with his tale. "I hesitated. Manfred saw it and said, 'Look, the odds that I fuck Monika are what? One out of sixteen, right? The chance you fuck your wife is three out of sixteen, am I right? And twelve out of sixteen—nothing happens. You'll get back home, and if she hasn't been shared, you will still have lived through the angst, and the two of you will know what it would have felt like. Then you might repeat the game next time or decide not to do it ever again. Your fantasy remains a fantasy, and never try living it through. Or just go ahead sharing her. Regardless of what you decide, you will have taken an informed decision. If Monika has been shared, well, it has happened. You will have dived into the deep my way.'

"'Hmm. Let us think about it,' I said.

"And do you know what Manfred said?

"He said, 'You feel butterflies in your stomach right now, don't you?'

"Both Monika and I nodded yes.

"He said, 'Your butterflies represent fun or fear, but you won't know what it is until you see them fly out. Why don't you let them fly out and find out what they represent? Otherwise, you'll always wonder what it could have been if we had gone ahead with this, and, well, you'll never know.'

"Monika and I thought for a while, and in the end, we agreed to be blindfolded, drew cards and were taken to the rooms. I waited for about half an hour. The most agonising thirty minutes of my life and the most exciting at the same time. Then Klaus came back and asked me to put my clothes on. Whatever had happened in the other room, if anything had happened, I had not been part of it. He led me out of the room. He did not tell me where he was taking me. When he removed my blindfold, we were at the bar, and there was my wife.

"Klaus removed her blindfold and said, 'The cards you drew are in your pockets. Check them when you get home.'

"Monika briefly smiled at me, I smiled back, and then we both looked away from each other. We did not want to be guessing answers by looking for clues in our facial expressions. We would find the answers at home anyway.

"Klaus called a taxi for us and accompanied us to the gate. Monika and I sat in the back seat and continued not speaking and avoiding looking at each other. I glanced at her once, but she was stubbornly looking away from me, staring outside through her window.

"I couldn't read her face, but the way she had crossed her legs gave me a pause for thought. *Why is she squeezing her thighs together like this? Could it be a subconscious action? Protecting her pussy after it had taken a cock? Or being chafed? Fuck! Manfred looked quite endowed. Could it be? Could he have. . . ?*

"I did not want to torture myself, perhaps for nothing, so I forced myself not to look at her. Thus we travelled in silence, not looking at each other. It was only a thirty-minute drive, but it felt like hours. Regardless of our angst and trepidation, we resisted speaking or checking our pockets until we got home. However, as soon as we shut the door behind us, we looked at each other and kissed. Then we took out the cards.

"Both Monika and I had drawn spades. Manfred had fucked my wife.

"We continued visiting the club for about a year twice a month. Mainly Manfred fucked Monika, but also Klaus and another guy a few times. I only watched in the beginning, but at one point, I started to participate.

"Manfred became our favourite bull and remained a permanent member of our relationship.

"Years later, he admitted that he had swapped the cards once we had been blindfolded, and there had been only spades in the two decks he had given us to draw from. Monika and I were not angry at him for his deceit. We were thankful. As he had said, the best way to manage through the emotions of doing it the first time, both for wife and husband, is to not know what is going on or at least to pretend not to know."

We finished our drinks in silence, reflecting on what Gerhard had just told us. It was becoming busy as more and more hotel guests were flocking to the pool, so we headed back to the sun loungers.

POOL VOLLEYBALL

Ella and I were pretty tipsy and lay down on our loungers to sunbathe but also to sober up. Gerhard took his book to read and soon fell asleep. Ella also seemed to drift off, and it wasn't long before I followed her into the land of Nod.

Ella woke me up to ask if I wanted to join her at a dance class; it was about to start in the swimming pool. I wasn't keen on jumping around in the water, but Ella went and joined the dance group that had already gathered in the pool. The dance class consisted mainly of women, so I got up and prepared to feast my eyes on all those bodies.

Gerhard had also woken up and offered to bring me a beer from the poolside bar. I gladly accepted his offer.

When he came back with our beers, Ella and the others were already dancing in the water, rocking their bodies, and waving their arms as directed by the dance instructor at the poolside.

Gerhard gave me my glass and sat down on his lounger.

He looked at the dancing women in front of us and then, leaning toward me, said, "Would you mind if I ogled your wife?"

I stared at him for a second but then burst into laughter. "Ha-ha! Be my guest, Gerhard! Watching's free!" I raised my glass. "Cheers!"

He raised his glass too. "Cheers!"

We drank beer and watched the women dance. Ella was the prettiest woman and had one of the sexiest bodies.

Not taking my eyes off the dancing women, I leaned to Gerhard and asked him, "How's the ogling going on?"

Not taking his eyes off the dance class either, he replied, "Excellent!"

"Which of them do you fancy the most?" I asked.

"Your wife," he said straight away. "I fancy her the most."

I looked at him at the same time he looked at me. Our eyes met. He smiled. The old man wasn't joking. He fancied my wife.

"Right," I said. "So given a chance—"

"And capability," Gerhard said, "yes, I'd fuck her." He grinned at me shamelessly.

I held his gaze for a few seconds before I murmured, "I'm sure you would," and drank from my glass.

We resumed watching the women dance in silence.

The dance class finished at 11:30. Ella went to the swim-up bar for a drink. A Caucasian guy with dark hair and a goatee beard, probably in his mid-forties, began chatting her up. She laughed at a joke he probably said to her. The bartender—a black guy in his thirties, slightly shorter than the average Cape Verdean—also threw a joke, and Ella and the bloke with the goatee beard laughed. The barman had to attend to other clients but occasionally interjected a comment or two in the conversation between Ella and her bearded friend. It was clear that the two men were hitting on my wife.

"Your wife's on a roll," Gerhard said.

"Yeah. She is," I agreed with him.

"And?"

"And what?"

"Would you let her?"

"Let her what, Gerhard?!" I asked him abruptly, knowing very well what he was asking about and feeling annoyed by his directness.

He leaned closer to me and whispered, "Let her get fucked by another man."

"I'm not the one letting her do anything, Gerhard," I said, raising my voice. "She's the one who lets or not. I don't possess her!"

"Sorry! I didn't mean to wind you up," Gerhard apologised.

"Why? Why are you so keen to know?"

"Sorry, I just—"

"You just what? Curious? Or you want to fuck her yourself?"

Gerhard stared at me for a few moments, then said quietly, "You're getting pissed off. Let's not talk about it!"

"No, tell me!" I insisted. "Why? Do you want to fuck her?"

"Yes, I'd gladly fuck her given the chance, as I already told you, but that's not why I asked you. I just wanted to find out if you are ready to embrace the lifestyle."

I looked away from Gerhard. I was pissed off, indeed. I took a deep breath and exhaled. I moved my gaze to Ella and watched her for a while as she giggled with the two men, and then I thought: *It's not Gerhard's fault that I have a cuckold fetish, or that he wants to fuck my wife. Who wouldn't?* I sighed to myself, looked at Gerhard and said, "Sorry. I shouldn't have lashed out at you. I'm a little nervous, you know."

"Oh, I know." He waved his hand. "You are on the brink of a massive lifestyle change. But it's a change for good, Nick."

I put my long-empty glass on the ground. "To answer your question: I won't stand in the way if she decides to go for it. OK?"

"That's the most sensible approach, Nick!"

Ella finished her drink, said goodbye to the stranger at the bar and the chatty bartender, and joined Gerhard and me at the loungers.

"How was it, hon?" I asked her.

"Great! You should have joined me," she chirruped.

I grinned at her. "In the dance class or at the bar?"

Ella stared at me, unsure if I had turned jealous, but then pointed at the bar over her shoulder and said, "Oh, those guys? They were just, you know, commenting on my dancing."

"Like, how you danced?" I asked. "How sexy you looked?"

"Umm, yeah," Ella mumbled. Then she asked me rapidly, "Are you jealous, Nick?"

I smiled. "No, of course not. I just wanted to hear it. You know how proud I am of you."

Ella smiled, finally realising I enjoyed hearing she was an object of attention. She said, "They said I danced well, said I looked well, yeah, you know how men are, nothing lewd, just suggestive. Apparently, the curves of my hips and bum were most impressive. You shouldn't leave me alone, Nick! Next time you should come with me."

I chuckled. "He-he! Sure I will! Both to the dance class and the bar!"

Gerhard interjected, "Ella, the truth is, you look great!"

"Thanks!" Ella chirped and took her towel to dry herself.

She had just sat down on her sunbed when Johan and Mikkel came out of the poolside bar.

Gerhard waved at them to join us, and they walked up to us.

"Hello," Mikkel and Johan said almost simultaneously as they stood before Ella and me.

"Hi!" I greeted them.

Gerhard nodded. "Hello, there!"

"Hi," Ella said briefly and looked away. She must have recollected the events of the previous night and felt a little embarrassed looking at the guys who had not only flirted with her, but one of them had groped her boobs.

"There will be a pool volleyball game," Johan said. "Mikkel and I will play. Would you like to join us?"

"Um, no," I declined. "I drank too much."

"He-he!" Gerhard chuckled. "I'm afraid I drank too much too, but, Nick, it is a good way to burn through the alcohol! Shall we?"

"I don't know," I replied.

"Ella?" Johan turned to Ella. "Come play with us and set an example for your husband!"

Ella had been stubbornly looking away but now looked at him and blushed.

Johan knew why she was embarrassed and chuckled. "He-he! Don't be shy, Ella! We won't be taking photos or anything! It's just a volleyball game! You'll like it, come!"

Ella shook her head from side to side. "No, thank you, Johan. I've never played volleyball."

"Oh, it's easy! I'll teach you!" Johan squatted in front of her. He put his hands on her knees and looked up at her face.

Ella smiled shyly. "You'll waste your time with me. I am a slow learner."

"Oh, that's rubbish!" Johan slid his hands up her legs. "You'll learn in no time. Hitting the ball comes naturally."

"I don't think so," Ella said.

"Oh, come on, Ella!" Johan tilted his head to the side and smiled. "It's like dancing. Remember yesterday?! How we synced up on the dance floor? Imagine I am a ball. And we dance and move together." His hands crept further up Ella's thighs.

She blushed big time and, smiling, said, "I'll need a lot of imagination, Johan!"

Johan's hands continued to slide up Ella's legs and now reached her mid-thighs.

He persisted in his attempt to talk her into joining the volleyball game. "It's all about syncing your upper and lower body movements. It starts with the legs. Imagine you are receiving the ball. You have to adjust your body posture for balance. And how do you do that? You slightly bend the knees and spread the legs a bit."

Johan grinned at her, and his hands slipped down between Ella's legs, on the inside of her thighs. He gently nudged her to open her legs a little, and, to my surprise, Ella did. At that moment, I realised she was more than tipsy, and her inhibitions had been lowered.

Johan kept staring her in the face, whispering, "You see. The leg movement is key."

Ella was holding his gaze. She was not saying anything and looked like she was in a trance. Her chest was moving up and down rapidly, and her breathing was becoming louder. She felt Johan's hands on her legs but seemed unable to stop them from moving up her thighs; she kept staring at him and blushing.

Johan continued to explain, "If you watch the ball, the leg movement comes naturally: acceleration, level changes, deceleration."

His hands slipped dangerously close to the triangle of Ella's bikini bottom that covered her pussy.

Gerhard, Mikkel and I had fixed eyes on Ella's cameltoe as Johan's hands were moving ever closer to it.

The tips of Johan's fingers brushed the outline of her pussy lips, which were puffed up, clearly discernible through the fabric of her bikini briefs.

He whispered, "It's like having sex; the moves come naturally, and you play—"

"No, thanks!" Ella said abruptly, grabbed Johan's hands and pushed them away from her pussy. She closed her legs. "I'll watch you guys play." She turned to me. "Nick, you can play if you want."

Her face was flushed red out of embarrassment but even more out of arousal. Johan's hands crawling up her thighs so close to her private parts had turned her on too much. She didn't want to show it, didn't want to blush, but she couldn't stop it. The alcohol in her blood wasn't helping either.

"Are you sure, Ella?" Johan asked her as he stood up. He had a boner.

Ella's gaze fell on the tent in his trunks, but she pretended she did not notice his erection and only said, "No, thanks!"

Johan looked at me. "You coming?"

I said, "I'll watch too."

"OK." He shrugged. "If you change your mind, come join us. It's a fun game. They don't count the number of players in the teams; as long as it is not too overcrowded, you can join at any time."

Johan and Mikkel headed for the pool.

Ella, Gerhard, and I watched silently the two teams gather on the opposite sides of the net. A guy from the hotel's entertainment team turned on some music and began shouting instructions about the game from the poolside using a megaphone. It became loud, so Ella, Gerhard and I had to raise our voices to hear each other.

"You know, it's none of my business," Gerhard said, with his gaze on the pool, "but, sometimes, it's worth giving it a go. Even if you are a little scared. You know, those butterflies in the stomach I talked about? They are a huge part of having fun."

Ella and I looked at Gerhard.

She asked him, "Why do you want us to do it, Gerhard?"

Gerhard knew precisely what my wife was asking him about and said with a playful twinkle in his eye, "Because I know you both want to have a taste of it and need a little encouragement to make it happen. I believe in letting those butterflies fly out. Give in to the temptation! You can always pull back if you feel things are getting out of hand, but you cannot pull back from something if you haven't started it, you know. And how will you know if you like it if you've never tried it? Even a little? Just a little fun?"

Ella looked at Johan and Mikkel. Johan immediately caught her gaze and waved at her. She did not wave back, just smiled and, still looking at him, said, "Fun is never free, Gerhard. It always comes at a cost. There are consequences."

"Life itself comes at a cost but is worth living, isn't it?" Gerhard said. "Please give the old man some joy to watch you play with the boys! Dip your toes in the water a little!"

Ella wasn't saying anything. She was watching Johan, who was warming up by stretching his arms, showing off his physique.

Mikkel waved at Ella. She waved back at him.

"They are willing to help you play," Gerhard said. "Take up on their offer!"

Ella turned her head and looked at him.

"Why not?" Gerhard shrugged his shoulders, smiling. "It's just a game, Ella." He stood up and stretched out his hand, inviting her to take it. "I'll play if you play too."

Ella was not taking his hand. She stared at him until a smile curved her lips, and she said, "Volleyball. Right?"

Gerhard nodded yes. "Volleyball, Ella. That's what I am asking you to do. To play a little volleyball with the boys."

"OK!" Ella finally took his hand and stood up. "Nick, will you play?"

"Yes, let's play some fun volleyball!" I said and rose.

The game was about to start, but Johan saw us heading for the pool and raised his hand, signalling his mate, who was about to serve, to wait for us. All eyes turned to us as the players waited for us to join them in the pool.

Ella, Gerhard, and I reached the pool ladder, and Gerhard put his hand on the small of my wife's back.

He said to her, "You do realise that every man around is leering at you because you are unbelievably hot, Ella!"

"You're making me self-conscious, Gerhard!" Ella said and blushed. She slowly looked around and appeared intimidated for a second but then giggled. "Hi-hi! They are indeed!"

I looked around and caught quite a few guys ogling my wife. Ella's cheeky bikini bottom provided a medium bum cover, and the black fabric contrasted against her white skin, making her firm buttocks stand out. The V-shape cut of her cheeky bottom was designed to attract lustful looks and not only showed plenty of bum cheek but accentuated her long legs. Ella's firm ass definitely attracted most of the attention, but many eyes also wandered up to her nicely shaped breasts, slightly spilling out at the edges of the cups of her bikini top.

Gerhard lowered his head to her ear and said, "But you like feeling butterflies, don't you?"

Ella moved her head back and looked at him. "It turns out I do, actually."

Gerhard's hand slipped down from the small of her back, just a little, but enough for his fingers to end up on her bottom. "You see? You've just discovered something new about yourself."

A mischievous smile flickered across Ella's face before she said, "And something new about you!"

Gerhard raised his eyebrows. "About me?"

"Yes, about you." Ella leaned her mouth to his ear. "Your hand on my ass tells me something about you."

Gerhard removed his hand from her butt and pulled his head back to look at Ella's face. He smiled apologetically and shrugged his shoulders. "Well, I'm a man, after all."

Ella grabbed the handrails of the pool ladder. "Let's not keep everyone waiting for us!"

She climbed down into the pool, and Gerhard and I followed her.

Another couple had gathered the courage to play and entered the pool from the other side, joining the opposing team, and the game finally started.

Gerhard hadn't really intended to play because he leaned his back against the pool wall and prepared to watch us play. He had only wanted to make Ella and me join Johan and Mikkel.

I tried to play for the first five minutes, even spiked the ball once and scored a point, but I realised that it was not a competitive game but more of a fun party game. Four or five people in each team were actually playing; the rest seemed to be watching or fooling around. Johan and Mikkel were in the group that was fooling around. And the two Danes were fooling around in all senses of the word. And they were doing it with my wife.

Mikkel had managed to assume the role of Ella's volleyball teacher, to the great dissatisfaction of Johan. I was not sure whether Mikkel lied about having played in a volleyball club as he was claiming—he was not tall enough for this sport—but certainly, he was competent enough to exude the confidence of a coach.

I heard him saying to Ella, "First, you learn how to pass the ball."

"Yeah, let me show you," Johan said, taking her hands in his. "You put your hands like this to receive."

Mikkel stepped behind Ella and, pressing his chest against her back, grabbed her hands from behind and forced Johan to let go of her.

"You bend your knees a little," Mikkel said and hooked his chin over her shoulder. "Push your bum against me, Ella!"

Ella smiled shyly and hesitated. Mikkel held her wrists in one hand and placed his other hand on her stomach. Ella giggled and looked at me.

I smiled and nodded. She knew this was my signal that I wanted to watch her flirt with Mikkel and Johan.

She looked at Gerhard.

He smiled at her, too, and gave her a thumbs-up. He also wanted to watch her flirt with the two Danes.

And Ella was going to give us what we wanted. She looked ahead of her and pushed her bum out, inches away from Mikkel's crotch.

Mikkel pressed his hand tighter against her stomach. "Half-squat, Ella! Push your bum against me, don't be shy; that's how you learn to play."

I stopped playing at all because my twitching cock did not allow me to think of anything else but what my wife was doing. I walked up to Mikkel, Johan and Ella. I had to be closer and watch!

Someone from the poolside tossed four or five balls into the pool. One landed in front of Johan, and he took it.

"Mikkel, let me show Ella how to strike," Johan said and turned to Ella. "I will—"

Mikkel cut his friend off, "Don't interfere! She needs to learn to receive first." Mikkel added something in Danish, and Johan stepped back.

"Stand by, Johan!" Mikkel switched back to English. "When I tell you, pass the ball into her hands."

Johan was visibly not happy to be bossed around by Mikkel, but when the latter shouted something in Danish again, Johan held the ball and waited for instructions.

Mikkel whispered into Ella's ear, "Now, try to relax your shoulders!" Then he looked at Johan and ordered him, "Throw!"

Johan tossed the ball into Ella's hands, and, helped by Mikkel, she hit it.

"Yeah!" she squealed in delight and started to jump with excitement, forcing Mikkel to let go of her.

I looked around, concerned we were obstructing the game, but

I saw the game had disintegrated into smaller groups of people playing between themselves.

"Let's do it again!" Mikkel grabbed Ella's hands from behind. "Squat a little! That's it!"

Johan had picked up the ball and prepared to toss it to Ella.

"Push your bum out, Ella!" Mikkel said as he pressed his chest against her back.

Mikkel was a different person when sober: confident, smiling, and charming.

"A little more! Don't be afraid to touch me, Ella!" he encouraged my wife, and she pushed her bum out.

Ella giggled when her butt touched Mikkel's crotch.

"Get ready to receive the ball!" Mikkel instructed her. "Push your bum out a little more!"

Ella giggled again but did not push her ass further out.

"Don't be afraid, Ella!" Mikkel said. "Stick it out! It's an underhand bump rather than a hit. You need to do it in a controlled manner with minimal arm swing. The easiest way is if you have flexibility in your knees. And the way to achieve it is to squat a little. Push your bum out a little more! Don't be shy! We are learning a game!"

Ella pushed her bum further out. She was pressing her backside tightly against Mikkel's crotch.

"Now look at the ball and grind your butt!" Mikkel said.

Ella stayed still. She was reluctant to follow Mikkel's latest instruction.

He chuckled. "He-he, Ella! Gyrate your bum while watching the ball! All volleyball players do it. Grind your butt against me as if we are having sex!"

Ella looked at Mikkel over her shoulder and laughed. "Ha-ha! Mikkel, I can't do that!"

He smiled at her. "Of course, you can! That's how we are learning to pass."

"God!" slipped through Ella's lips, and she looked ahead. "OK!"

She gyrated her butt against Mikkel's crotch a few times, then suddenly stopped and again looked at Mikkel over her shoulder.

"What?" Mikkel asked, smiling, then said, "I know, I know. I have a hard-on, but would you blame me?"

Ella burst into laughter. Mikkel laughed too.

She looked at me.

I gave her a thumbs-up. "Come on, hon! You're doing great! Learn to play! Have fun, and let those butterflies fly!"

Ella shook her head, smiling, looked ahead, and ground her ass against what I assumed was Mikkel's erection since I could not see under the water.

Johan threw the ball, and, with Mikkel's help, Ella bumped it and, of course, squealed in delight.

"Let's do it again!" Mikkel said and took Ella's hands to guide her strike again.

I looked at Gerhard. He was watching with great interest as Mikkel was feeling up my wife. The old man caught my gaze, walked up to me and said, "Let her have fun!"

I looked back at Ella and Mikkel and thought: *Gerhard wanted this to happen! All this time, he wanted it. He knew something like this could happen or maybe had arranged it in advance? Perhaps he had talked to Mikkel and Johan. That's why he was so insistent on Ella playing volleyball. Because he had promised them to talk her into doing it so they could flirt with her and grope her.*

"We'll bump the ball real hard this time!" Mikkel said into Ella's ear as he hooked his chin over her shoulder and pressed his body tight against her, holding her hands in his.

And then he kissed the side of her neck.

Ella froze for a second, but when Mikkel kissed her again, she giggled and asked him, "Mikkel, are you sure this is part of the lesson?"

She was not pulling away from Mikkel, waiting for an answer to her question. At the same time, she stared at Johan, smiling with a flirtatious twinkle in her eyes. She was flirting with both Mikkel and Johan! Ella was drunk, and her inhibitions had gone out the window. That was true. However, she knew very well what she was doing. And she was doing it because she enjoyed being the subject of sexual attention by Mikkel and Johan, and even more, she liked teasing them and making them fight each other over her.

"No!" Mikkel finally answered her question. "I got distracted!"

Ella looked at me, still smiling.

I said, smiling too, "Your teacher is very passionate about the game!"

Ella laughed. "Ha-ha! Yes, my teacher is passionate about the game. And maybe about something else!"

I shrugged my shoulders. "Well, a passion is a passion."

She looked back at Johan and ground her ass against Mikkel's crotch, deliberately and provocatively, and giggled. "Hi-hi! Let's play!"

Johan was fuming and was not happy with Mikkel, not at all!

As for me, I didn't give a toss about the feelings of the two Danes toward one other. I was in a world of my own. My cock was now throbbing and twitching. I was drunk with excitement.

These two are fighting over the right to flirt with my wife, I thought. *This is such a turn-on to watch!* Then I said to myself: *I am probably too drunk if I enjoy watching my wife flirt with these two men. But who cares?*

"Let's try blocking!" Mikkel said and let go of Ella's hands. "Strech your arms up, Ella!"

Ella stretched her arms up, not taking her eyes off Johan, who continued to look sad and pissed off.

Ella loved teasing him. She enjoyed it very much when the two men fought over her. So much so that she pushed her chest up, deliberately making her nipples poke through her bikini top.

It did not go unnoticed by Johan, who smiled and, shaking his head, said, "You like to play, don't you, Ella?"

"Hi-hi!" Ella giggled. "Yeah, I do. I find volleyball fun!"

Johan was about to say something, but Mikkel cut him off, "Stop distracting Ella, Johan!"

Johan's smile gave way to a frown, but he did not say anything and prepared to throw the ball.

"Ella, raise up to your toes!" Mikkel said and wrapped his arms around Ella's stomach from behind.

Ella giggled yet again and raised up to her toes.

And then Mikkel slid his hands up and cupped her breasts over her bikini top.

I thought Ella would pull away, but she didn't! My wife seemed to have decided to taste the fun Gerhard had talked to us about.

I didn't intervene, but Johan did! He had had enough. He dropped the ball in the water, walked up to Ella, and grabbed her by the waist. He pulled her away from Mikkel. The latter did not expect this move from his friend, and taken by surprise, he let go of my wife.

"Enough volleyball for today, Mikkel!" Johan said. "You'll confuse her if you teach her more than one main move at a time."

"Really?!" Mikkel squeaked and tried to grab hold of Ella's shoulder to take her back from Johan.

However, Johan pushed Mikkel in the chest and pulled Ella closer to himself. "Yes! Volleyball is taught one move at a time!"

Mikkel cast an angry look at his friend. "So now you know

volleyball better than me?"

Johan was undeterred. "Yeah, I do!"

He stood next to Ella, put his hand on the small of her back and lowered his mouth to her ear. "Let's have a drink!"

Ella looked over her shoulder at Mikkel and, smiling softly, almost apologetically, said, "You'll teach me some more tomorrow!" She let Johan lead her away.

Ella was playing a game, and that game was not without risks. It could easily turn into something more than just a teasing game. True, she was drunk. However, she surely knew what she was doing and knew the risks, but at that very moment, she seemed to have completely given in to the temptation. The temptation to let go and let the butterflies fly out. After receiving my tacit approval, she had gathered the courage to do it. She had decided to have a little of the fun Gerhard had been advocating for during the past two days, implicitly as well explicitly.

I thought to myself: *I didn't know she had it in her. But you know what? I like it! I know I shouldn't let this happen, but I like it too much to stop it!*

3. TEMPTATIONS

PAULO

Mikkel and I stood next to each other and watched Ella and Johan get out of the pool. They went to the poolside bar and took seats at the counter. Johan wrapped his arm around Ella's waist. She did not push him away and giggled at whatever he whispered in her ear.

"So what?" Gerhard's voice came from behind Mikkel and me. "You two are going to let Johan have all the fun?"

Mikkel and I didn't bother responding to Gerhard. We headed to the bar, and the old man followed us.

The poolside bar was usually full of people, but not this time because of the volleyball game in the pool. Most hotel guests were on their loungers sunbathing or cooling down in the water and drinking at the swim-up bar as they watched the show in the pool. Thus Gerhard, Mikkel and I had no problem finding empty stools. We took one each and brought them to the bar counter to join Johan and Ella.

Johan and Ella squeezed to make room for us, and Johan ended up hugging my wife even tighter. I sat next to Ella, while Mikkel and Gerhard had to sit next to Johan.

The barman turned up. He was a tall black guy with a handsome face. He was not only tall but very fit. The man had an impressive physique and quite some muscles to show. Bare-chested, with broad shoulders, he was a sight to reckon with. And yeah, he had a massive bulge in his shorts, indicating that in addition to his envious figure, this Cape Verdean man was very hung!

His fitness and charming smile did not go unnoticed by Ella. She smiled friendly at him when he asked her what she wanted to drink. He seemed to like her because when she asked him what cocktail he would recommend to her, he readily grabbed the cocktail menu and, pointing at each cocktail photo, described what was in the mix in great detail.

Ella was unsure what drink to get.

She closed her eyes, murmuring, "What shall I go for? Umm... Pina Colada, Gin Martini, Daiquiri, Mojito, Sex on the Beach, what else? Bushwhacker. Hmm. I like Pina Colada and Sex on the Beach, but I've never tried Bushwacker or Gin Martini. Which one shall I try...."

Johan whispered in her ear, "Sex on the Beach!"

His lips touched her ear lobe, and Ella giggled, still not opening her eyes.

"Sex on the beach," he whispered again and slid his hand from Ella's side to her stomach, placing his palm on her belly button.

Ella's stomach muscles shook, and goosebumps rose on her neck as she felt his touch. My wife was aroused and excited. She was letting herself loose for the first time in our married life and discovered she liked it very much. It seemed that Gerhard had been right. Exploring these new sensations—dipping a toe in the water, as he had said—seemed fun indeed! And not only for her. I liked the fun too, and I liked it very much! My cock was hard, pushing up the waistband of my trunks, and with no sign of standing down!

Johan ran his lips over Ella's ear. "Ella, go for Sex on the Beach! I'll go for it too, and we'll both have sex on the beach!"

Ella opened her eyes and laughed. "Ha-ha! You wished!"

"Oh, I wish! A lot!" Johan chuckled. "He-he! Let's have sex on the beach, Ella!"

"Ha-ha!" Ella laughed again. "Johan, you go for Sex on the Beach and have it on your own."

She looked at the bartender. The black man smiled at her. He assumed she and Johan were a couple and watched them with amusement as they fooled around.

And that was when Gerhard said, "Ella, ask your husband! He's sitting right next to you." He pointed at me. "Nick, help your wife! Choose a cocktail for her!"

Ella's face turned crimson red. She was caught off guard by Gerhard's untimely intervention. Whether he revealed on purpose or accidentally that I was her husband was irrelevant. It became crystal clear to the bartender that she was flirting with another guy in front of her husband.

I rubbed her hand reassuringly. "Whatever you choose, honey! It's your drink. Your fun, your choice! I'd say go for something you haven't tried before!"

Ella did not turn her head to look at me. She was not taking her eyes off the black man in front of her.

He smiled at her reassuringly. "Your husband's right! Try something different! Have you tried Gin Martini? It's really good. The way I make it is unique."

"OK, Gin Martini it is!" she chirped.

"Oh, what a shame!" Johan exclaimed. "I'm gutted to miss out on having sex on the beach with Ella!"

"Ha-ha!" The bartender laughed. "Who wouldn't be!"

The black man was brazen. He stared Ella in the eyes intensely, provocatively, and she blushed yet again.

My wife had decided to play a little teasing game to test the waters, as Gerhard had urged her. She had chosen Mikkel and Johan to do it with. But now, there was a handsome, chatty, fit and hugely endowed man she had just met, and that man had admitted in front of her that he would gladly fuck her given a chance. She must have remembered Gerhard's words about the unintended recipients of the women's signals. But was the black man in front of her an unintended recipient of her signals? Or had she not wanted him to read her signals?

In any case, intended or not, her signals had been received by the man with the athletic body. And he had responded. His implicit declaration of intent had been registered by Ella, too. She was looking into the man's eyes and biting her bottom lip as if contemplating something.

The playful bartender smiled and, as if he hadn't made his desires clear enough, holding Ella's gaze, said quietly, "I would have been gutted too to miss out on having sex with Ella."

Ella couldn't hold his gaze any longer and looked away.

"Beer for me," Johan said coldly. The smile on his face had disappeared. He didn't like the unexpected competition from the man behind the bar.

The rest of us also ordered beers.

The frisky bartender went away to get the drinks, showing off his firm butt and pronounced back muscles.

I touched Ella's hand, and she looked at me with a worried look. She realised I had caught her eyeing up the barman's body and smiled shyly.

Johan put his hand on her leg and gently squeezed her thigh. He wanted to remind her he was still in the competition. Without looking at him, Ella grabbed his hand and pushed it away.

She reached for my hand and took it. "You're OK, hon?"

I smiled. "You're letting those butterflies fly free, aren't you?"

"Um, a little bit, yeah!" she said. "Or shall I not?"

"Oh, no!" I stroked her knuckles with the pad of my thumb. "I enjoy watching them fly free and high."

A smile replaced Ella's worried look. She was relieved that I was OK with her fooling around.

She cocked her head to the side and, still smiling, murmured, "How high do you want to see them fly?"

I let go of her hand and tapped her nose. "As high as it's safe."

"Hi-hi! OK then!" Ella giggled. "Watch and enjoy!"

Gerhard overheard us, and a grin of satisfaction spread across his face. His metaphors and teachings seemed to have taken root in our minds, and, of course, he was happy about that.

"What butterflies?" Johan asked.

"Don't mind us, Johan!" Ella waved off her hand and giggled again. "Hi-hi! We're fooling around."

Gerhard clarified for Johan, "It's about the flutter people feel when trying something new. In English, it's called butterflies in the stomach."

"Butterflies? Where?" Johan put his hand on Ella's stomach. "Here?"

Ella's stomach muscles trembled at his touch, but she did not remove his hand. Instead, she laughed. "Ha-ha! Yeah, there."

Johan put his other hand on her thigh. "Do you also get goosebumps?"

Ella looked at his hand. She did not answer his question.

He moved his hand up her thigh. "Do you?"

She said, "Yes!"

Johan slipped his hand between her thighs. "How much?"

Ella's breathing became heavier and faster. His fingers touched her pussy over her bikini bottom.

She grabbed his hand and removed it. "A lot, Johan! A lot!"

Johan tried to put his hand on her leg again, but she pushed him away, saying, "Don't play with fire!"

He chuckled. "He-he! I thought I was playing with goosebumps and butterflies!" He made a funny face.

Ella stared at him, barely suppressing her laughter.

He made another funny face.

Ella laughed. "Ha-ha!" She slapped him playfully on the shoulder. "Stop it!"

The black guy with an impressive physique brought us the drinks.

Instead of returning to help his colleagues, he sat at the bar across from Ella and said to her, "I make Gin Martini my special way. Let me know if you like it!"

Ella took a sip and put the glass on the bar counter. "Wow! It's really good!"

The barman chuckled. "He-he! I'm glad you like it! I made it using my secret mix, especially for you!"

The muscles of his chest contracted, and his abs stiffened. His biceps bulged, and his forearms tightened up. He was strong and masculine!

Ella took her time to appreciate his body. Her eyes wandered from his chest to his six-pack, to his big hands, up his powerful arms and broad, muscular shoulders until she looked up at his face and, smiling, said, "I like how it has this zesty but smooth flavour. You have to tell me how you make it!"

"I put orange bitters, but the proportions are key to getting the right flavour," the sexy black man said proudly, and another smile covered his face.

"May I?" Johan reached for Ella's glass.

Ella nodded yes, and he took a sip from her cocktail.

He put the glass back on the bar. "Yeah, it's good!"

The bartender smiled proudly. "It's my special recipe!" He leaned towards Ella and whispered, "Don't tell my boss this, but I have secretly changed the cocktail recipes on the menu! Mine are way better." He nodded towards a woman busying herself behind the bar on the other side of the poolside restaurant.

"Hi-hi!" Ella giggled and tapped the black man's arm. "We won't tell her, don't worry!"

The handsome barman kept his gaze on Ella. He was smiling friendly and was not taking his eyes off her. He wanted to make it obvious that he was interested in her. He was showing he liked her more than just a customer.

Ella liked him too and couldn't help but openly gawk at him. Her gaze moved between his strong arms and firm abs a few times before it finally settled on his face.

"What's your name?" she asked him, tilting her head to one side and smiling coyly.

"Paulo," he replied.

Ella's glance fell again on the well-developed abs of his stomach.

Paulo caught her gaze, and an even broader smile spread across his face. "I always do some extras for my clients, but I don't want my boss to know."

"Why not?" Johan asked.

Paulo leaned over the counter even closer to Ella and Johan and whispered, "She's jealous because customers like me. She doesn't get it. It's all about customer care. I always go the extra mile for the clients. Whatever my clients ask for, I do it for them. They want to have drinks on the beach; I bring them drinks on the beach! They want extra towels; I bring them extra towels. They want a massage; I give them a massage."

"You work as a masseur in the spa, too, don't you?" Gerhard jumped into the conversation. "I saw you at the spa the other day."

"Yes." Paulo nodded. "I finish here at two, have a thirty-minute lunch break and then start my shift in the spa at two thirty. I like it there because it's not too busy. And the manager is a very laid-back guy. He doesn't mind if I pop out for a drink or a client pays me privately to massage them in their room."

Paulo's boss shouted something, and he said, "I'd better go!"

The bartender walked away, and Ella did not miss the opportunity to eye his body up and down again. His firm butt, shaped thigh muscles, strong back and triceps, and black skin glistening in the sun were making a strong impression on my wife. And I couldn't blame her for appreciating his athletic body. The guy was simply the epitome of masculine power!

"You like black men, don't you, Ella?" Johan said.

Ella looked at him, and a mischievous smile flickered at the corners of her lips. "I like black men, yes! They always smile and are so polite."

Johan chuckled. "He-he! And they are so well-built."

"And they have huge cocks!" Mikkel interjected.

"Some of them," Gerhard threw in before Ella could scold Mikkel for his inappropriate remark. Looking at Paulo, who was arguing with his boss about something at that moment, Gerhard added with a lamenting voice, "But yeah, this Paulo is something, alright?"

Ella followed Gerhard's gaze and watched Paulo take a cocktail shaker and pour ingredients, murmuring something under his nose, visibly unhappy with his manager.

Johan moved his mouth to Ella's ear and whispered, "Have you been with a black man?"

"Johan!" Ella squealed and pulled her head back abruptly to look at him. "It's none of your business, but: No. I haven't."

I noticed from the corner of my eye how Johan's hand moved from her belly to her hip, hooking his fingers under the waistband of her bikini bottom.

He cocked his head to the side. "Never had sex with a black guy?"

"No, I told you already," Ella said. "Have you?"

"Ha-ha!" Gerhard burst into laughter. "She got you, didn't she?"

Mikkel smiled, amused with Ella's wit.

Johan laughed too. "Ha-ha! I haven't, no. But you know, Ella, what people say? They are good in bed! Better than white men! If I were gay, I would have tried a black cock!"

"We should stop talking like this, guys!" Gerhard interjected. "It's racist!"

Johan shrugged his shoulders. "What?! Everyone knows it! They have bigger dicks." He nodded in Paulo's direction. "And that one has a really big one!"

"Stop it!" Ella looked sternly at Johan and pointed her finger at him, trying to look serious, but the smile curving her lips said otherwise.

Johan grinned at her enticingly. "Well, Ella, you know. He is something, as Gerhard said. That one over there"—he glanced at Paulo—"is something! He's got all he needs to bring the big 'O'. And he seems keen on you. You sure you don't want to give it a go?"

"Ha-ha!" Ella burst into laughter. "OK, I get it! This is a classic projection. You desperately want to have sex with a black guy." She waved her hands in Paulo's direction. "Go! Talk to him, Johan! Come out of the closet!"

Ella didn't mind when Johan's hand slid inside her bikini bottom and squeezed her buttock.

He lowered his mouth to her ear and whispered, "You're naughty, aren't you?"

Ella chuckled. "He-he! Naughty is my second name!"

"Yeah, you are. But not as much as that girl!" Johan nodded at a young woman making out with her boyfriend on a sun lounger. She had put her hands in the guy's trunks and was feeling his cock.

"Umm, . . . no," Ella said. She grabbed Johan's hand and pulled it out of her bikini bottom. Then she got up from her stool and stretched her hand to me. "Let's go to our room, hon!"

I knew what she wanted us to do in the room—have sex—so I jumped off my seat and took her hand.

Ella looked at Johan and said, "But maybe I can be as naughty as that one!" She nodded at a woman standing on the footbridge over the smaller part of the pool.

The woman had leaned her back against the parapet and was engaged in heavy kissing with a man. The guy had wrapped his arms around her waist. His hands had slipped down her buttocks, squeezing her butt cheeks left bare by her G-string thong. The woman was teasing him by grinding her crotch against him.

Johan got up and looked at the woman and the guy.

"Nah!" He waved his hand off dismissively. "If you are as naughty as her, why aren't you wearing a G-string for a start?"

"Hi-hi!" Ella giggled. "Because my ass looks good in a classic bikini bottom!"

"Not so much classic!" Mikkel interjected and grinned at Ella. "Rather a cheeky bikini bottom!"

She stuck her tongue out at him. "Fine! Cheeky bikini bottom! But it is good enough! I don't need a G-string to show what I have."

"True to that!" Johan said. "But still! Your bum will look better in a G-string thong!" He gently slapped her butt.

Ella slapped his butt in return. "No, it won't!"

"Have you ever tried a G-string?" Johan asked her before turning to me. "Have you seen your wife in a G-string, Nick?"

Ella wore G-strings, mainly as underwear with short denim shorts or similar outfits and sometimes in bed before having sex with me. So I knew how she looked in G-string thongs, but I decided to play along with her and shook my head from side to side. "Nope! I haven't."

Johan stepped in front of Ella. "Let's show Nick how you'd look in a G-string, and he'll tell us what he thinks."

He wrapped his arms around her waist and pulled her into him. Ella let go of my hand and put her hands on his chest.

She pushed him playfully in the chest. "Nick likes me very much in my current bikini bottom, Johan."

"I do," I confirmed.

"Yeah, but still," Johan said and pulled her in closer to him.

"Still what?" Ella asked with a flirtatious glint in her eyes.

"Shall we show him?" Johan's hands slipped to her buttocks, and he hooked his fingers in the legs of her bikini bottom.

Ella did not say anything; she just giggled.

And then Johan pulled her bikini bottom into her ass crack, completely baring her ass cheeks.

"Do you like her more?" he asked me and nodded at her bum.

I pretended to look at Ella's butt and said, "She's always sexy!"

"You see?" Ella chirruped." My husband likes me with or without G-string!"

Johan's hands slipped to Ella's ass, and he squeezed her bare buns. It was so erotic to watch him do that that my hard-on became painful, and I adjusted the boner in my trunks. I knew doing that exposed me. It showed I was excited watching my wife in the hands of another man, but I didn't care.

"There are kids around, Johan! Stop it!" Ella whispered but did not push his hands away.

"There aren't any kids. Kids are not allowed at a bar where they serve alcohol," Johan said, grabbing her bikini bottom by the sides and pulling it further up her ass. "G-strings are worn tight to show a cameltoe!"

Ella giggled. "Hi-hi! I don't know what they show, but I know they chafe!"

"Do they?" Johan pulled her bikini briefs up higher, staring her in the eyes. "Are they chafing you right now?"

Ella was not saying anything; she just held Johan's gaze, and the mischievous smile continued to dance on her lips.

Johan smiled. "No?"

She said quietly, "Not yet."

"Good. 'Cos that's how a G-string thong is worn," Johan whispered, pulling her briefs even higher. "Tight! The cameltoe effect is stunning!"

Ella giggled. "Hi-hi! There's no cameltoe effect. It's only in your imagination, Johan!"

"Oh, it's not only in my imagination," he said. "There is a cameltoe effect. I'm sure there is."

Ella shook her head. "No! There isn't!"

A lustful grin spread across Johan's face. "May I have a look?"

Ella laughed. "Ha-ha! No! There are people around! You can't look at my crotch!"

The grin stretched Johan's lips thin. "But I can feel it, can't I?"

Ella did not answer his question.

Johan held her bikini bottom up with his left hand and placed his right hand on her stomach. "Can I?" he whispered.

Ella's smile faded away as they held each other's gaze. Her breathing accelerated. Johan slid his hand down her abdomen, and his fingers touched the waistband of her bikini bottom. His hand kept moving down. He and Ella stared at each other in a standoff. Johan's hand slid over the fabric of her swimsuit, and Ella was still holding his gaze. Her chest was moving up and down rapidly. She was biting her lips; her cheeks were red. Johan's hand slid down between her legs, and he cupped her pussy. Ella trembled. Another man had his hand on her most private part!

"I think there is a cameltoe effect," he said, not taking his eyes off hers. "Am I right, Nick?"

I squatted and looked at my wife's groin, just in time to see his fingers trailing over the thin fabric of her bikini bottom along her bulging pussy lips.

Before I could say anything, Ella grabbed his hand and moved it away.

She pushed Johan in the chest and stepped back. Ella pulled her bikini bottom out of her ass crack.

I stood up, and Ella and I looked at each other. She reached her hand to me, and I took it.

"We have to change for lunch," she said and pulled on my hand for us to go.

I knew she wanted us to go to our room to fuck, and I let her lead me away.

However, we had barely taken ten steps when Gerhard shouted, "Hold on! Let's have lunch at the grill restaurant. I have a surprise for you after lunch."

Ella and I stopped walking and turned around.

"What surprise?" Ella asked.

"I'll tell you after lunch," Gerhard said and turned to Johan and Mikkel. "You two are also invited."

Ella and I looked at each other. I shrugged my shoulders. Sex could wait for later in the afternoon.

"OK," Ella said. "Take us to lunch then, Gerhard! And tell us about your surprise!"

SURPRISES

Ella hooked her arm under my left arm, and we headed to the restaurant where we had had lunch on the first day. Mikkel and Johan almost tripped over each other as they rushed to walk on Ella's left side. Mikkel won the race by a slim margin. Johan was not happy, but there was nothing he could do other than join Gerhard and trail behind Ella, Mikkel and me.

I expected that Mikkel would try to flirt with Ella in his usual crude style. However, it seemed he had figured out that when he behaved like a gentleman, he scored more brownie points and was surprisingly well-behaved. During the 500 yards walk to the restaurant, he made sure Ella felt he was genuinely interested in her as a person. He asked her how often she visited her home country of Croatia, about where exactly she grew up, and if she had relatives there. He said he had heard of Croatia's beautiful coast and would love to visit its beaches. It turned out Mikkel knew a lot about Ella's home country. He mentioned places that even I didn't know about, which surely scored him the brownie points with Ella he so desperately wanted. As they talked, he wasn't missing an opportunity to put his hand on the small of her back. Ella did not mind that. In fact, she liked that he flirted with her subtly rather than subjecting her to crude comments, which he had often done when drunk.

The grill restaurant operated a buffet service during the day, so we grabbed food and sat at a table. We opted for draft beer, and even Ella, who is not a beer fan, went for it.

"Cheers!" Gerhard raised his glass. "To letting butterflies fly out!"

Ella and I giggled and raised our glasses.

"What are these butterflies you guys keep talking about?" Johan asked as he raised his glass.

"Well, it's a little secret between Ella, Nick, and me!" Gerhard replied.

"All right!" Johan said. "Cheers then to Ella, Nick, and Gerhard's butterflies!"

Mikkel raised his glass, too, and we drank up.

Gerhard put his glass on the table. "I like beer! But I must be careful with my intake of liquids."

"Why? Prostate troubles, old man?" Johan asked.

"Like what?" Mikkel jumped in. "You can't pee or can't get it up?"

Gerhard smiled. "A bit of both!"

"My grandpa suffers from it," Johan said. "You need to pee often, several times during the night, right?"

Gerhard nodded. "Yes, that's my problem."

"And it's limp, isn't it?" Johan continued asking his intrusive questions.

"Most of the time," Gerhard replied.

"What about Viagra?" Mikkel asked.

Gerhard laughed. "Ha-ha! No way! Viagra would kill me!"

"Why? High blood pressure?" I asked.

"No, thank God, my blood pressure is OK," Gerhard said.

Johan raised his eyebrows. "So, why not then? Once in a while, with the right woman, you know, take a pill and rock her world! "

"Yes, but no, thank you!" Gerhard drank from his glass and put it on the table. "My problem is that it doesn't go up when I want it to go up, but when it does, it stays up for ages! Can you imagine what would happen if I had taken Viagra? Walking around all day with a hard-on! I am an old man; you youngsters can do it! I can't!"

We all burst into laughter.

Then Johan said, "I wouldn't mind having a hard-on all day

long!"

"Me too!" I said and looked at Ella. "You'd also love it, wouldn't you?"

Ella slapped me on the shoulder. "Stop it!" Then she giggled. "Hi-hi! Let's say I wouldn't mind it!"

Mikkel looked at Gerhard. "You see, Gerhard? You can use Viagra! Women don't mind people with erections! Take the pill, and a lucky woman will be happy to help you with your hard-on!"

"Ha-ha!" Gerhard laughed. "I wouldn't bet on that. Where will I find a woman interested in an old bloke like me?"

"It all depends on what that old man can offer!" Johan said and winked at Ella. "Am I right, Ella?"

Ella giggled and, shaking her head from side to side, pointed her finger at Johan. "Stop it!"

Mikkel tapped Gerhard's hand comfortingly. "Sorry, old man!"

Johan made a sad face. "Poor Gerhard! She says 'No'!"

Johan and Mikkel were mocking Gerhard, and Ella didn't like it.

She stuck her tongue out at Johan and Mikkel. "I didn't say 'No'. Gerhard is a nice guy and a friend! Why wouldn't I help him?"

"Oh-oh!" Johan grinned and pointed at Gerhard. "Someone's in luck!"

"Ha-ha!" Gerhard laughed. "You see? Never write off an old man who knows a few things about women!" He reached over the table and stroked Ella's hand. "Thank you, darling! Thanks for putting these youngsters in their place!"

"You're welcome!" Ella said.

Gerhard let go of Ella's hand and raised his glass. "Cheers, Ella!"

After that, the conversation moved to discussing business opportunities in Cape Verde. It appeared Gerhard had given some serious thought to starting some business on the island, so it was interesting to listen to him.

When we finished lunch, Gerhard said, "Now, my surprise for you!"

"What is it?" I asked.

"I have reserved the private Jacuzzi!" he announced.

"Gerhard!" Ella squalled in surprise. "It's expensive!"

"Did you really do that?" I asked. "Ella and I looked at it yesterday and decided to give it a pass. It's very expensive!"

"Seriously, Gerhard, did you really book it?" Johan also asked.

Gerhard smiled. "Yep! I did. It's ours! The private Jacuzzi in the open is ours from 2 pm until 4 pm!"

The old man was gleaming with delight. He was happy he could give us a pleasant surprise. At times I hated him that he had befriended us and gotten under our skin, planting dangerous ideas in our heads. At times I loved him for the same reason I hated him—planting the ideas—but also for doing us these small favours and making us feel appreciated and cared for.

By the smile on Mikkel's face, it was clear he also appreciated Gerhard's gesture but still felt obliged to say, "Gerhard, we can't accept your offer without paying. How much do we owe you?"

Gerhard waved Mikkel off. "Nothing."

"It's not fair," Mikkel insisted. "You're doing this for Johan and me. How much do we owe you?"

"No!" Gerhard said firmly. "I already owe you for the turtle tour. We're quits!" He turned to Ella and me and explained, "These two talked me into joining them on a private turtle-watching tour on Thursday night. Me, the old man! Never mind!" Gerhard stood up. "It's five to two, so we'd better get going now!"

"Thank you, Gerhard!" Ella chirped. She stood up and hooked her hand under Gerhard's arm. "Take me to the Jacuzzi!"

Johan said wistfully, "This is how an old man gets a young woman!"

Ella looked over her shoulder and stuck her tongue out at him. She pressed her body closer to Gerhard and kissed him on the cheek. "Let's go, shall we?"

A few minutes later, we were standing next to a large Jacuzzi in the private suite. The place itself was not big. Practically, it was just the Jacuzzi. The hot tub was in the open, situated next to the main pool, but separated by a wall for privacy. There was a door to the main pool area in case someone fancied popping into the pool or going to the swim-up bar. To ensure only people who had hired the Jacuzzi could enter the private area, the door was operated by a key card they had given to Gerhard.

"I'll join you in a minute," Gerhard said, finally letting go of my wife's hand. "I have to pee."

Johan laughed. "Ha-ha! Ella, let the old man tend to his enlarged prostate!"

"You laugh, but prostate enlargement is unavoidable. With age, every man gets it," Gerhard said. "You'll get it too. It's like cellulite in women! After giving birth, all have it!"

"That's not true!" Ella squealed. "I've given birth and don't have cellulite!"

"You don't?" Gerhard asked.

Ella shook her head. "No, I don't."

"Let me see!" Johan said.

He stepped in front of Ella and put his hands on her shoulders. He spun her around, making her face away from him. Ella giggled, standing with her back turned to him.

Johan bent over, pretending he was examining my wife's thighs for cellulite and ran his hand along the back of her leg.

Ella trembled at his touch. "You see? I have no cellulite!"

"Maybe it's further up," Johan said and pulled her bikini bottom into her ass crack as he had done at the bar.

He ran his hand over her exposed ass cheek, and Ella giggled again.

Mikkel squatted in front of her. "Maybe there's some here."

He ran his hand along the inside of her thigh.

Ella tilted her pelvis forward. "You see? There isn't any!"

"Let me check! Let me check!" Mikkel nudged her to spread her legs further apart.

Ella spread her legs, and Johan slipped his hand between her thighs from behind and cupped her pussy.

"Ha-ha!" Ella laughed and reached behind her, grabbed Johan's hand, and pushed it away from her labia. "You don't check for cellulite there, Johan!"

"You sure?" Mikkel ran his hand along Ella's inner thigh, up to the crease between her leg and pussy. "Maybe you have some up here!" He ran his finger along the crease.

"No, I don't have any!" Ella shook in laughter. "Ha-ha! Look!"

She spread her legs further apart and pulled her bikini bottom to one side, exposing more of her groin, just short of showing her pussy lip.

"May I see too?" Johan asked. He walked around her and squatted in front of her, pushing Mikkel aside.

Ella pushed her pelvis forward. "See? I don't have any!" She pulled her bikini bottom further aside. However, she pulled it further than she intended to and bared her shaved pussy.

Realising she was flashing herself, she squealed, "Oops!" and pulled her bikini bottom back over her pussy.

"Let me see! Let me see!" Mikkel shouted, pushing Johan away, and squatted in front of Ella.

Ella laughed. "Ha-ha! You're late, Mikkel! The show's over!"

My wife proved to be a brilliant teaser. All four of us had tents in our trunks, including Gerhard! Yes, the old man was sporting an erection!

Ella saw what was going on around her and laughed even more. "Ha-ha! Ha-ha! I'm going in the Jacuzzi before someone has a stroke!" She loved playing her teasing game.

She got into the hot tub and sat down with her back pressed against one of the jets.

She looked at us. "Are you coming or what?"

Hurriedly, Johan, Mikkel and I got into the Jacuzzi and sat in the hot tub seats. I sat next to Ella. Mikkel sat on her other side while Johan took a seat across from us.

Gerhard did not follow us into the hot tub but headed to the door to the main pool area.

He was about to scan his key card on the door card reader when he stopped, turned around and said, "I'll get us some drinks from the bar on my way back from the loo. What would you like to drink?"

"Gin Martini, please!" Ella chirruped.

Johan giggled. "Hi-hi! Paulo's cocktail!"

"He's not at the bar," Mikkel said. "His shift finished at two, remember?"

Johan slapped the edge of the hot tub theatrically. "Darn! What a shame! Isn't it, Ella? You like his Gin Martini so much!"

"Ha-ha!" Mikkel laughed. "She likes not only that!"

Johan reached over and tickled Ella in the stomach. "What else do you like from Paulo's brand?"

Ella wriggled, giggling, and slapped his hand away before saying, "Everything!" She stuck her tongue out at him.

"You like black men, don't you?" he said and grinned at her.

Ella stopped giggling and stared at him for a few seconds before she shrugged her shoulders. "I don't know. I don't know if I like black men per se!"

"But she likes Paulo," Gerhard jumped into the conversation.

Ella looked at Gerhard, appearing somewhat surprised by what he had said.

I touched her hand. "You like Paulo, don't you, hon?"

She turned to look at me. She bit her lips a few times, thinking over her answer, before saying, "Umm. . . . Well, he's nice, sweet, talkative."

"With broad shoulders," I added.

"And abs to dream about!" Mikkel threw in.

"Oh, yeah, he's got muscles," Johan said. "Even I am getting some hots for him!" He continued to name Paulo's physical qualities: "Tall, with long, strong legs and a firm ass. And big feet. I saw them! You know what they say about guys with big feet? They have big cocks! I bet he's got a big one!"

"I might ask him to show it to us if I see him," Gerhard threw in casually.

Ella looked at the old man. She was not sure if he was joking or not.

We all looked at Gerhard. Was he serious?

He shrugged his shoulders. "What?! He said he goes the extra mile for his clients."

We stared at Gerhard, still unsure what to make out of his words.

He smiled. "What I'm saying is you need to read between the lines!"

"Go find him and ask him!" Johan said.

"Stop it!" Ella squeaked. She looked serious. "They'll kick us out of the hotel!"

"Why? Asking doesn't hurt!" Mikkel said. "The man knows what he can and cannot do."

"I am not looking at another man's cock!" Ella said, raising her voice. It was hard to tell whether she was faking frustration or was genuinely frustrated. She added in a lower voice, "You go and look at his cock yourselves!"

"OK, OK! Sorry!" Gerhard raised his hands. "I was joking! I have to go before I pee myself. What do the rest want? Beers?"

The two Danes and I nodded yes.

Gerhard disappeared behind the door to the swimming pool.

"We'll pay Paulo a visit at the bar tomorrow and ask him to show us his thingy!" Mikkel said.

"Stop it!" Ella squealed. This time she smiled and slapped his shoulder. "I mean it!" She leaned against the tub's wall, closed her eyes, and murmured, "I love back massage with jets!"

I wrapped my arm around her shoulders.

We stayed silent, enjoying the massage of the water jests. It was soothing and relaxing.

Probably fifteen minutes had passed before Mikkel broke the silence. "What does it take Gerhard so long?"

"Yeah," I said, "he's been away for quite a while."

"Shaking it!" Johan said.

Mikkel giggled. "Hi-hi! And milking it!"

"Shh!" Ella shushed us without opening her eyes.

Johan ignored her and continued to joke. "It must be taking a while to shake off his hard-on! Did you not see it? Ella gave the old man a massive hard-on!"

"Stop it!" Ella scolded Johan, raising her voice but still keeping her eyes closed. "He's ordering drinks. There must be a queue!"

"Yeah!" Mikkel said. "It's called a queue, all right? Hiding in the toilet and waiting for his hard-on to pass."

Johan giggled. "Hi-hi! It may take a while in his condition!"

A brief smile curved Ella's lips, but she still refused to open her eyes.

Satisfied they had managed to bring a smile to my wife's face, the two Danes stopped talking, and we continued to relax.

Another five minutes or so passed, and the door from the pool finally opened.

We heard Gerhard's voice. "Drinks are here! Ella, your special drink is here too!"

Ella opened her eyes and looked at Gerhard. We all looked at him. He was holding the door open for someone to come in.

It was Paulo!

Paulo was carrying a tray with drinks. He was wearing only swim briefs.

Gerhard must have paid him to bring us drinks here, I thought. *'Going the extra mile'!*

The bulge in Paulo's briefs was huge. It was even more pronounced than what we had seen in his shorts at the bar. The guy had a massive cock; there was no doubt about it.

We all watched him with unhidden admiration as he climbed into the Jacuzzi, balancing the tray with care.

He walked up to Ella and lowered the tray for her. "Your Gin Martini, Ella!"

Their eyes met, and they smiled at each other. Ella blushed.

"Made especially for you," Paulo said, not taking his eyes off Ella's.

She took her glass. "Thank you, Paulo!"

"You're welcome, Ella!" he said and finally turned his attention to the rest of us.

We took our glasses, but Paulo was still not leaving. He stood in the middle of the tub with an empty tray in his hand.

What Gerhard said explained Paulo's behaviour. "I asked Paulo to tell us about his bodybuilding exercises. We all talked about how fit he looked, and I thought it would be helpful if we found out how he manages to do it. He told me he's got a unique way of maintaining a great body with less than a thirty-minute workout in the morning, and he's happy to share it with us."

Gerhard sat down.

Paulo stepped in front of Ella and me without waiting for a further invitation. "May I squeeze between the two of you?"

Ella and I moved slightly apart from each other.

Paulo put the tray on the edge of the tub and sat between us.

"So, my routine starts in the morning with twenty-five push-ups," he said. Then he went on to explain the various exercises he did without using any equipment. After he talked for about five minutes, he finished his lesson by saying, "This is how I maintain my fitness. Abs are hardest to build and maintain, but I think they are worth the effort."

He turned in his seat to face Ella and asked her, "Ella, do you want to feel them?" He tightened up his abs and smiled invitingly.

Ella blushed but placed her hand on his stomach and blushed even more.

"Impressive!" she said as she ran her hand over his abs.

"Can I feel your biceps?" Gerhard asked and rose from his seat.

"Sure!" Paulo replied and pumped up his muscles.

Gerhard walked up to him and felt his biceps.

"Ella, feel him!" Gerhard said before quoting a famous movie line, "'The force is strong in this one'!"

"Hi-hi!" Ella giggled. "OK!"

She felt Paulo's arm and smiled. The black athlete smiled back at her.

Gerhard asked Ella, "Ella, have you ever felt another man's

muscles like this in front of your husband?"

Ella shook her head, saying, "No, I haven't," and looked at me. She smiled shyly, and her face flushed red again.

I smiled encouragingly. "Feel his chest, hon! I'm a man and don't admire men's bodies, but when it comes to this man, I do."

I reached my hand to Paulo's chest and felt his chest muscles.

Ella also ran her hand over his chest.

"Do you take steroids?" Mikkel asked.

"No," Paulo replied straight away. "I've always wanted to build my muscles naturally. I am a bodybuilder without steroids."

"Steroids shrink your cock, don't they?" Johan threw in.

Paulo smiled. "That's what they say. But you see. I've never worried about that."

"'Cos you have a big cock, right?" Mikkel said, and a somewhat mischievous smile spread across his face.

"Ha-ha!" Paulo burst into laughter. "You can say that! Ha-ha! You can say that!"

"Can you show it to us?" Johan asked.

Paulo stopped laughing and looked at Johan.

Johan shrugged his shoulders with an innocent smile on his face. "Curiosity."

Paulo shook his head. "No."

"Please, don't listen to him, Paulo!" Ella said, blushing profusely.

Paulo wrapped his arm around her shoulders and turned his head to look at her. "Of course, I won't! These horny men forget there's a lady present, don't they?"

Ella smiled appreciatively. "Tell me about it!"

Paulo let go of her and stood up. "I'd better get going!" He turned around and asked her, "Would you like me to bring you another cocktail?"

He reached for the empty glass in her hand, but she turned down his offer, "No, thanks, Paulo! I've already drunk a lot." She placed her glass on the edge of the tub.

"Why did you want to become a bodybuilder?" Gerhard asked Paulo.

Paulo said, "I wanted to be fit. Also, I need an athletic body for my profession."

"Your profession? A bartender?" Mikkel asked.

Paulo looked at him. "I am a professional stripper."

Mikkel's eyes went big. "A stripper?!"

All of us looked at Paulo in surprise, except Gerhard, who just smiled.

Paulo shrugged his shoulders. "Yeah. I'm a male stripper."

"Nick!" Gerhard called my name, and I looked at him.

"Have you ever taken your wife to a male striptease show?" he asked me.

"No," I said. "Should've I?"

Gerhard smiled. "Well, she's missed a lot. I took Monika once, and she said there was nothing like the butterflies she felt when she slid her hand into the stripper's briefs and touched that warm, masculine flesh."

Blushing profusely, Ella shook her head from side to side and whispered, "They are awful, Paulo!"

He looked at her and said, "They sound awful, but they are well intended. They are having fun and want you to have fun too."

"Paulo," Gerhard said. "Would you let Ella feel your cock?"

Ella's eyes went big. She had not expected Gerhard to go that far.

She expected even less to hear Paulo say, "Sure! If she wants to. Do you want to, Ella?"

Without waiting for Ella's answer, Paulo took her hand and

placed it on his stomach.

"Just snuck it in," he said.

Ella pulled her hand away and looked at me, red-faced.

"Go for it, hon!" I said with an encouraging smile.

She hesitated. Paulo took her hand again and again placed it on his stomach. This time he did not let go of her hand and, holding it, began slowly pushing it down.

Ella was staring at me, biting her lip nervously. I smiled at her. Her fingertips touched the waistband of Paulo's briefs. There was absolute silence. Only the slushing of the water could be heard. Everyone was waiting to see if Ella would do it.

Paulo kept pushing her hand down, slowly but steadily, until her fingers slid into his briefs. Ella's breathing became fast and urgent. Her gaze was fixed on me. She was like in a trance.

Paulo let go of her hand and stood still.

Staring at me, Ella continued to slide her hand down on her own until it disappeared completely into Paulo's briefs. Then she swallowed nervously, and her hand stopped moving down. Paulo trembled. The fabric of his briefs stretched around Ella's hand; the outlines of her knuckles became discernible. It was clear: Ella had wrapped her hand around Paulo's cock!

Her face was flushed red. Ella was holding another man's cock in her hand! For the first time in our married life! And I was watching her do it. My cock was hard; my balls were tingling. I found the sight of my wife staring at me while her hand gripped someone else's penis very erotic. There was something special in the expression on her face—a mix of lust, submission, surrender, shame, embarrassment, and guilt—all this made me want to see more.

Gerhard stepped behind Paulo and whispered something into his ear. Paulo nodded, grabbed the waistband of his briefs, and pulled them down, revealing a massive cock, semi-flaccid.

This was the largest cock I had ever seen. Paulo's penis was circumcised, which was strange because, as far as I knew, Cape Verdeans did not generally practise circumcision. However, I did not have time to delve into this oddity since my attention was drawn to Ella's hand wrapped around the shaft in the middle. She was unable to close her fingers around the girth. This made the bulbous head and thick base of the cock look even more impressive. The sack with the balls hanging below reminded the onlooker of the potency of the organ my wife was holding in her hand.

If there could have been any doubt whether she was holding Paulo's cock while he had had his briefs on, now there was no doubt. Ella knew we were all looking at her as she held his dick in her hand. That was why I expected she would let go of Paulo's cock, but I was wrong. She didn't. Instead, she turned her head to look at it.

"You can put it into your mouth," Paulo whispered.

Ella stared at his manhood for about ten seconds, and then, slowly, as if in a trance, she lowered her head, and Paulo's cockhead touched her lips. She opened her mouth and took his cockhead in, spreading her lips wide around it.

Suddenly, she seemed to realise that what she was doing was too much, pulled Paulo's cock out of her mouth and stood up.

She grabbed my hand and said, "Nick! Let's go to our room!"

I stood up. I knew what Ella wanted. She wanted me to fuck her in our room.

Ella tugged on my hand to lead me out of the hot tub when an idea came to me. A bold idea. An idea that I did not have time to think through or to assess how rational it was, but I was too drunk with lust to think straight.

So, I blurted out, "Let's do it here!"

Ella whispered, "Nick?!"

I took my hand out of hers and pulled down my trunks. My erect cock sprang out. I couldn't help but look at Paulo's dick. It dwarfed mine, and I felt intimidated. What Paulo had was extraordinary.

He is a stripper! I told myself. *It's OK to be beaten in the cock department by a male stripper.*

I looked back at Ella.

She was biting her lip, contemplating my proposal.

Ten, maybe twenty seconds, passed, and she looked around us.

She saw four horny men.

Two of them were sitting, and the other two were standing, but all four were watching us intently. They wanted us to do it.

I sat back in my seat and whispered, "They won't be able to see much in the water."

I pulled Ella to step closer to me, and she did. She stood in front of me.

I put my hands on the waistband of her bikini bottom and slowly began pulling it down.

"Nick, you're sure?" she whispered.

The way Ella slurred her words, her slow movements, dilated eyes, and engorged bottom lip showed me how horny she was. She was so horny that her thinking was muddled, and I knew she would follow me on the audacious adventure I was taking her on.

So, instead of answering her question, I pulled down her bikini bottom to her knees, baring her ass and pussy.

Ella looked around at the men staring at her, moving her gaze from one to the other.

I stroked her buttock. "They want us to do it, hon. They want to watch us!"

Paulo and Gerhard stepped back. Paulo's cock was rock hard.

Gerhard pulled down his trunks. He didn't have a full erection, the poor guy. But still, his cock had hardened enough to allow him to stroke it.

Johan and Mikkel suffered no such constraints. They stood up, pulled down their trunks, grabbed their fully erect cocks and started to wank.

Ella bent over, showing her naked butt and pussy between her legs from behind. She stepped out of her bikini bottom, put it on the edge of the tub and straddled me, facing me. Then slowly, very slowly, she lowered herself onto my cock.

I gasped as I felt her warm pussy engulf my manhood.

"Shout when to get off you," Ella whispered, then crossed her arms around my neck and began riding me, slowly in the beginning but gradually increasing the pace of her thrusts.

Paulo, Mikkel and Johan were wanking vigorously. Poor Gerhard stepped back and leaned his butt against the edge of the Jacuzzi. His cock was not cooperating and had gone completely limp. He resigned himself to watching only.

Ella began moaning, and it didn't take long before I shouted, "Now, Ella, now!"

She jumped off me, letting my cock slip from her pussy and watched me shoot my cum in the water.

She took her bikini bottom, but before she put it on, she looked around. The three able men were jerking off with jets of cum shooting off their cocks.

Ella smiled. It was a smile of pride. She had made three men wank and ejaculate watching her have sex with her husband.

She put her bikini on and said, "Nick, the party's over. We can't stay in this water." She pointed to the streaks of cum floating in the water.

Johan tucked his emptied cock into his trunks. "Why not? You can't get pregnant from staying in the water. The semen—"

"Yeah, that's what they say until it happens," Ella cut him off and took my hand. "Let's go take showers!"

I stood up, pulled my trunks up, and Ella and I proudly walked out of the hot tub.

We got out of the Jacuzzi area, hurried to the sun loungers, grabbed our stuff, and ran down the stairs off the pool complex.

We headed straight to our hotel block. We walked fast, almost running.

"Did you enjoy it?" I asked Ella as we took the central walkway.

"Yes," she said.

"Did you like feeling Paulo's cock?"

Ella hesitated, but after a few seconds, she said, "Yes!"

"Gerhard must have paid him," I said.

"Probably," Ella agreed with me.

We turned onto the walkway to our hotel block, and I asked her, "Did you like his cock in your mouth?"

Ella did not answer my question, so I asked her again, "Did you?"

"I was only curious," she finally said.

"Would you have fucked him?"

"I only fuck my husband, Nick!"

"I know, but theoretically?"

"Theoretically? Yes!"

We kept walking in silence. Ella was in the lead and was in a hurry. And we walked faster and faster. As if we were trying to run away from something.

We entered the corridor leading to our room, and, at that point, we were running.

I grabbed Ella's hand. She stopped, turned around and looked at me.

"Why are we running, Ella?" I asked her.

Ella was panting. She took a deep breath and exhaled slowly. Then she looked around us to make sure no one was listening to us and said, "I don't know, Nick."

"Are we running away from temptation?" I asked.

"Temptation? Of what?"

"Of fucking Paulo?"

"No!" Ella squeaked. "I told you: I fuck only my husband!"

I stroked her shoulder. "But still; you said theoretically—"

"Honey! Have you not seen the size of that cock? It's huge! I barely fitted its tip into my mouth! How do you imagine that thing penetrating me?"

"But you enjoyed taking it into your mouth."

"I. . . . I. . . . Honey! I think we should stop this whole thing!"

"Like? . . . Like what thing, honey?"

"You know what thing!" Ella said abruptly. "Paulo, Gerhard, Johan, Mikkel. All this! It's madness. We'll lose control. We've already lost control!"

"Do you regret that we've already lost control?" I asked.

"Yes!"

"Why?" I took her hand and rubbed her knuckles with the pad of my thumb.

"Because it's not us!" Ella said in an almost pleading voice and pulled her hand out of mine. "It's not us! We've never done anything like this! If we keep going like this, where will it all end?!"

"So, it's the temptation that we've been running from?"

"Yes!" Ella cried, on the verge of bursting into tears.

She put her hands between her thighs. Instinctively, without realising it, she began rubbing her pussy while staring at my face.

"And more than anything, the black temptation. Right?" I asked her.

"Yes!" Ella cried again and squeezed her legs together with her hands between them.

I looked around us, and after I assured myself no one was in the corridor, I said, "But when Paulo—"

"Please, can we stop talking about it?" Ella pulled her hands from between her legs, grabbed my hand and squeezed it. "And dial the whole thing down? Like, dial it down a lot?"

"Like how much?"

"Like, stop it! Completely!"

She let go of my hand, and we resumed walking down the corridor.

We reached our room, and I took out the key card to open the door when Ella stood before me. I looked up at her.

She placed her hands on my chest and said, "Nick, you do realise I am a human being, don't you?"

"Yes," I said, taken aback by her words. "Why are you telling me this?"

"I am vulnerable to temptations. I can give in to temptation."

"Of course, you can. I realise that."

"Then you should not put me in the way of temptation."

"I know," I said quietly.

She stepped out of my way, and I unlocked the door. I held it open for her. She entered the room. I followed her and shut the door behind me.

Ella turned around and grabbed my hands. "Nick, can you? Can you keep me out of temptation?"

"How?" I asked.

"Let's not see them again!"

"Umm. . . . Yeah. OK. Let's try to do that. But what if we can't? We'll be bumping into them. We're in the same hotel, after all."

Ella let go of my hands. "Then we'll solve this problem the way you solved your food problem. Remember how you lost weight? You learned how to slow down your eating. Starting with a starter, fully enjoying it, moving to the main meal but eating half of it, and not eating the dessert at all. You always pushed the dessert aside while dieting. Remember? That was how you controlled your food temptation. Can the two of us do that with this temptation?"

I chuckled. "He-he! Like, stop just before the dessert comes?"

Ella smiled. "Yes! We'll keep the dessert for ourselves!"

"And the dessert, in this case, being?"

Ella poked me in the ribs playfully. "You know what the dessert is!"

I lowered my mouth to her ear and whispered, "The dessert is your pussy. We won't give it to anyone to fuck it!"

"Hi-hi!" Ella giggled and pushed me in the chest. "You're lucky I like your dirty talk, you know?"

"Ha-ha!" I laughed. "I know!"

"So, are you helping me?"

"Yes!"

"Good! I'm going to take a shower now!"

Ella took her bikini off and went into the bathroom.

I was happy that my wife's mood had improved after she had appeared minutes before, overwhelmed by remorse and regret for playing the game Gerhard had enticed us to play.

SAVING THE DESSERT

I took a shower after Ella, and we called the kids and her mum in London. After chatting for almost an hour, we closed the video call and turned on the TV. We watched a movie until, at about 5:30, Ella and I both felt sleepy and lay down for a nap. We overslept and rushed for dinner because it was half past nine when we woke up, and dinner closed at ten.

We didn't see any of the guys in the restaurant. We finished dinner, but instead of leaving, we ordered a second glass of wine, to the frustration of the waitress, who was keen to clear the table and prepare it for breakfast, but still smiled and served us.

When we left the restaurant, we decided to go to the lobby bar. The idea was to have a couple of drinks and go to the late show at eleven o'clock afterwards, trying to avoid seeing Johan and Mikkel at the earlier show.

Ella liked the bartender—a young black guy in his early twenties—and after I hinted to her I was OK if she flirted a little with him, she chatted him up. The man seemed to be in a good mood, and since there were not many people at the bar, he had plenty of time for us. Thus, Ella and I got involved in some banter with him. We kept talking and joking, and he kept offering us drinks to try. Relaxed by the alcohol and enthused by the pleasant company of the young barman, Ella and I became horny again. I was joking with her, teasing her, tickling her and, frankly, trying to feel her up. She was pushing my hands away, of course, not wanting us to behave obscenely in front of the young man and the other people hanging around in the lobby, but she was giggling and tickling me back.

Ella and I stayed at the bar longer than we had planned, and by eleven thirty, we had had several rounds of drinks. So when we finally went to watch the late show, which was already well in progress, we were pretty drunk.

We sat in the end row, where there were a few empty seats.

"I can't see any of them," I whispered in Ella's ear and slid my hand down her back to her bum.

"Hi-hi!" she giggled, grabbed my hand, and pushed it away before whispering back to me, "Good! 'Cos I'm saving the dessert for you."

"Hi-hi! I know, right!" I giggled too.

I signalled a waiter, who was going around and collecting orders from the bar, and I ordered Ella a cocktail while I opted for a pint of lager.

Just when our drinks arrived, Mikkel turned up from nowhere.

"Hello, my friends!" he greeted us. "I've been looking for you all night!

To my surprise, he did not look drunk.

"May I sit next to you?" Mikkel pointed to the empty seat next to Ella.

She looked at me and smiled. Her smile was mischievous. I knew what her smile meant: she wanted to tease Mikkel. My wife was more than tipsy, and the alcohol had diminished her resolve to resist temptation. And not only her resolve but mine too.

I said with a drunken smile, "We'll pull out before the dessert arrives!"

She said, "Oh, the dessert has arrived," and giggled, then grabbed my hand and, staring me lustfully in the eyes, placed it on her thigh. "I have the dessert on me, honey, don't you know?" She giggled again and dragged my hand up her thigh, pushing her skirt up.

"Oh, yes," I said, "I keep forgetting that technically you are the one who serves the dessert!"

"And I'll serve it to you only!" She pushed my hand away and added, "But later!"

She pulled her skirt down to cover her upper thighs and looked up at Mikkel.

He was patiently waiting for her answer, looking a little confused by our weird behaviour.

Ella did not answer his question; she just smiled at him and tapped on the seat next to her.

Mikkel sat down.

We watched the show in silence for about five minutes before Mikkel whispered something in Ella's ear, and she giggled.

"Where?" she asked.

Mikkel lowered his mouth to her ear again, and this time I heard him say to her, "If you look at the lower left corner." He put his arm around Ella's shoulders and pulled her towards him. "Do you see it now?"

"Ha-ha!" Ella laughed. "I see it now, yes!"

I didn't care what they were looking at. Perhaps some wardrobe malfunction of one of the performers or something. I was much more interested in what Mikkel was doing to my wife. And he was onto something.

His hand slid from her shoulder to her side. A second later, his fingers touched her side boob, which was peeking through her tank top's armhole.

They stayed like this for a minute, supposedly watching the show. And then Mikkel slipped his hand under her top and cupped her breast.

Ella let him be. She did not object at all, just looked at me.

I winked at her, and she smiled.

During the next ten minutes, Mikkel kneaded, squeezed, felt, and massaged my wife's breast. She let him play with her boob as much as he liked.

The show ended, and Ella finally pushed Mikkel's hand off her tit.

She stood up and straightened her tank top, making sure her breasts were covered.

She looked at me. "Shall we go?"

I rose up, as did Mikkel. He had a tent in his shorts.

He looked at me and smiled with a guilty smile.

I said, "Ella and I will call it a night."

Ella hooked her hand under my arm and smiled coquettishly at Mikkel. "Good night, Mikkel!"

"Good night!" he replied.

Ella and I left the auditorium and took the walkway to our hotel block. We had turned around the corner when we heard Mikkel's voice behind us, calling my wife, "Ella!"

Ella and I stopped walking and turned around.

Mikkel had followed us and now stepped forward to Ella.

"What is it, Mikkel?" she asked him as she let go of me.

He cleared his throat. "Hmm. I was wondering if you fancy having a drink."

"No, thanks," Ella said.

"Yeah, thanks, Mikkel," I also said. "Ella and I will be having fun in our room!"

"Nick!" Ella squeaked and slapped my arm lightly. "How could you?!"

Mikkel giggled. "Hi-hi! I see." He looked at Ella, then me, then again at Ella before placing his hand on her hip and saying, "Would you like me to join you and Nick?"

"Hi-hi!" Ella giggled. "Why not?!"

"Really?!" Mikkel was so surprised by my wife's response that he let go of her hip and stepped back.

He stared at her face, unable to believe his luck that Ella had agreed to let him join us and have sex with her. Because he knew very well what we meant by 'fun'.

Ella was holding Mikkel's gaze and smiling. She loved teasing the guy, and I liked watching her manipulate him. Well, I was also turned on to hear my wife agree for another man to join us to fuck her, of course, knowing too well she was just cock teasing him.

"Ha-ha!" Ella burst into laughter and tapped his shoulder. "I was kidding, Mikkel! I was kidding!"

"Ha-ha!" Mikkel laughed too. "I get it!" He kept his gaze on her face for a while, then asked, "Though, are you sure? I can help you have fun! Real fun! I am good at it!"

"I have high expectations, Mikkel!" Ella said, smiling. "Very high!"

Mikkel chuckled. "He-he! I have what it takes to meet them, Ella!"

"Do you have what Paulo has?" I interjected.

"Nick!" Ella squalled and pushed me on the shoulder. "You and your dirty mind!" She turned to Mikkel. "Don't listen to him! My husband drank too much tonight!"

Mikkel stepped closer to Ella. "Well, I may not have what Paulo has, but I work hard! Ella, I stayed sober all day for you!"

He wrapped his arms around her waist and pulled her to him.

Their eyes met.

"I think you've misunderstood something, Mikkel," Ella whispered.

"Have I?" Mikkel whispered back and leaned his face towards hers.

"Mikkel, don't!" Ella murmured but did not pull her head back when Mikkel planted his lips on hers. Instead, she let his tongue enter her mouth, and they kissed a deep, French kiss.

Ella broke the kiss and put her hands on Mikkel's chest. "That's enough fun, Mikkel!"

"You sure?" he asked. "We've just started!"

Ella's face turned serious. "Started what?"

"You know what, Ella!" Mikkel pulled her closer to him.

Ella spread her palms on his chest and gently pushed him back. However, he didn't let go of her and again pulled her closer to him.

"What do you want from me, Mikkel?" she asked him.

"You know what I want," he replied. He briefly looked at me, then looked back at Ella.

Ella's chest was moving up and down fast. She kept staring at the emboldened Dane, who was holding her around the waist.

"No." She shook her head. "I don't know."

"You know, Ella!" Mikkel said. They stood silent for a few seconds, holding each other's gaze before he whispered, "I want to fuck you. That's what I want."

Ella did not say anything. She only pushed him away, forcing him to let go of her, turned around and grabbed my hand.

"Let's go, hon!" she said and pulled my hand to follow her. "I want you to fuck me! Now!"

We walked away in a hurry, leaving Mikkel behind. He was not going to have more fun with my wife that evening.

Ella and I reached our hotel block, ran through the corridor, and rushed into our room.

The moment I shut the door behind us, I grabbed Ella by the waist and pulled her skirt down. Then I pulled down her knickers. She stepped out of her clothes.

I took a condom out of my pocket, took off my shorts and briefs, and pushed Ella to lie on her back on the bed.

I unwrapped the condom and rolled it over my erect cock.

Ella dragged her butt to the edge of the bed and spread eagle her legs, opening her pussy wide open for me.

"Fuck me hard, Nick!" she shouted. "Hard!"

"Call me Mikkel while I'm fucking you!" I said and stepped between her spread legs, leaning against the edge of the bed.

I grabbed her ankles and pushed her legs up, guiding my cock towards her pussy only by moving my pelvis. My cockhead touched her wet vulva.

"Fuck me hard!" Ella shouted again, and then a second later, she cried, "Mikkel, fuck me hard!"

I pushed my cock in, and it slid smoothly into her vagina.

I began thrusting straight away, and within less than a minute, Ella was moaning and shouting, "Fuck me, Mikkel, harder!"

A couple of minutes later, she began shaking in orgasm.

Ella reached down and grabbed my ass cheeks. She pulled me deeper inside her, digging her fingernails into my flesh, and cried, "Stay still, Mikkel!" Then she groaned, "Urgh! Stay still! I wanna feel your cock against my cervix!" A second later, she screamed, "Oh, God! Oh, fuck! Paulo! Fill me up! Paulo! Fill me up with your big cock!"

Her words pushed me over the edge, and I began cumming, standing still with my cock buried deep inside her pussy.

We groaned and moaned for about a minute until our orgasms passed. Ella let go of my ass, and I pulled my still-erect cock out of her.

"Ella, this was amazing!" I said, panting, as I removed the condom. "We haven't had such passionate sex for a long time! Maybe since we were newlywed. Don't you think?"

"Yes," she said and sat on the edge of the bed. She ran her fingers over her pussy and landing strip.

"Can I admit something?" I asked her.

"Sure!"

"I think I know why it's been so passionate."

"Why?"

"Thinking of Mikkel and the others fucking you makes me extremely horny, like crazy. That's why I fuck you so well! I'm insatiable for you and want to fuck you all the time!"

"Same with me, Nick!" she said and paused. She bit her lips a couple of times and then began shaking her head from side to side. "No! No! No!" She grabbed my hand and stared me in the eyes. "Nick! We can't go on like this! We have to stop this madness. We have to! You do realise where it will end, don't you? Role-playing and fantasising is one thing. We can get away with that. Teasing and goofing around? Maybe we can still get away with that. But where is this going? No! We can end up in a place where we shouldn't be. It's dangerous. Irreversible! We shouldn't go there. Can we pull the brakes now? Before it's too late? Can we?"

I sighed, and after thinking for a bit, I said, "We can try, but I'm not sure we'll be able to."

Ella tugged on my hand. "Nick, we have to!"

"I don't know, honey. Do we?"

"Nick! You and I are leading each other on. And with Gerhard muddling our minds, this will end up God knows where. We have to stop it now! Before it's too late!"

I took a deep breath, exhaled, and said, "OK! Let's try!"

Ella let go of my hand. "Good! Thank you!"

"But how? How do we stop it?"

"By staying away from temptation! Forget about the dessert thing! It won't work! It doesn't work! We've got to stay away from temptation!"

"We'll bump into them. They are at the bar, at the show, in the—"

"We won't go there!"

"But, honey," I said, "they are at the pool. All the time! There's no way we—"

"We won't go to the pool!" Ella interrupted me again.

I smiled and shook my head. "Honey! We came here for the sunshine and the pool. We might as well pack our bags and go home!"

"No! We'll be going to the pool, but we'll be going early. And before they come, we'll go to the aqua park. If someone comes there, we'll leave! And come back for coffee. We'll change our schedule to avoid them and still enjoy our holiday."

4. RUNNING AWAY

TO THE BEACH

The next morning, Ella and I woke up early and skipped breakfast. We didn't talk about the previous night but reminded ourselves we had to change our routine to avoid bumping into Mikkel and Johan. After we visited the toilet and brushed our teeth, Ella quickly shaved down there and put on her floral Brazilian-style bikini with side string ties while I opted for swim trunks. She shoved two beach towels into the beach bag along with a bottle of sunscreen lotion. We also put our clothes, phones, and my wallet into the bag. Ella and I planned to go to the pool first, have a quick drink at the pool bar once it opened and then go to the water park. The plan was then to spend the rest of the morning in the aqua park, change in the changing rooms there and go for lunch in Santa Maria to avoid meeting Johan and Mikkel in the hotel. Ella took her sun hat, I grabbed the beach bag, and we left for the pool at ten past seven.

Our plan seemed to work because there was no one at the pool except Gerhard, of course. Having put his towels on four other sunbeds, he was lying on his back on a fifth sunbed and was reading his book.

Ella and I stopped next to the towel kiosk.

"He's planned for Mikkel and Johan to spend the day with us," I said to Ella.

"Yeah, it looks like it," she said.

We stood silent for a few seconds, thinking what to do, before Ella said, "We shouldn't join him! He talks me into things and muddles my mind!"

I put my hand on her shoulder. "You sure?"

"Yeah! We should stop him while we can. Today we should go to the beach!"

"The beach?"

"Yeah! The beach!"

"OK!"

We turned around to walk down the stairs to the walkway leading to the hotel's back gate, which was the exit to the beach.

However, we had barely taken a couple of steps when we heard Gerhard shouting to us, "Ella! Nick! Over here! Come!"

We turned around. Gerhard had put his book on his stomach and was waving at us.

Ella and I looked at each other, and after some hesitation, I said, "It will be rude if we don't go to at least say hello."

Ella sighed. "Yeah, it will be."

We walked up to Gerhard, and he did not miss the opportunity to ogle my wife's body as we stood next to his sun lounger.

He put the book away and sat up. "You look gorgeous, Ella! As always!"

"Thank you," Ella said.

Gerhard turned to me. "You have a beautiful wife, Nick!"

"Thank you!" I replied, while Ella only smiled.

"Come on! Grab one each!" Gerhard nodded to the sunbeds on his right. He held his gaze on Ella for a while before adding, "Mikkel and Johan turned up earlier—surprise, surprise! So early!—and said they planned some special fun with you today."

"I have no idea what they're talking about," Ella said.

"He-he!" Gerhard chuckled. "Mikkel said yesterday evening the two of you had a special chat or something"—the old man winked at Ella—"about having a fun challenge. I think he and Johan came up with an idea for a fun game to play with you today. Mikkel said I am invited to watch if OK with you?"

Ella frowned. "Gerhard, don't take this the wrong way, but I have to say it. Nick and I enjoy their company, but we're not sure we want to follow the path that I think you and they want us to take."

"Yeah, we're not sure," I said in support of my wife.

Gerhard was taken aback by Ella's and my bluntness. None of us spoke for a few seconds.

The old man kept his gaze on Ella for a while, glanced at me, then looked back at her and finally said, "You, see. You're never sure until you try it." He sighed. "Sometimes we get scared and don't do something that we later regret not doing."

Gerhard reached his hand to Ella's thigh and stroked it. Ella's stomach muscles trembled.

He continued to whisper, "But we should not be scared. I know of the wisdom of resisting temptation, but sometimes temptation is good. Temptation is what makes us try new things. That's what life is all about. Trying out new things. 'Cos if we don't try new things, life is too dull, isn't it?"

Gerhard's hand moved from the front of Ella's thigh to her buttock, left uncovered by her Brazilian bikini bottom. Ella's chest began moving up and down faster. I saw goosebumps rising on her skin.

Gerhard continued to rub her butt cheek, his fingers touching the hem of her bikini bottom.

He smiled at her. "That flutter in your stomach, Ella, tells you that your body likes temptation. You want the newness Johan and Mikkel bring." His hand slid under the hem of Ella's bikini bottom. Gerhard cupped her ass cheek and smiled again. "What I am saying is: don't run away when your body wants something. Because your body knows best what you need. You also know it on a subconscious level, but you are afraid of admitting it to yourself. Give it a try! Respond to what your body wants and see how it goes."

Ella bit her bottom lip, looked around as if she was concerned someone would overhear her and said, "I am a married woman, Gerhard."

Gerhard pulled his hand out of her bikini bottom. "I know. But you live your life only once." He nodded towards me. "Your husband knows it. He also lives his life only once and wants to try something new, and the good thing is he wants to try that something new with you. Not without you. With you. Think about it!"

Ella looked at me.

I didn't say anything.

Gerhard took his book, lay on his back, and flicked through the pages to find the page he had stopped reading at.

Ella and I were still standing silent.

Without taking his eyes off his book, Gerhard said, "Why don't you lie down and wait for the boys, see how you feel around them, what your body and mind tell you, Ella. I know what Nick wants, so I am not talking to him. It's up to you, really. You're the one who has to decide."

Gerhard continued reading his book.

Ella and I lay down on the sunbeds and enjoyed the sun until, about an hour later, Mikkel and Johan turned up.

"Hi, Ella! Nick! Would you like to have a drink with us?" Johan asked. "They've just opened the bar!"

"No, thanks!" Ella said.

Mikkel sat down on the edge of her lounger. "Why so, gorgeous?"

"Hi-hi!" Johan giggled. "A hangover from yesterday?"

Ella smiled. "Yes."

She sat up on the sunbed next to Mikkel.

I sat up too.

There was tension in the air. Ella knew these three men had

planned something to up their game with her, and she was nervous.

"It was too much yesterday, wasn't it?" Mikkel said and wrapped his arm around her waist. Ella's stomach muscles contracted, feeling the palm of his hand on her belly button.

Gerhard now sat up, too, and looked at Ella and Mikkel. "Too much booze or too much fun?" the old man asked. A mischievous smile spread across his face.

"Too much booze," Ella said. "I'll give it a rest today."

Johan squatted in front of her. He put his hands on her knees and looked up at her. "So, you had too much alcohol but not too much fun. It means we can have fun today, right?" He began slowly spreading her legs apart, not taking his eyes off hers and smiling seductively.

Mikkel's hand slipped to Ella's lower abdomen. His fingers touched the front string of her bikini bottom.

"Johan and I have planned a fun game for today," Mikkel said.

He slid his fingers under the string of Ella's bikini bottom where her pussy landing strip was. At the same time, Johan started to slide his hands up her inner thighs.

I had a perfect view of Ella's cameltoe. I was getting a hard-on just by thinking about how close their hands were getting to my wife's pussy.

Ella's face flushed red. Her breathing accelerated. She was getting aroused and worried at the same time. She was worried that she might not resist the temptation.

She still tried to act cool and forced a nervous giggle. "Hi-hi! What's that fun game?"

Johan's hands reached the creases between her pussy and her thighs. Mikkel's hand slipped further into her bikini bottom, right between her thighs, his knuckles pushing up the fabric. Ella gasped. Mikkel had cupped her pussy.

Johan looked at me and winked. "Nick, you'll join us, right?" He hooked his fingers under the sides of the front panel of Ella's bikini bottom and pulled the fabric up.

And I saw it. Yes! Mikkel's hand was right on her pussy. Gently moving up and down. Not inside her slit but rubbing her outer pussy lips.

Mikkel lowered his face towards her neck and planted his lips on her collarbone.

Johan looked at Ella. "Ella, Mikkel and I have been getting along very well with you and Nick. And we have been thinking of inviting the two of you to our room to play a game. We'll have fun, a lot of fun."

Johan tried to push Mikkel's hand off Ella's pussy so that he could touch it, but Mikkel did not let him do it.

Mikkel glared at Johan for a moment but then giggled. "Hi-hi! Johan and I are very competitive. We constantly fight over who's better in this or that. So, we thought you could help us solve our dispute. Nick is also invited to compete. You'll be the referee, Ella."

Ella's breathing was heavy. Her thigh muscles were shaking. Her pupils were dilated, and her lower lip had dropped. She was turned on like hell.

Mikkel looked at me. "Nick, tell your wife you're game!"

Ella looked at me.

I swallowed in panic. I panicked because I knew precisely what Mikkel was asking me. And I knew I had promised Ella to help her resist temptation. But she was struggling to resist. And I was struggling to help her. I was struggling because of my rock-hard cock. My heart was racing, and my balls were tingling. I wanted the two Danes to fuck my wife while I watched.

"Nick wants to play, Ella. You'll like it," Gerhard interjected.

Ella and I kept staring at each other.

"You'll like it, Ella!" Mikkel whispered. "Say yes!"

Ella swallowed nervously but did not say anything. She just kept looking me in the eyes.

"Nick, tell Ella you want her to do it!" Johan prompted me.

I could no longer hold Ella's gaze and looked at her crotch. I could see through the gap between her bikini bottom and her pussy, created by Johan pulling on the fabric, how Mikkel's hand was moving up and down, up and down, caressing her labia.

My cock began throbbing and twitching. It was too much for me. I couldn't resist temptation. I resigned to the fact that I wanted too much to see my wife fucked by these two men, and I accepted I was too weak to resist my urges.

I was about to open my mouth to say yes when Mikkel saved me from the disgrace of reneging on my promise to my wife: he slid his fingers into her slit and parted her pussy lips. That was too much for Ella. She closed her legs, grabbed his hand and pushed it away from her pussy. She jumped onto her feet, forcing Johan to let go of her bikini bottom.

"Maybe some other time, guys!" she said, raising her voice. "Nick and I have planned to go to the beach today." She adjusted her bikini bottom, making sure her pussy was covered, and reached her hand to me. "Nick, let's go!"

I grabbed her hand, took the beach bag and stood up.

"Yeah, we were about to head off to the beach," I said and, pushing Johan out of my way, I led Ella towards the stairs off the swimming pool area.

Johan and Mikkel did not stop us. Ella and I ran to the stairs, down the steps, and then along the central walkway.

We stopped running to catch our breaths only when we reached the turn to the beach gate. Both of us were panting. Not because of physical exertion. We hadn't run more than two hundred yards. But because we were both excited and alarmed at the same time.

"They got inside my head, Nick!" Ella said, struggling to catch her breath. "They really did!"

I dropped the beach bag on the ground. "They got inside our heads, Ella, our heads! Not only inside your head! But inside mine, too!"

Still panting, Ella said, "They just went on and on. Had we stayed there a moment longer, Nick, a moment longer. . . ." She did not finish her thought.

So I finished it for her. "You were gonna say yes."

"Yes. I think I was."

"Were you gonna let them fuck you?"

"Yes."

I opened my arms, and we hugged. Ella wrapped her arms around my waist. Her breasts pressed against me, and I could feel her heart pounding in her chest.

Her lips brushed against my neck, and I felt her warm breath on my ear as she whispered, "Nick, we've got to get out of here!"

"I know," I whispered back.

We stayed embraced for some time before Ella pulled her head back and looked up at me. "Nick, I think we should not be spending much time in the hotel, and we should never go back to that pool."

"Yes, hon, I agree with you!" I lowered my lips to hers, and we kissed.

We pulled away from each other, and that was when we saw Gerhard standing about ten feet away from us and watching us.

He walked up to us and said, "I am not stalking you. But I wanted to say this, and then I'll leave you alone. You know. . . . Hm." He cleared his throat. "You know what I learned through my career and life experience? I learned that almost every couple reaches a crossroads in their marriage when they have a choice to make. A choice to break certain taboos and embark on an adventure and fun. A chance to open the door to a wonderland of uninhibited, mind-blowing sex! Or, pass on the chance, and for the rest of their lives, wonder what it could have been had they taken the opportunity when it presented itself." He sighed. "Anyway. I hope we'll catch up later, but if we don't, I wanted to tell you that you have been the most fascinating couple I have ever met."

Gerhard turned around and headed back to the swimming pool.

I smiled a bitter smile at Ella. "To the beach?"

"Let me have my hat," she said, took her sun hat from the beach bag and put it on. "To the beach!"

I took the bag, and we resumed walking towards the beach gate.

We had escaped temptation!

JOAO

"No, thanks," my wife said and politely smiled at yet another guy, who was holding in his hand a laminated sheet of paper with a route of a tour drawn on it.

Ella and I had already declined several offers of tours that a bunch of locals were trying to sell to us. The black men, most of them young, dressed in boxers and t-shirts and wearing sandals or flip-flops, had gathered along the walkway leading from the back gate of our hotel complex to the beach. These local tour guides offered tours that undercut the big international tour operators in the hotels. The bargains were very good, and the offers were worth considering. The local men were eager to sell but were not too pushy. They were polite and always smiled. I liked the Cape Verdeans. They had a laid-back attitude and yet got things done. And for that, I felt they deserved our support and would have bought a tour from them if it weren't for an agreement between Ella and me. We had agreed prior to our holiday not to go on any tours. We had planned to stay in our luxurious hotel and enjoy the all-inclusive service and the pool bar. That intention, of course, had changed. After the recent events, we wanted to stay away from the hotel. But did we want to replace lying on a sunbed on the sandy beach with spending hours in a coach driving through the arid interior of the island?

"Sharks Bay?" another man shouted and began walking towards us.

"No, thanks!" Ella said and clamped her straw hat to her head with both hands to prevent a gust of wind from blowing it away.

I waved the guy off. "Thank you!"

He politely stepped aside, not missing the opportunity to eye Ella's body up and down again as we walked past him. His gaze was not intrusive but still noticeable. I couldn't blame him. We hadn't planned our trip to the beach, so Ella had not put on a beach dress or her wrap-up sarong, and her Brazilian-style string bikini revealed plenty of skin. She had perfect body proportions and looked stunning in her beach attire. Her firm ass, natural well-shaped round breasts, and her pretty face crowned with her shoulder-length blonde hair flowing down her shoulders ought to draw plenty of attention, so I knew that this guy was not the only one ogling her. All the men lined along the walkway were looking at Ella and saying to themselves: *'I'd love to fuck this white chick!'*

Just as we thought we had left behind us the improvised 'tour agency', a guy, who had stayed aside so far, talking on his mobile phone, finished his call, tucked his phone into his pocket and walked up to us.

"Where are you from?" he asked us.

Before I could open my mouth to respond, Ella chirped, "We live in London. However, I am Croatian, and my husband is Greek."

That was an unusually lengthy reply to a trivial question we used to get all the time from locals when they approached us to sell tours or souvenirs. Usually, we would either ignore such questions or just say, "The UK."

However, Ella had decided to provide a detailed answer to this twenty-five-something-old guy's question, maybe because the soft tone in his voice and his smile instilled trust or simply because she liked him. Or probably both. He was a handsome black man with smooth brown skin and a gentle, little mischievous smile. The man was taller than average, 6 foot 1 or 2 inches tall, with a well-built but slim body, muscular legs, broad chest, and arms with well-toned biceps. Since he was not wearing a t-shirt, Ella and I could appreciate his six-pack abs accentuated by his sunlit brown skin. His strong masculine physique contrasted with the delicate features of his handsome face and soft voice.

He kept his gaze on Ella's face and smiled. She smiled back at him.

"Have you been to Sharks Bay?" the guy asked.

Sticking to my agreement with Ella not to go on tours, I replied, "No, but we'll buy a tour from the hotel. Thank you!"

The guy's neatly shaved face stretched into another smile. "You know what you buy in the hotel, don't you? Overpriced tours led by people who are not from the island. They don't know Sal as the locals know it, its culture, the peculiar facts, the local stories. The big tour operators charge you eighty euros per person for a tour of the island, while I offer it for forty euros per person!"

What the guy offered was quite attractive, so I started considering his offer. "Does it include the salt mine?" I asked him.

The black man's chest muscles sprang up; his brown skin glistened in the sun.

"Of course, sir! Look!" He pointed at the brochure in his hand. "A day tour for only forty euros per person, a small group of up to six people! We start here, drive to Sharks Bay, the salt mine, the Blue Eye—"

"What about the desert mirage?" I asked impatiently.

"That one, too!" the man replied.

Ella put her hand on my shoulder. "Nick, I don't want to spend a whole day in a coach."

"That's not a problem at all!" the young man said before I could respond to Ella. He explained, "I'll customise your tour. We'll visit only Sharks Bay, the salt mine, and the desert mirage. I'll make it half a day private tour for you! A private tour for 100 euros for the two of you. I am free tomorrow. It's gonna be less windy. In a private tour, you don't have to hang around waiting for others to come back or wait for them to have lunch or whatever. Only the three of us in my pickup truck. When you say you want to leave, we'll leave. If you say, 'I don't want to visit this place,' we don't visit it. It will be your tour."

"What about the Blue Eye?" Ella asked.

"We'll visit it too, no problem," the black man replied enthusiastically.

Ella and I looked at each other.

I shrugged my shoulders. "Why not? We haven't seen anything of the island's interior. And we want to get away from the hotel."

"OK," Ella said.

"Tomorrow, 9 o'clock?" the man asked us.

"Yes," I replied, took my wallet out of the beach bag and paid him 100 euros.

He wrote a receipt and handed it to me. "Do you want me to wait for you here or at the main entrance of your hotel?"

I tucked the receipt into my wallet. "Umm... here?"

Ella rubbed my elbow. "Honey, why do we have to walk all the way down to here?"

"Umm..., yes, you're right," I agreed with her and put my wallet back in the bag.

Ella smiled politely at our newly hired tour guide. "At the main entrance, please!"

"OK. The main entrance it is," he said, smiling too, and stretched his hand to her. "My name is Joao, by the way!"

Ella took his hand and introduced herself. "Ella."

She let go of Joao's hand and blushed. Yes, she liked the handsome black guy smiling at her. I had no doubt about that. And he knew she liked him because his smile broadened into a wide grin. The glint in his eyes betrayed his thoughts, too. He liked Ella too.

What have we done? I asked myself. *We escaped one temptation only to stumble into another!*

I stretched my hand to Joao. "Nicholas. Call me Nick!"

For a few seconds, it looked like Joao was going to ignore my hand, standing still with his eyes fixated on Ella's face. Finally, he looked at me, and we shook hands.

"Are you going to the beach?" he asked.

"Yes," Ella replied, then looked at me with a bitter smile. "We thought going to the beach would be a safer option than hanging around the hotel pool."

I knew what she meant and smiled too. "Fewer distractors, right, honey?"

Ella smiled again. "Yeah, fewer distractors."

"I know what you mean," Joao interjected. "People drink too much at the pool bar, right?"

"You can say that," I said.

The wind blew off Ella's hat.

"I'll get it!" Joao shouted and ran after it.

Ella and I watched him as he caught up with the hat and bent over to pick it up from the ground, showing his firm ass and strong leg muscles. His butt was undoubtedly one of his assets that attracted women's attention. I looked at Ella. I was not wrong. She was staring at his backside.

Joao stood up straight and turned around, holding her hat in one hand and his laminated poster in the other.

I looked at Ella again and caught her gazing at his crotch. Only for a brief second before she moved her eyes to his face, but that was enough to tell me she had also noticed what I had noticed. This guy was very endowed. Judging by the massive bulge in his shorts, he had a cock to reckon with.

Joao walked back to us and handed Ella the hat, smiling. "Hold on to it! The wind likes to steal hats, Ella!"

Ella took the hat and smiled, too. "Thank you, Joao!"

Her smile was supposed to be friendly and polite, but it came out a little too friendly, even coy. Ella realised that and blushed.

Joao pretended he had not noticed her slight embarrassment. "You've picked the windiest month to visit our island, I'm afraid."

"What's the best time to visit it?" Ella asked.

"I would say: March to June," Joao replied, then thought for a second and added, "But that's based on my preference. It is the dry season. I don't like when it rains."

Ella grabbed her hat with two hands as the wind tried to steal it from her again.

"I think it's best to do away with it," she said and stuffed her hat into the beach bag I was diligently holding. She looked back at Joao. "What about September?"

He shook his head. "No. I wouldn't recommend it. July to October is the rainy season."

"How do the seasons go?" I asked.

Joao explained, "March to June is the dry season. July to October is the rainy season. November to February is a transition. Trust me! March to June is the best time to visit! It's windy but doesn't rain and isn't too hot."

"So we picked the best time then!" Ella chirped, smiling sweetly.

She definitely likes him, I thought. *Otherwise, she would never have indulged like this in a conversation with him.*

Joao giggled. "Hi-hi! Yes, Ella! You're absolutely right!"

"Thank you, Joao!" Ella said. "I feel vindicated. Nick wanted September, but I picked March!" She kept her gaze on Joao's face; a faint smile flickered at the corners of her mouth.

Joao was holding her gaze and smiling. There was a playful spark in his eyes.

Is there too much going on between these two? I asked myself, but then I thought: *Nah! It doesn't make sense. They've just met! And what was the point of running away from Gerhard and the Danes? For her to flirt with this chap here? Nah! She wouldn't do that. It must be my imagination! It must be my imagination playing after what happened at the pool.*

"All right!" I said. "We'd better go now."

Ella put her hand under my arm, and we walked away.

"Tomorrow, 9 o'clock," Joao shouted. "In front of the hotel!"

I looked at him over my shoulder and shouted back, "Yep, see you tomorrow at 9!"

We reached the wooden platform at the end of the walkway from where the sandy beach started. Ella and I bent over to take off our sandals before stepping on the sand.

I looked back at Joao. He was standing where we had left him and watching us. I had no doubt: he was staring at my wife's ass. A wide grin spread across his face, and he gave me a thumbs-up. I did the same: smiled and gave him a thumbs-up. Having shown me he had noticed my wife's curves, he finally turned around and joined his friends.

When Ella and I got on the beach, we found a free sun lounger, put our bag on it and sandals under it and went into the water.

However, as soon as the first wave splashed onto our feet, Ella squealed, "Oh, no! It's too cold!"

"OK," I said, "let's get out and sit down for a while."

We walked out of the water and came back to our sunbed. Ella put a towel on it, and we sat next to each other. We sat in silence and watched the sea in front of us, relaxing and enjoying the sun.

The other sunbathers around us were relaxing too. Some were chatting, some were reading books, others were lying on their loungers and taking in the sun rays, and some were sleeping.

One large guy had fallen so sound asleep that he was snoring. Of course, no one bothered to wake him up. People were too polite.

Ella reached her hand to mine. "It's so beautiful here—with the sun, the sea, and the palm trees—isn't it?"

I took her hand. "Yes, it's beautiful."

We interlocked fingers and continued to sit in silence, gazing into the distance, deep in thought.

I couldn't tell for sure what Ella was thinking about. However, I suspected she was thinking about Joao.

Have we run away from one temptation only to get tempted by an even stronger one? I asked myself. *What are the odds of meeting someone like Joao after the recent events at the pool? And after Paulo in the Jacuzzi? Meeting another charming young black guy who makes a strong impression on Ella. And who seems as hung as the Paulo guy! How odd is that?*

I kept thinking. *Maybe because we got so hooked on the idea. On Gerhard's idea! Huh! Maybe it's not a coincidence. Could it be that Ella is sending subconscious signals, as the old man said, and attracts them?! Like pheromones? Yes, it must be Ella. It's her! Not the men!*

I looked at Ella. She was watching the waves in the distance. She didn't even notice I was looking at her. Her face was sombre. She was thinking hard about something.

The more I watched Ella's face, the more I was getting convinced she was thinking about Joao. Ella liked him a lot, as a man —pure physical attraction—and as a person, despite her brief interaction with him. And I could not blame her. Joao was strong, muscular, endowed, and charming. And being black only added to the perception of exoticism and erotism.

"Joao seems a nice guy," I said.

"Yeah," Ella murmured, staring into the distance.

"We could have gone on a tour from the hotel, but his tour is cheaper. Though, there's a risk with him."

Ella turned her head sharply and looked at me. "Are you worried he might do something to us?"

"No, not that! They wouldn't have let these guys hang around at the hotel gate if they had done something dodgy. They would've been reported to the police and the hotel by now. No. We'll be safe with Joao. But he poses a risk to our fight with temptation, don't you think?"

Ella kept her gaze on me for a while, not saying anything. Then she sighed and looked at the sea again. I let go of her hand and wrapped my arm around her shoulders. I also looked at the waves splashing on the beach. It was soothing and relaxing.

We stayed embraced like that for several minutes until my gaze wandered off the sea and fell on a woman who was lying face down on a lounger a few feet away from us. I was looking at the woman for about a minute—she had a sexy butt—when she rolled over onto her back. She was topless and bared her breasts. Her boyfriend or husband squatted next to her and started applying sunscreen on her chest and boobs. Another guy, who was sitting in the sand next to the sunbed, stood up and said something to the woman, to which she laughed. Her boyfriend or husband also laughed. Apparently, the three knew each other. The guy that had stood up had a tent in his trunks. I saw out of the corner of my eye that Ella had also turned her head to watch the couple and their friend.

"We made the right choice with Joao, honey," I said quietly. "A cheaper tour with a local guy who knows the island."

The guy with the tent in his trunks now went and squatted on the other side of the bed opposite the man applying lotion on the woman's chest and put his hand on her stomach.

The woman giggled and pushed his hand away. The two guys looked at each other and laughed.

I stroked Ella's shoulder. "People are having fun. Maybe Gerhard is right, after all. As he said, we should embark on an adventure while the opportunity has presented itself. Maybe Joao is the right guy to open the door to wonderland for us."

Ella pulled away from me and looked at my face.

I said, "I am thinking, honey. Maybe it's karma that we met him just when we were running away from that same door. The one Mikkel and Johan wanted to open for us. Perhaps Joao is a better choice."

Ella stared at me without saying a word.

I caressed her arm with the back of my hand. "I mean, as a one-off." I lowered my voice as if someone could overhear me. "Like. No one knows him. We don't know him to feel conscientious or something. He doesn't know us either. He doesn't know any of our friends, family. He even doesn't know anyone in the hotel, you know, to talk about us and spread rumours. No one would find out. Only you and I would know."

Ella was now biting her lips, still not taking her eyes off me.

"I mean," I continued, "he's perfect for a no-strings-attached thing. To try it once and see how it is. We'll never see him again. He'll never see us again. It would be like nothing ever happened."

Ella pursed her lips and blew air out. "Don't know, Nick!"

She looked at the topless woman and the two guys playing with her.

SEA TURTLE

Ella and I watched in silence the topless woman and her two suitors. The man who had been applying sunscreen on the woman's tits passed the bottle to the other guy. The latter squirted lotion on his palm and spread the sunscreen on the woman's stomach. She suppressed laughter, and her abs muscles convulsed as she felt ticklish.

The guy who was now in charge of the woman's skin protection moved his hand from her stomach to her thigh, and she spread her legs apart.

Not taking my eyes off the woman and the two men, I lowered my mouth to Ella's ear and whispered, "Is it me, or are there too many people into swinging in this resort?"

Ella did not answer my question but pulled her head back and looked at me, somewhat surprised by my question.

"What?!" I shrugged my shoulders. "That's what it feels like, isn't it?"

Ella burst into quiet laughter. She looked around to check whether she had drawn attention, and when she saw no one was interested in our conversation, she leaned to me and whispered, "Did you look at the small print on the web page when you booked this holiday?"

"Hi-hi!" I giggled. "There was no small print." I paused before adding quietly, "I'm sure I haven't booked a swinger resort, hon."

"In that case, threesomes are simply on the rise, honey!" Ella giggled. "Hi-hi! That's the explanation! Let's go with it!"

The woman being serviced by the two guys squealed, and Ella and I looked at her. One of the guys was tickling her, and she was laughing. This time the behaviour of the mischievous triplet attracted the attention of the other sunbathers, and the woman lowered her voice but continued to giggle, pushing the hands of the intruder away.

Ella reached her hand to mine. "Let's go back to our room!"

I took her hand and asked her, "Why?" although I knew the answer.

Ella leaned her mouth to my ear. "'Cos I am horny!"

"We should so much go back to our room!"

"We'll sneak in. Without the others seeing us."

"Yes, we'll be super stealthy!"

"Nick, just the two of us, right?"

I smiled. "Yes, just the two of us!"

We got up, put the towel in the beach bag, grabbed our sandals and left the sunbeds area. When we got on the wooden platform at the end of the sandy beach, we brushed the sand off our feet, put our sandals on and headed back to the hotel following the same walkway we had used to get to the beach.

We reached the place where the local tour guides were hanging out. There were now more people coming to the beach, so it was pretty crowded.

We saw Joao, who was busy talking to a couple, and we thought he would not notice us and were about to walk past him when he waved at us. "Hey, Ella! Nick! Did you like the beach?"

We stopped walking, and I said, "Hi, Joao! Umm, yeah, it's beautiful out there."

"The water was cold," Ella said and smiled somewhat apologetically.

He smiled, too, and held up his hand. "Just a sec!" He turned to the couple and handed them a receipt. "Monday, 9 am at the main entrance!"

The couple nodded yes and walked away.

Now Joao was able to focus his full attention on Ella and me. "Did you go in the water at all?"

Ella said, "Ankle-deep was more than enough!"

"Ha-ha! Ankle-deep!" Joao laughed. "That's why you found the water cold! The trick is to dive straight into the water. The pain lasts a few seconds, and you're fine after that! You can swim for hours."

Ella giggled. "Hi-hi! No, thanks! Not into this freezing water." She shook her head energetically, and, smiling sheepishly at Joao, she hugged herself and imitated shivering. "Brr! No, I can't do that!"

Joao smiled again. "But that's the way to do it, Ella. That's how I always do it and never feel cold!"

Another smile flickered across Ella's lips as she cocked her head to the side. "Never?"

"Never!" Joao shook his head from side to side, smiling, not taking his eyes off her.

Gosh! I thought. *These two are cracking smile after smile! If that's not flirting, I don't know what is!*

"Let me show you how I do it!" Joao said with a burst of energy.

He walked up to the foot-tall and half-foot-wide stone parapet separating the paved walkway from the sandy beach ground and picked up a bag. He put his tour brochure, pen and receipt book into the bag, put the bag down and got up on the parapet, facing away from the walkway. He looked over his shoulder at Ella and me and smiled. Then he turned to look back in front of him, leaned forward as if he was about to dive headfirst and jumped onto his knees in the sand.

"Ha-ha!" Both Ella and I laughed.

"That's how you do it!" Joao said. He stood up and walked backwards, preparing to get up on the parapet and demonstrate his diving technique again.

Ella took my arm and hugged it. She swayed her body back and forth, watching Joao and smiling. She had such a playful glint in her eye.

Joao demonstrated another 'dive'.

"You see?" he said as he got off the ground and spread his hands. "You can learn so much from a local!"

Ella stopped swaying her body and let go of my arm.

She continued to look at Joao and smile in amusement. She didn't try to hide that she found him funny and entertaining.

Ella rubbed her clavicle, not taking her gaze off him, and hesitated for a second but then said, "Joao, may I ask you something?"

"Sure! Ask me anything you want!" he replied enthusiastically, stepped over the parapet, and walked back to us.

Ella said, "Do you know where we can see sea turtles?"

Before Joao could answer her question, one of the guys who had come to listen to our conversation said, "I'll show you a turtle! Come with me! I have a turtle in my house. Fifty euros!"

Joao pushed the guy gently in the chest to step back and said something to him in Creole.

The man stepped back but said to Ella, "March is not a turtles season, but for forty euros, I'll show you my turtle."

"Shut up, Tiago! I'll show her a proper turtle!" Joao said in English to the intruder and then turned to Ella. "Ella, it's not the turtles season, but I can take you to the sanctuary." He nodded towards an area fenced with green mesh around fifty yards from us on the sand dune. "They keep rescued turtles there."

"Thirty euros, and I'll drive you to my place and will show you my turtle!" the Tiago guy said. He took his phone out of his pocket and started scrolling through his photos. "Let me show you a photo of my turtle. It's huge!"

Joao ignored Tiago and explained to Ella and me, "When they rescue turtle nests, they bring the baby turtles to the sanctuary and release them into the sea when they are strong enough to survive on their own. Sometimes, they rescue adult turtles too. Mauled by dogs, boat propellors. They keep them until they recover. I have a friend at the sanctuary. He told me he would be releasing some turtles today. Come with me! I'll ask him to show you some. He might give us one to release!"

Ella hesitated for a second, but Joao smiled at her invitingly and took her hand in his. "Come with me! You'll like it!"

He was about to lead Ella and me to an exit on the side of the walkway from where we could walk over the sand towards the sanctuary, but Tiago stepped in front of us.

"Here!" he said and showed us his phone screen with a photo of a turtle. "For twenty euros, you can hold a huge turtle! See?"

Joao let go of Ella's hand and scolded his colleague in Portuguese or Creole—I couldn't quite tell the difference—then turned to Ella and me and said, "It's illegal to keep turtles at home!"

Joao reached his hand to Ella, and she took it.

Tiago got pissed off and shouted, "OK, lady! Go with him! The turtles he'll show you are tiny! Rescue turtles. Sick! They're not worth it."

"Don't listen to him," Joao said. "They are not sick and are not tiny. I'll show you good size turtles. For free!"

"Really? For free?" Tiago shook his head in disappointment.

Joao gently tugged on Ella's hand. "Yeah! For free! Come! You'll see. My turtles are of good size!"

"Ha-ha!" Tiago suddenly burst into laughter. "He'll show you, lady, good size, all right? His turtle is very big indeed!" Tiago scrolled hurriedly through the photos on his phone and showed a photo to Ella. "Here! This is Joao's turtle! Ask him to let you hold it! Ha-ha! Ha-ha!"

Ella's and my jaws dropped. Tiago was showing us a photo of a white woman's pussy and a huge black cock with a tattoo of an anchor on the shaft pointing at her pussy. The face and the upper body of the woman were not in the photo, but her spread thighs, pussy and stomach were. And that black cock was huge. I was aware that some pictures could be taken from an angle that exemplifies the size, but that was not the case with this photo. It was clear that the cock was huge because there was a basis for comparison. There was another cock in the picture. It was a white cock, erect, lying on the woman's stomach. Apparently, the photo was of a woman being fucked by two guys – a black man and a white man. By comparing the two cocks, it was clear the black cock was twice as big as the white cock.

Joao pushed the vulgar man in the chest and shouted at him in their local language, then turned to Ella and me. "Ignore him! Let's go!"

He pulled on Ella's hand, and we followed him.

Joao led us off the walkway onto the sand dune. We had to walk around the green fence for a while until we reached the entrance to the fenced area.

Joao called someone, and a guy turned up.

"This is Domingos," Joao introduced his friend, then nodded to us. "Ella and Nick."

Domingos nodded hello, and Ella and I nodded back.

Joao and Domingos exchanged a few words in Creole before Domingos said to Ella and me in English, "Give me a minute! I'll give you one to release."

Joao and his friend went into a shanty shack, and Ella and I waited for a couple of minutes before Joao returned with a turtle. It wasn't small at all. There were some scars on its shell.

"Oh, my God!" Ella squealed excitedly. "It's so beautiful!"

Domingos came out of the shed and said, "It was mauled by a

propeller but healed well. She's ready to go back into the sea."

Joao stretched his hands, holding the turtle towards Ella. "Do you like it?"

"Yes, I do!" Ella squeaked again, all in smiles. She touched the turtle's shell.

"Be careful!" Domingos warned her. "Turtles bite!"

Joao held the turtle for Ella to touch it again. I also brushed the turtle's shell.

"Let's go and release it!" Joao said and headed for the ocean.

Ella and I thanked Domingos and followed Joao.

As we walked through the beach grass, Joao explained that when turtles come to the shore to lay eggs, if there is a major settlement nearby, they get confused by the lights and lay their eggs in places that are not safe for the hatchlings or themselves. That is when the conservationists most often come to the rescue.

Joao told us he volunteered in turtle rescue during the egg-laying season, but off-season, he concentrated on his tours business.

I listened to Joao and couldn't fail to notice that he was well-educated, caring, and polite. He was nice to be around. I liked him. Ella liked him too, although in a different way, judging by how she eyed his body up and down as she followed him.

As we walked, I reflected on her behaviour around Joao. *The signs in her body language when she talked to him at the sanctuary and earlier at the tour guides' place were more than obvious. The little glint in her eye and the way she smiles at him whenever he looks at her; the way she plays with her hair when his gaze falls upon her face for a little longer; swaying her body back and forth as she watches him showing his 'diving technique'. These are unmistakable signs that she is sexually attracted to the guy. I also caught her several times, glancing at the sizeable bulge in his shorts.*

Before coming to Cape Verde, I thought she was not into large cocks. She's always told me size doesn't matter. But our experience with Paulo, and her glances at Joao's crotch, make me think otherwise. Maybe she is not a size queen, but she definitely likes large cocks, or at least is curious about them. Perhaps Ella has been telling me size is unimportant, not to make me feel insecure. My cock is just about average size, after all! Or, maybe she has been honest with me. She's been only with one man before me, and she has told me he is about my size. So, she didn't know how a big cock looked like or felt before we arrived at this resort, where she developed an interest in large penises. Such an explanation makes the most sense. Gerhard's 'teachings' and the Danes constantly hitting on her have helped her open up to sexual experimentation. And then, for the first time in her life, she encountered large cocks for real. First, Paulo's truly enormous penis—feeling it in her hand and taking it into her mouth must have been an eye opener—and now, the enticing contours of Joao's sizeable member in his shorts. It has been a journey of discovery for her.

We reached the sea, and Joao stopped, turned around and said, "Ella, hold the turtle on each side of the shell; otherwise, it can bite you!"

He held the turtle with the head away from Ella so she could pick the animal up safely.

"Well done!" Joao praised her once she was holding the turtle. Then he removed his sandals and said, "You are in swimming gear, but I don't want to get my shorts wet."

And before Ella and I realised what he was about to do, he took his shorts off.

He wasn't wearing briefs underneath, and his cock swung out! It was a massive cock! And it had a tattoo of an anchor on its shaft! The black cock in the photo Tiago had shown us was Joao's!

Both Ella and I stared at Joao's penis. It was a nine or ten incher and was thick, really thick, with a wide base like Paulo's—maybe a tad thicker or thinner. It was hard to say. And like Paulo's, his cock was circumcised and had a prominent cockhead. I couldn't blame Ella for staring at Joao's manhood. It was impressive. A giant black cock, flaccid and hanging down between his muscular legs.

Joao caught Ella's gaze and smiled. "Let me help you release it!"

He stood behind Ella and put his hands under her elbows. He glued his chest to her back and pressed his crotch against her butt.

Ella kicked her sandals off, and they slowly walked into the water in a choo-choo train style—Ella holding the turtle and Joao supporting her arms from behind.

Huh! I thought to myself. *With his cock behind you, the water doesn't feel so cold, honey, does it?*

When they were knee-deep, Joao whispered in her ear, "Let go of it! Slowly!"

They're only knee-deep in the water! I thought. *There was no need to take his shorts off. It was an excuse to show off his impressive cock!*

Hugging my wife from behind, Joao lowered her hands and nudged her to bend over. Ella bent over and pushed her butt back against his cock.

She let go of the turtle.

"Yay! I released a turtle!" Ella squealed in excitement as the turtle swam away.

"Yes, you did!" Joao said and let go of her elbows, but instead of stepping back when Ella stood straight, he wrapped his arms around her waist from behind and placed his hands on her stomach.

"Let's watch it swim away!" he said and hooked his chin over her shoulder, brushing his cheek against hers and pressing his cock against her bum.

Ella giggled and did not push him away.

WIFE TRIES SOMETHING NEW

The turtle disappeared, and Joao finally let go of my wife. They turned around and began walking back to the shore.

Joao's cock was now semi-erect, proudly swaying from side to side.

God! I thought. *These Cape Verdeans have cocks to show! Are all of them so hung?!?* I couldn't help but compare what I was seeing between Joao's legs with what I had seen between Paulo's. *Whose is bigger? Hm. It's hard to tell if I can't see them side by side!*

"Nick, did you see me? I released a turtle!" Ella chirruped as she put her sandals on.

"I saw you, honey, I saw you. You did great!" I praised her and went to her.

I put my arm around her shoulders, and we watched Joao put his shorts and sandals on.

"Let's go back!" he said once he had tucked away his impressive tool.

We headed back to the walkway, walking through the sand dunes.

"You know that your hotel is the best hotel in Sal?" Joao said as we walked around a bunch of dune grass.

"Is it?" I asked.

"Yes!" he replied. "I visited it once and loved it! It is truly luxurious there!"

"It is," Ella agreed with him.

"It's too expensive for folks like me," Joao lamented.

"How did you get to visit it?" I asked.

Joao said casually, "Tiago and I were invited to spend the night with someone's girlfriend, but we got kicked out after a couple of hours. Things got messed up. Otherwise, I would have gladly stayed much longer."

Ella and I stopped walking and looked at each other. *Wow! The photo, and now this?*

Joao stopped walking, too, and smiled. "You know, some tourists come to swing. A one-night stand, things like that. The guy wanted to share his girlfriend with black guys." Joao shrugged his shoulders, and his smile stretched wider. "What?! Life is about having fun, isn't it?"

"You sound so much like someone else," I said.

Joao raised his eyebrows. "Like whom?"

"Never mind!" I waved him off and resumed walking.

Ella and Joao followed me.

We walked in silence for a while before I said, "It is you in that photo, isn't it?"

"Yes," Joao confirmed.

I asked, "Who took the photo?"

"Tiago," Joao replied, but when he saw Ella's disapproving look, he clarified, "He took it only because she and her friends asked him to do it."

I raised my eyebrows. "Her friends?"

Joao giggled. "Hi-hi! Yeah. Her friends. Tiago and I, her boyfriend and his friend gangbanged her."

"Joao!" Ella squealed. "That's awful!"

"No! It's not. They had fun. We all had fun," Joao said. "Only at the end, the boyfriend went sour."

We didn't talk until we reached the place on the walkway where Joao's colleagues were hanging out.

We got on the paved path, and Joao picked up his bag from the parapet. We prepared to say our goodbyes.

"Are you going back to your hotel?" he asked.

"Yeah, we are going back to our room," I said.

"Oh, I see!" He smiled, somehow guessing that Ella and I

intended to fuck.

Ella blushed and found herself at pains to convince him otherwise. "We'll shower, relax, have a coffee from the minibar. We'll watch TV. We'll call home. That's what we'll be doing. We need to kill time."

"Kill time?" Joao squeaked. "It sounds like you're bored! You are on holiday in one of the best hotels on this island! Do something! Have fun!"

"Yeah, we did that," I said. "We had fun, and things were never dull, but, well, they got out of control." I looked briefly at Ella, and she smiled, blushing. I continued, "Joao, the thing is we are trying to avoid the lobby, the pool, the aqua park, the hotel restaurants, . . . well, everything." I sighed. "Don't ask me why!"

"Well, in that case," Joao said thoughtfully, "would you like me to take you on your tour today? I am free."

"Oh! Can we do it today?" I asked.

"Yeah, we can," Joao confirmed.

I looked at Ella. "Honey?"

"Umm. . . don't know." Ella placed her hand on her chest, thinking for a few moments. "Maybe we could do it today." She shrugged her shoulders. "We'll be away from the hotel."

"Yeah, let's do that then," I said and turned to Joao. "Joao, would you wait here while we go change in our room?" I looked at my watch. "Let's say. . . fifteen minutes to our room, five minutes to get changed, fifteen minutes—"

"Nick! Nick!" Joao interrupted me. "Don't change now! You need to wear swimsuits for Sharks Bay and at the salt mine, anyway. That's where we are going first. You'll change into your clothes afterwards." He nodded at the beach bag in my hand, where he could see my shorts, t-shirt, and Ella's light summer dress and thong.

I thought for a second before agreeing with him. "Actually, yeah, you're right. We'll change afterwards."

Joao looked at his watch. "If we leave now, we'll be able to do Sharks Bay and the salt mine before lunch. We'll have lunch in Palmeira, the fisher's village. Then we'll drive up to Buracona - the Blue Eye Cave, and on our way back, we'll stop at Terra Boa for the desert mirage. We'll be back by five o'clock. What would you say? Shall we?"

Ella and I looked at each other.

I shrugged my shoulders. "Why not? We wanted to be away, didn't we? Let's do it!"

"OK, let's go," Ella agreed with me.

"My pickup is parked over there!" Joao pointed at several pickup trucks parked about a hundred yards from where we stood.

He went ahead, and Ella and I followed him.

5. THE ISLAND TOUR

SHARKS AND RAZORS

Joao took us to a Toyota Land Cruiser pickup truck and unlocked it. "Where would you like to ride? In the back or the cab?"

"In the cab," Ella replied.

"In the back," I said.

Ella looked at me. "Nick, are you sure? It's windy!"

I chuckled. "He-he! It's just fresh air, honey!"

She shrugged her shoulders. "OK! You know better."

Joao lowered the tailgate door for me. "Tap on the roof if you want to come inside. OK?"

I nodded yes and got on the truck's flatbed. There were two benches lined along the side panels, and I sat on one of the benches. Joao secured the tailgate door and went to open the passenger side door for Ella to get in the cab.

She got in the passenger seat, and he closed the door for her. Then he opened the back seat door and tucked his bag under Ella's seat, closed the door and went to the driver's side of the truck.

He looked up at me. "Ready to go?"

I gave him a thumbs-up, and he got in the driver's seat.

We departed at 10:30.

Within less than five minutes, I regretted my decision to travel in the back of the truck because it was indeed windy. Nonetheless, I persevered watching the mostly barren scenery for a while before my attention shifted to what Ella and Joao were doing in the cab. I could not hear what they were talking about, but I watched them through the truck's back window and figured out that Joao was throwing jokes because Ella kept smiling and laughing.

Fifteen minutes into the trip, Ella and Joao seemed to be getting along really well. She was giggling almost nonstop, and at one point, she turned in her seat to face him, despite the seat belt. He told her a joke or something that made her burst into laughter. He chuckled too, and while he kept his eyes on the road, he reached his hand and rubbed her thigh.

They joked and talked for another five minutes or so, and Ella turned further to face him. She put her feet on the seat and hugged her knees to her chest, exposing a good portion of her butt cheeks. She kept giggling as he continued to throw joke after joke. And then he reached his hand and put it on her buttock. He said something, and Ella's reaction was to spread her legs apart and look down between her thighs. Joao's hand moved between her legs, slipped up on the inside of her thigh and stopped about an inch away from her cameltoe. Shaking her head and laughing, she opened her legs as wide as possible and pointed with her finger at the crease between her thigh and pussy. Joao slid his hand further up, and his fingers touched her labia over the fabric of her bikini bottom. Ella burst into laughter, grabbed his wrist, and pushed his hand away. She closed her legs, still giggling.

I had had enough of watching them without knowing what they were talking about. Also, the wind had become unbearable, and my ears got blocked, so I knocked on the cab roof. Joao looked in the rearview mirror and gave me a sign he would pull over.

A minute later, I was sitting in the back seat behind him.

"Did you freeze out there?" Ella asked me.

I smiled. "Freeze? No. But my ears started to ache; it's too windy."

"I told you!" Ella said, happy she was proven right.

I fastened the seatbelt. "How far to Sharks Bay?"

"We'll be there in ten minutes," Joao said. "We'll go off-road here. It's a shortcut to Sharks Bay that only the local guides know about."

Seconds later, we were driving off-road.

Joao looked at me in the rearview mirror and said, "Nick, before you joined us, Ella and I were arguing about whether women should shave or wax when wearing a bikini. Your wife says that shaving is the way to go. I'm saying that waxing is better if you want to be sure no pubic hair sticks out. Not that I mind it, but just for the argument's sake. What's your take on this issue?"

"Umm. . . ." I thought for a second before saying, "I tend to agree with Ella."

"Ha-ha!" Joao laughed. "Husband-wife solidarity!"

"No. It's not that." I waved my hand. "I just think that shaving is enough. I mean, waxing is probably smoother, but it's too traumatic to the skin, and as far as bikini goes, shaving is just good enough."

"Absolutely!" Ella now chimed in. "Shaving is healthier."

"Well, that depends," Joao said. "As I was saying earlier, my ex-girlfriend switched to waxing after she got tired of razor burn." He smiled and glanced at Ella briefly before looking back at the road. "There's no way to shave yourself down there without cutting yourself or getting razor burn."

"That's not true!" Ella squeaked, smiling and shaking her head from side to side. "I showed you already! I shaved this morning and have no razor burn or cuts!"

"Yeah, because it's just the crease. But if you got further in, . . . how to say this. . . ." Joao looked at Ella again and smiled shyly. "I mean, the labia. The skin is delicate. And there's curvier. That's where you get razor burn. You can't avoid—"

"No!" Ella squealed. "You absolutely can! I can. I use a special razor and completely shave. . . ." She stopped midsentence, hesitant to reveal too much detail about her private parts.

I had no such qualms and said, "Yeah, Joao, Ella shaves her labia bare. OK? And granted: she's not hairy down there, but she still regularly shaves her pussy lips and leaves only a landing strip. And I've never seen razor burn."

"Yeah," Ella confirmed and looked between her legs, spreading them apart again and using her hand to pull her bikini bottom to one side so she could better inspect the crease between her thigh and pussy.

Joao kept his eyes on the road but watched her in his peripheral vision. He shook his head slowly from side to side, smiling.

Ella saw him doing that and got a little irritated but still smiled. "What?! You don't believe me?!" She stared at him, holding her legs apart.

Joao shrugged his shoulders. "Look! As I told you, my ex-girlfriend—"

"Your ex-girlfriend didn't know how to shave her pussy, Joao," I interrupted him. "I assure you: Ella has no problems!"

"OK!" Joao said, glancing briefly at Ella's crotch and looking back ahead at the road.

A mischievous smile spread across his lips.

"Trust me! Ella shaved this morning, and her skin is absolutely smooth!" I said, getting caught up in the argument myself but also turned on by the discussion about my wife's private parts.

"Yeah, OK. I believe you. All smooth down there!" Joao said, and his smile broadened.

"It is smooth!" Ella squealed. She looked between her legs again and pulled the fabric of her bikini bottom further, revealing her crease all the way to her pussy lip. "Look, Joao! No razor burn, no bumps, no ingrown hair!"

Joao slowed the pickup down and looked at what Ella was showing him. "Yeah, Ella, as I said, there's OK, but the area with more sensitive skin?"

"It's pretty sensitive skin down here, Joao!" Ella said, smiling and shaking her head. "You just don't want to believe me, do you?"

Joao shrugged his shoulders. "As I said: when you shave your labia, and I mean your. . . ." He paused, trying to find the words for 'pussy lips' in English or just not sure if he should use those words.

I said them for him, "Pussy lips."

"Yeah." He nodded. "They are curved, and it's much harder for the razor—"

"Show him, hon!" I said to Ella, cutting Joao off mid-sentence.

Joao looked at me in the rearview mirror, unsure if he understood correctly what I was asking my wife to show him.

Ella also turned her head to look at me and whispered, "Nick!"

I said, "Hon, show him! He won't believe you unless he sees your skin down there."

Suddenly there was silence. Only the tyres could be heard rumbling on the pebbly ground.

Joao slowed the truck almost to a standstill. He had been driving off-road, so there were no cars around and slowing down was not a problem.

Ella kept staring at me, sitting with her feet on the seat and her legs spread apart, holding her bikini bottom pulled to one side.

She swallowed nervously. She was hesitating.

Joao stopped the pickup completely and turned in his seat to look at Ella's crotch.

Ella looked at him. She was not smiling anymore. She was nervous and hesitant, biting her lips. Her chest was moving up and down fast. *'Shall I do it or not?'* was written all over her face.

Joao smiled at her softly but didn't say a word.

Ella's face turned red. She hesitated for another five or ten seconds, then smiled briefly and pulled her bikini to one side, showing her entire pussy. Her labia were on full display, and my already hard cock twitched in excitement as I watched her show her most intimate parts to the stranger sitting next to her.

And as if seeing my wife's pussy was not enough for Joao, he reached his hand between her legs, and his fingers touched her labia majora.

Ella trembled at his touch, and her face turned crimson red as she looked at the hand, feeling her pussy. Joao ran the pads of his fingers over her outer pussy lips from her clitoral hood down to her swollen pink inner pussy lips. Ella's vaginal hole was wide open and glistening. She was wet and aroused. Talking to Joao about her private parts had undoubtedly turned her on. Ella was aroused even before he had touched her. But now, feeling his hand on her pussy, brought her to a whole new level. Her breathing turned heavy, her pupils dilated, and she began biting on her bottom lip, watching Joao's hand as he traced her labia.

She was tense and aroused at the same time. I could hear her heart beating in her chest as she held her bikini bottom pulled to one side.

Joao ran his fingers over her pussy lips again, then withdrew his hand, and Ella pulled her bikini bottom back, covering her pussy.

"Yeah," Joao said. "My ex-girlfriend apparently didn't know how to do it!"

"Ha-ha!" I laughed. "I told you, didn't I?"

Ella smiled. "It's smooth, isn't it?"

"It's gorgeous, Ella!" Joao said. "Your pussy's gorgeous!"

As if Ella wasn't blushing already, Joao's compliment about her pussy made her blush twice more.

Joao adjusted the tent in his shorts, evoking a giggle from Ella.

"You've got to teach me how to shave ladies down there, Ella," he said, "in case my next girlfriend also doesn't know how to do it!"

"Ha-ha!" Ella laughed. "I'll write you instructions!" She turned to face ahead. "Are we going to Sharks Bay or not?" A smile of superiority flickered at the corners of her lips.

Ella had enjoyed her little striptease show. And moreover, the sense of power it had given her, power over a stranger she had met barely two hours earlier. She liked how much he had become mesmerised by her sex appeal. And, of course, she knew I had also loved her performance since she had seen me adjusting my erect cock in my trunks.

Joao put his foot on the accelerator.

We travelled in silence. Each one of us was reflecting on our little frivolity.

It turned out we were not far from Sharks Bay because, within a few minutes, we saw the beach and the sea, and Joao turned to drive along the shore a few feet away from the splashing waves.

He slowed down and pointed at the sea. "Can you see the shark fins?"

Ella and I looked in the direction he was pointing at.

"These are mature sharks," he clarified.

We saw a few dorsal fins popping out of the water thirty or forty yards away from the shore.

"I see them! I see them!" Ella squeaked excitedly.

I joined her, shouting, "I see them! Yes!"

"Big sharks are dangerous," Joao explained. "Lemon sharks are not aggressive towards humans but will bite if they feel threatened. You can walk or swim to them but not too close. However, baby sharks are safe to approach. They are over there!"

He pointed in the distance down the shore. Ella and I looked in that direction and saw parked cars, groups of tourists, and people walking in the shallows.

Joao continued to explain, "Baby sharks stay in the shallows to avoid getting eaten by their mums and dads—the big sharks. Sharks are cannibals; they eat their own, given the opportunity.

I'll park where you see the tourists and the shacks. I am not allowed to take you to the baby sharks in the water. You need to hire a guide there. It costs only five euros. I'll wait for you on the shore. Don't be scared if a baby shark brushes against your ankles! They are just curious and won't bite you!"

Joao might have fooled around with Ella minutes earlier, but now he behaved professionally as a proper tour guide. He stopped the truck and waited about a minute for Ella and me to finish watching the sharks through the pickup's windows. Then he drove down the beach to the place where the baby sharks were.

He parked and cut the engine. "Let's get you water shoes to put on. There are sharp rocks in the bay; you need water shoes. You have to hire them for 3 euros per pair. The guide will show you the baby sharks first, and if you are up to it, ask him to take you to the big sharks. You can safely go to within twenty-thirty meters of them. Look at that group!" Joao pointed at a group of tourists and a guide wading waist-deep in the water a few yards away from the dorsal fins of the larger sharks. "That's how close you get to the larger ones. Do you want to do that?"

"Yes. I'd like to see them more closely," I said.

"OK, then!" Joao said. "Let's go! You'll have to wade deeper in the water in that case. It's good you have your swimsuits on. As I told you."

The three of us got out of the truck, and Joao took us to a shack where they rented out water shoes. Ella and I hired shoes of our sizes and put them on. We were approached by a guy whom Joao knew and introduced as Miguel. Miguel was our shark tour guide. We paid him five euros and followed him into the water.

We waded knee-deep and soon saw the first baby sharks. We were joined by another group of tourists. Their guide put a bag with food in the water to attract more sharks, and Ella and I had the pleasure of standing amongst a shoal of baby Lemon sharks, attracted by the smell of food.

After spending about ten minutes with the baby sharks and, of course, plenty of excitement, Miguel took us further into the ocean until we were wading chest deep. Along with a few other brave tourists, we watched five or six grown-up sharks from a distance of approximately twenty meters for about five minutes before we followed Miguel back to the shore.

Joao was waiting for us and took us back to the shoe rental shack, where we returned the water shoes and put on our sandals.

Ella looked at her wet bikini and frowned. "Joao, I can't stay in wet clothes! Sorry! Where can I change?"

"Over there!" Joao pointed at another shack where a man was selling souvenirs. "Let me give you the bag!"

"I'll change, too," I said, and we followed Joao to the truck.

He unlocked it, and I took the beach bag with Ella's and my clothes. Joao took us to the shack with the souvenirs. There was a 'room' in the back of the cabin, and Ella and I went inside. There were clothes and bags. Perhaps this was a shack that some guides used to change and keep their stuff in while they were at work with tourists.

It was pretty dirty and miserable in the shack, so Ella and I quickly dried our bodies with our beach towels and changed, taking special care not to drop our clothes on the floor.

THE KNICKERS INCIDENT

We were back in the pickup truck five minutes later, and Joao drove off, heading to the salt mine.

He glanced at Ella. "You know that the lake in the salt mine is saltier than the Dead Sea, and you can't sink in it. You'll be floating on your back."

She looked at him. "Oh, do you mean we have to change again?"

Joao smiled. "Yes, unless you want to go nudist?"

"No!" Ella squeaked.

He laughed. "Ha-ha! I'm joking! But, yeah, if you want to go in the water, you must wear a swimsuit."

"I don't have another one," she said.

"Neither I have," I added.

Ella sighed. "I hate putting on a wet bikini!"

Joao looked at her and, smiling, shrugged his shoulders. "Well. You don't have to go in the water, but I recommend you do. It's a unique experience."

"I'll go in," I said.

Ella sighed again. "Argh! Hate it!"

As Joao drove, he provided us with details about the salt lake. It was formed inside a volcanic crater; they used to mine salt there, but nowadays, the mine is a tourist attraction. He advised us not to stay in the water for more than five minutes and to protect our eyes because of the high mineral and salt content. Then he went on to explain the history of the mine, and by the time he finished his history lesson, we arrived at the site.

We bought tickets and walked for about hundred and fifty yards until we reached a terrace in front of the salt pools, where there were some dubious changing rooms and showers.

Ella and I changed into our wet swim gear in the changing rooms while Joao waited for us outside. Then he took us to one of the salt pools.

Ella and I were initially reluctant to go into the water, but after encouragement from Joao, we went in. It was fun to lie on our backs and relax, floating on the surface of the super salty water.

Ten minutes later, Ella and I took showers—we had to pay the lady supervising the showers to turn them on—and after that, we went into the changing rooms to change back into our dry clothes.

And while we were changing, Ella dropped her thong into a puddle of dirty water.

"Shit!" she cursed as she picked up her thong from the mud.

"Go pay the lady to open the showers again and wash it," I suggested.

"No!" Ella squeaked as she looked again at her soiled knickers. "God knows how many germs are in this mud. I need to wash it properly. With soap!"

She inspected her thong again. It was pretty soiled.

"Shit!" she cursed again. "What shall I do now?"

"Well, go commando, honey!" I said as I successfully put on my shorts without incident.

"How's that gonna work, Nick?!" She shook her head. "With all this wind, everyone will see my butt."

I giggled. "Hi-hi! Not only your butt, hon!"

"Oh, stop it!"

"You'll be in the truck most of the time. Just hold your dress tight when outside."

Ella looked at her knickers yet again. Even pissed off, my wife looked sexy, standing naked in the semi-dark changing room, trying to figure out what to do.

I said, "When you're in the truck, you may not bother hiding too much! Joao already saw plenty!"

"Oh, shut up, Nick!" she cut me off, raising her voice. "Just hold it!"

She passed me her dirty thong and took her light summer dress out of the beach bag.

I took my t-shirt out and put her soiled knickers, the towels, and our wet swimming gear into the bag. I put my t-shirt on while Ella slipped into her dress without incident.

We went outside, where Joao was waiting for us.

He nodded in the direction of the salt lake. "Did you like it?"

"Yes!" I said.

Ella frowned, not saying anything. There was a gust of wind, and she had to quickly grasp the bottom of her dress and hold it down to avoid flashing Joao and me.

Joao looked at her blushed face. "You're OK?"

"My wife went commando!" I said.

"Nick!" Ella squealed.

"She dropped her knickers in the mud," I said.

"Nick, please!" Ella scolded me.

Joao nodded at the changing rooms. "Yeah. It's quite dirty there, I know."

We headed to the pickup truck. I carried the beach bag, and Ella held the hem of her dress, fighting the incessant wind that seemed to be blowing nonstop on the island.

She sighed in relief when she took a seat in the passenger seat. I sat in the back seat, and Joao sat behind the wheel.

He shifted in his seat to face both Ella and me. "Ready for the Blue Eye?"

"Yes," I responded enthusiastically while Ella only nodded.

"Well, do you know what it is and how it works?" he asked.

Ella and I shook heads.

Joao explained the physics behind the phenomenon of the Blue Eye. He also explained that the time of the day to visit it was important and assured us he had chosen the best time for us to see it in its best colours.

He warned us to be careful when walking near the cliffs because a fall onto the rocks in the ocean was a certain death. He said, "You really need to hold onto the safety railing to avoid slipping or being blown out by the wind. It can be very windy up there on the cliffs."

"I won't be coming out of the truck with all this wind," Ella said and held her dress in a subconscious move.

Joao smiled. "Ella, you've got to see the Blue Eye if you are in Sal!" He reached his hand to her knee and stroked her leg reassuringly. "You'll be fine! It's windy only on the cliffs and close to the natural lava pools next to the cave. To be fair, we shouldn't go anywhere near the pools on a windy day like today. But walking down to the observation platform of the Blue Eye is okay because the cave's hole is well-shielded from the wind. You have to lean just a little over the parapet to see the Blue Eye. Nick and I will hold you by your sides while you hold your dress. You'll be fine! Shall we go now?"

Ella nodded yes.

Joao said, "OK, then. We'll stop in a small fisherman's village called Palmeira for a quick lunch on our way to Buracona. Buracona is where the cave of the Blue Eye is located."

He turned to face ahead, started the engine, and we drove off.

Ella's mood had improved slightly after hearing Joao's assurances but was still somewhat sour, and he put an effort to cheer her up by telling a funny story about one of his tours that had gone wrong a few years back. As she listened to him, the frown on her face gradually disappeared, and she began to smile and even laughed at the end of the story. Encouraged by his success, Joao told us another funny story about his parents and their herd of goats on his home island, Santiago, and Ella and I laughed a lot. He continued to work on improving Ella's mood with jokes about goat herders, and by the time we were driving through Espargos about ten minutes later, Ella had forgotten about her incident at the salt mine. So much so that, at one point, she stopped holding her dress down.

Joao seemed to be on a roll, and as we neared Palmeira, he was cracking joke after joke while Ella and I were giggling and laughing nonstop. Ella had forgotten entirely about her wardrobe predicament and had brought her feet up onto the seat, hugging her knees to her chest. And, of course, while giggling and laughing, she was spreading her legs apart, completely exposing her naked butt and pussy to Joao, who kept glancing at her. Realising she was baring her pussy, she was closing her legs and hastily pulling her dress down to cover her private parts, only to flash him again the next time she laughed.

OVERCOMING FEARS

We arrived in Palmeira, and Joao parked the truck on the street in front of a restaurant.

"Let's grab something to eat!" he said.

Ella looked at the people eating at tables outside the restaurant and hesitated. "Umm, I'm not sure."

Joao shifted in his seat to face her. "It's not windy here, Ella. Look! The trees are not moving. The wind has gone down. Come on! Let's go!"

"Umm!" Ella looked at the restaurant again. "I don't want to."

She was still hugging her knees to her chest, balancing her feet on the edge of her seat. Her dress had hiked up to her waist. She had covered her pussy in front, but her thighs and buttocks were exposed. Joao put his hand on her bare thigh and rubbed it. Ella seemed not to mind his hand, even when it made its way up her inner thigh under her dress. She kept looking at the people in front of the restaurant.

"Ella, let's rehearse here for the Blue Eye," Joao said. "Nick and I will walk by your sides and protect you! We'll walk into the restaurant, buy a sandwich and a drink, and—"

"And pee!" Ella interjected, smiling shyly at Joao. "I have to pee!"

He laughed. "Ha-ha! And pee, yes. We don't want 'her'"—he nodded at her crotch—"to suffer, do we?" His hand slipped further up, pushing Ella's dress up and baring her pussy. His fingertips made contact with her pussy lips.

Ella trembled. She stared him in the eyes, and her breathing became heavier.

Joao held her gaze. "After lunch, we'll go to see the famous tuna fisherman's sculpture before we leave for Buracona. Trust me!

There won't be any incidents! 'She'"—he again nodded at her crotch—"will be protected!" His hand slipped further up, and he cupped her pussy.

Ella finally gripped his wrist and slowly pushed his hand away from her labia. "OK! Let's see how it goes!"

She closed her legs, put her feet on the floor and pulled her dress down.

She turned and looked at me. I smiled, and she smiled back.

We got out of the pickup truck. Joao and I walked on each side of Ella while she held her dress down—despite that the wind had slowed down, but just in case—and we had no problem walking into the restaurant. We took turns visiting the loo and after that bought sandwiches and drinks. We sat at a table inside upon Ella's insistence out of concern about indecent exposure at the outside tables. She was careful to keep her legs closed while we ate, and there were no wardrobe malfunctions. We finished lunch and went outside. We walked a few yards down the street to the fisherman's port. Feeling much more confident, Ella agreed to pose with me in front of the fisherman's sculpture, and Joao took a photo of us.

We returned to the pickup truck. Ella sat in the passenger seat, and I sat in the back seat as per what seemed to be an implicitly agreed sitting arrangement.

Joao turned on the engine and looked at Ella. "So, was it scary?"

"No," she said and giggled. "Hi-hi! Just a little!"

"Ha-ha!" he laughed. "A little? Like why? It wasn't that windy in Palmeira. No one saw anything."

"No, no one." Ella shook her head. "But I had the feeling people were staring at me all the time. How can I say this?" She paused for a moment before adding, "Knowing you are without underwear makes you conscientious, you know!"

"Ha-ha!" Joao laughed again. "Conscientious? Why?"

"Why?!?" Ella squeaked. "Joao! Have you walked without knickers in a village full of strangers?"

"Well, I just did that," he said, smiling with mischief. "I've got nothing under my shorts. Did you not see me when we released the turtle?"

"Oh, yes, she did!" I jumped into the conversation. "And not only see you. I think she felt you quite well." I turned to Ella. "Didn't you, honey? In the water?"

Ella blushed profusely but did not answer my question. She drew her feet up onto the seat and hugged her knees to her chest. Her dress slipped up her legs, baring her thighs and buttocks.

She stared into the distance, and it looked like the conversation was over.

Joao drove off, and we were out of the village a minute later. He took a desolate dirt road without any cars on it.

Ella had been looking through the windshield, deep in thought, but now she suddenly turned and looked at Joao. "Why don't you wear underwear, Joao?"

"Because it chafes me," he said.

Ella kept looking at his face. "Your underwear chafes you! Really?"

Keeping his eyes on the road, he smiled and shrugged his shoulders. "I'm too big down there and chafe!"

"Ha-ha!" I laughed. "It's true! Both Ella and I saw you. You are hung! Although, I doubt that is a reason to chafe. I know many men who are hung but don't chafe, and they wear underwear."

"Well," Joao said, "that's because their skin is thick. The skin of my penis is more delicate than that of other men and chafes. Remember? I'm black."

"Ha-ha!" I laughed again. "Nice try, but don't play the racial card! Your skin is not more delicate than that of any other man, Joao!"

"You don't believe me!?" He looked at me in the rearview mirror and grinned. "Sneak your hand into my shorts and check for yourself!"

I smiled, shaking my head. "Nice try again! But I'm not gay."

And then Joao made his most brazen move. He glanced at Ella, then looked back at the road, and a mischievous smile curved the corners of his lips before he said, "Ella, you can check and tell your hubby if I am lying or not!"

"Joao!" Ella squealed, and her eyes went big. Yet, a second later, she giggled. "Hi-hi! Nick can feel your cock for himself if he wants to!" She looked at me and stuck her tongue out. "You brought this on yourself, honey!"

Ella liked our little teasing game. Her eyes were full of mischief but also lust. She was horny. She spread her legs, completely forgetting, or ignoring, that she wore no knickers, and bared her pussy.

Her action did not go unnoticed by Joao. He slowed down the truck, looked at her pussy and asked, "Would you check it for Nick, Ella?"

Ella knew he was looking at her pussy but did not close her legs. She just smiled. "Umm.... would I?"

Joao smiled too. He looked at the road, slowed down the pickup truck further, and then looked back at her. "Checking is believing, Ella."

"Is that so?" Ella ran her tongue seductively over her lips. "Umm.... Checking is believing... checking is believing."

"That's right!" Joao pushed his pelvis up, showing the tent in his shorts.

Ella closed her legs and opened them again, staring at Joao with a playful smile. She was teasing him and enjoying it.

"Umm,... maybe I should...." She reached her hand to his crotch but did not touch it. She hovered her hand over the bulge of his manhood for a couple of seconds before pulling her hand back and bursting into a giggle. "Hi-hi! Hi-hi! You wished, Joao, you wished, but no!"

Joao smiled and shrugged his shoulders. "Why not?" He looked back at the road. "Checking is believing, Ella."

"Honey!" I said. "He's right. Someone has to check. As I said, I am not gay. Plus, I'm sure Joao will prefer your hand over mine. Right, Joao?"

Joao looked at me in the rearview mirror, then looked at Ella and smiled as he nodded. "Yes, I prefer Ella's hand!"

Ella stuck her tongue out at him. "Yeah, nice try!"

"What try?" Joao asked her and reached his hand to her crotch.

She watched his hand approaching her pussy, and her smile froze on her face, but again did not close her legs or push his hand away.

Joao now slowed the truck down to a stop and looked at her face, holding his hand in the air, with his fingertips inches from her pussy.

"I prefer your hand, Ella!" he said quietly. He moved his hand forward and cupped her pussy. "And not only your hand."

Ella trembled at his touch but again did not push his hand away.

She looked at me and bit her bottom lip.

I mouthed, "Go for it!"

"Go for what exactly, Nick?" she whispered.

Joao ran his hand over her pussy. "You may use something else to check my skin's texture. Something other than your hand."

Ella looked at him.

He parted her pussy lips.

That was too much for her. She grabbed his hand and pushed it away. She closed her legs and put her feet on the floor.

Suddenly there was an uncomfortable silence.

Joao resumed driving.

A minute passed before he said, "So, you don't want to feel it?" He did not look at Ella, just opened his legs invitingly. The tent in his shorts was massive. "Have you ever held a black cock in your hand, Ella?"

Ella swallowed and looked at me.

Joao whispered, "A cock that huge?"

I said, "Let the butterflies fly, hon!"

Ella looked back at Joao's crotch.

She stared at it for a few seconds and then did it! She shifted in her seat to face Joao and slowly reached her hand to his stomach. He trembled when he felt her fingers touch him just above the waistband of his shorts and leaned back in his seat, spreading his legs as open as he could in the driving position. Ella waited a few seconds, then slipped her fingers underneath the waistband. She hesitated again, but after another five or six seconds, she slid her hand deeper into Joao's shorts.

His body trembled.

Looking at the shape of his bulge, I became certain Ella had wrapped her hand around his cock.

She gripped his shaft for about ten seconds, not moving, then slowly began moving her hand up and down. She was stroking his cock. Joao did not look at Ella. He stared straight ahead, driving.

Ella stroked his cock for a few seconds, and a moan escaped his lips. The sound of his voice woke her up from her trance-like state, and she quickly pulled her hand out of his shorts.

"How was it?" Joao asked her, still keeping his eyes on the road. "Big?"

Ella turned in her seat to face forward and, with a few seconds' delay, said, "Big. Very big."

There was complete silence after her admission. The three of us were looking ahead at the road as if there was something to look at. It was barren terrain and a road that could barely be called a road. Only dirt and dust.

A minute or so passed in silence before Joao said, "It's big, and it fucks very well."

Now he looked at Ella. He wasn't smiling. She looked at him but did not say a word. Her face was sombre too.

Joao alternated between glancing at the road and looking at Ella.

She finally said, "I am sure it does," and turned her gaze to the road.

I put my hand on her shoulder. "You're OK, hon?"

She nodded yes but did not turn to look at me; she just stared ahead.

There was silence for another couple of minutes before Joao broke it. "Nick, how would you like the sight of black on white skin?"

"Joao!" Ella squealed. "Stop it!" She turned and looked at him. "Stop it, now!"

"What?!" Joao threw his hands in the air but quickly grabbed the steering wheel again before looking at Ella. "You're reading too much into my question. I'm asking Nick because he might want to take a picture of you and me together at the desert mirage. Some of my tourists ask me to pose with them. That's why I asked."

"Yeah! As if!" Ella pursed her lips and stared at him with a rather hostile look on her face.

Joao held her gaze, and a smile flickered across his face. He wasn't looking where he was driving and veered off the road.

He stopped the truck and said, "No, seriously. I asked for a photo.

What else did you think I had in mind?"

They kept staring at each other for a while until Ella's lips curved into a smile, and she giggled. "Hi-hi! Yeah, that's what you asked for! A photo! I believe you!"

"He-he!" Joao chuckled. "It's true, Ella!" He leaned towards her and put his hand on her thigh, exposed by her hiked-up dress. "A photo!"

He looked at me over his shoulder, holding his hand on Ella's leg. "Do you like black-on-white skin, Nick? For a photo!"

I smiled and shook my head from side to side. "Joao, Joao, you know that whatever I say will be deemed racist, don't you?"

"Well, I can say it, though," he said. "So, how do you like the contrast?"

I chuckled. "He-he! I like it."

He rubbed Ella's thigh and looked at her. "Ella, did you hear that? Your husband likes it. Would you like a photo with me?"

Ella smiled coquettishly. "I'll think about it!"

Joao let go of her leg. "OK, think about it! The two of us in a photo at Terra Boa!" He looked at me in the rearview mirror. "Nick, you'll have a chance to watch your wife with a black man!"

"Stop it!" Ella squeaked, barely suppressing her laughter. She slapped him playfully on the shoulder. "I warn you!"

"What?!" Joao looked at her with an innocent smile. "I'm talking about a photo, Ella!" A second later, he laughed. "Ha-ha! We'll be together in a photo. That's all! What else did you think of?"

Ella smiled. "Yeah! In a photo."

"Yeah! In a photo. You and me. Together. Skin to skin!" Joao looked at me in the rearview mirror. "Nick, would you like to watch your wife's skin gliding against mine?"

"You're impossible, Joao!" Ella shook her head in faked disappointment.

"I'd love to watch!" I said.

"Nick!" Ella squealed and looked at me over her shoulder, smiling. "You are awful!" She turned to face ahead and, laughing quietly, added, "You're both awful! I won't speak to either of you!"

Joao resumed driving. He kept glancing at Ella, but she pretended to ignore him, looking into the distance.

At one point, he opened his mouth to say something. "Ella, are you—"

"Not talking to you, Joao!" Ella cut him off, raising her hand to wave him off. A few seconds later, she giggled. "Hi-hi! You're a bad boy!"

Joao shook his head in amusement, looking at the road ahead. Ella stubbornly stared outside but did not lose the faint smile playing on her lips.

We travelled in silence for a few minutes before Joao put his hand on Ella's thigh and said, "Well, we're arriving at the Blue Eye. Are you sure you're still not talking to me, Ella? 'Cos we need to talk to each other if we're going to the cave!"

Ella giggled. "Hi-hi! OK, in that case! I'll speak to you! But I'll file a complaint with your boss that you harass your clients!"

"Ha-ha!" Joao laughed. "I am my boss, Ella! I am the whole company. You need to complain to me about me!"

Ella pushed his hand away from her leg. "Well, I will! Prepare yourself for a fervent complaint about yourself!"

Joao smiled and looked around for a place to park.

IT'S A MAYBE

He parked, and we got out of the truck. It was very windy, so Ella had to hold her dress down as we walked to the ticket office and bought tickets. It was even windier in the open on our way to the cave. Joao and I had to walk on each side of Ella in case the wind blew her dress up. As Joao had said, once we walked down the few steps to the cave, we were shielded from the wind, and Ella let go of her dress. We were lucky that there were no other tourists—the only benefit of visiting Buracona on a windy day. We went straight to the viewing platform overhanging the hole in the cave where the sun shines into the cave and illuminates the sea, forming the appearance of a large blue eye.

"Let me hold you while you look down at the Blue Eye!" Joao said to Ella when we stood at the parapet of the platform.

He stepped behind her and wrapped his arms around her waist, gently nudging her to bend over the parapet.

"Can you see it?" he asked her and, at the same time, slipped his hands up her stomach, shamelessly cupping her breasts.

Ella didn't mind his hands.

Instead, she squealed in delight, "Oh, yeah! I see the eye! It's beautiful!"

Joao held her for about a minute, squeezing her tits through the flimsy fabric of her dress before he helped her step back from the parapet.

He let go of her and offered his hand to me.

"Ha-ha! No, thanks!" I laughed. "I don't have titties!"

Joao laughed too. Ella blushed but still laughed with us.

I had a quick look at the blue eye, and we returned to the truck, Ella taking precautions not to have her dress blown up.

"Did you like it?" Joao asked after we sat in our usual seats.

"Yes, very much," Ella said.

"Absolutely," I concurred with her.

"Right! Off to Terra Boa! The desert mirage!" he said, started the engine and drove off the car park.

A couple of minutes later, we had left Buracona behind us and approached a junction. There was the main road and a dirt road that, as far as I could see, disappeared after a few yards.

Joao nodded towards the dirt road. "It's a shortcut! Would you be happy for some more off-road to save time, or do you want me to stay on the main road?"

"Let's take the shortcut!" I said.

Joao took the dirt road, but it became pretty bumpy after a few hundred yards, and he stopped the truck. "Is it too bumpy, Ella? Nick?"

"No, that's OK," Ella said.

"I'm fine," I added.

He was about to resume driving but then stopped himself. He turned to look at Ella and asked her, "Have you decided?"

"Decided what?" she asked back and sat on her side, facing him.

He put his hand on her stomach. "Nick to take a photo with you and me at the desert mirage?"

Ella smiled. "Maybe!"

The front tie of her dress was undone—probably by Joao when groping her breasts at the cave—and a good portion of her boobs could be seen.

He slipped his hand into her cleavage. "Nick said he would like a photo of my black skin against yours."

He cupped her left breast and used his other hand to flip open the front panel of her dress. Her boob popped out, and he squeezed it. Ella looked down at her breast and watched him roll her hardened nipple between his fingers.

Joao glanced at me. "Do you like the contrast, Nick?"

"Yes," I said quietly and adjusted my hard cock in my shorts.

He looked back at Ella. "Ella, do you like it?"

Joao continued to knead her breast. Ella's breathing became heavy and urgent. She looked at me, and I smiled.

Keeping her gaze on me, she said quietly, "Yes."

Joao pressed his palm against her breast. "Ella, have you been with a black man?"

Ella bit her lips and blushed, not taking her eyes off me. She swallowed nervously.

"Have you?" Joao asked again.

She whispered, "No."

He gently squeezed her breast. "Would you like to be with one?"

Ella was staring at my face, but my eyes were drawn to her chest, where Joao's hand was working on her boob. He was kneading and squeezing her breast, rolling her erect nipple between his fingers, and brushing her areola with the back of his knuckles.

His whisper filled the silence. "Would you like to be with a black man?"

Ella was feeling his hand and hearing his voice. Pleasurable sensations were taking over her body, and at the same time, her adrenaline was pumping up. I could literally see her heart beating in her chest.

Joao reached his other hand and tried to squeeze it between Ella's legs, but she closed them. The audacious man did not give up. He pushed his hand gently, and Ella opened her legs slightly. His hand slid in between her thighs, and she trembled. He had touched her pussy. She closed her legs around his hand.

I looked at Ella's face. It was gripped with tension, sexual tension.

Joao lowered his mouth to her ear. "Do you want to be fucked by a black man?"

Ella was not saying a word, still not taking her gaze off my face. She was breathing heavily, and her bottom lip was hanging down.

My cock was throbbing in my shorts. I was helpless to do anything other than stare at her.

"Do you?" Joao whispered again.

"Maybe," Ella whispered.

"Would you let me fuck you?" he asked her quietly.

She was not answering his question.

"Maybe you should, hon," I murmured in Greek.

My voice seemed to wake Ella up from her trance because she suddenly grabbed Joao's hands and pushed them away. She squeezed her legs tight and put her breast back in her dress.

"You're crazy!" she murmured in Croatian.

She turned to face ahead, looked at Joao and said sternly in English, "No!"

Joao smiled. "OK. If you change your mind—"

"Drive!" Ella ordered him.

"Sure!" Joao said and drove off.

A minute passed, and Ella looked at me over her shoulder.

"Nick, are you sure?" she asked me in Croatian.

I nodded yes.

Ella did not say anything and turned to look ahead at the road.

There was a tense silence for about five minutes before Joao said, "Ella, I'm sorry if I overstepped a boundary."

Ella said quietly, "It's OK!"

WIFE TRIES SOMETHING NEW

She pulled the bottom of her dress down, trying to cover her legs as much as she could.

"I had to try," Joao continued to explain himself. "You know. You are very pretty. No! You're beautiful. And sexy. Very sexy. And I thought Nick would want me to."

Ella was not saying anything; she just listened to Joao and watched the road ahead.

Joao said, "I'm sorry if I ruined your day. I probably misread the whole thing." He sighed. "I am stupid, you know. When I like a woman as beautiful as you, I should cherish her presence. Not ruin everything. I lost my judgement. I am sorry. I shouldn't have asked you such a stupid question. When I asked you—"

"Maybe!" slipped through Ella's lips.

Joao sighed again. "I am sorry, Ella. When I asked you, I—"

"I said maybe!" Ella said, raising her voice, still staring outside.

Joao looked at her and slowed down the truck.

Ella was still not looking at him. She bit on her bottom lip and put her hand in her hair.

Joao murmured, "Ella, I—"

"It's a maybe!" Ella said again and began playing with her hair while staring through the windshield.

Joao stopped the truck completely because he was not taking his eyes off her, and it had become dangerous to drive, even if we were off-road.

A playful smile flickered at the corners of Ella's lips as she kept looking in front of her and playing with a strand of her hair.

A few seconds passed in silence, and Ella said, "The answer to your last question is maybe, Joao!"

She let go of her hair and turned to look at him. "To be clear, Joao: I haven't decided yet. So it's a maybe!" She looked at me. "Nick?"

I said quietly, "It is maybe from me too, honey!"

Ella looked back at Joao, who seemed caught by surprise. She leaned over to him, took his cheeks in her hands and pressed her mouth against his. He grabbed her by the shoulders and pulled her closer into him. He pushed his tongue between her lips, she parted them, and they had a long French kiss.

Ella broke the kiss and pushed him in the chest. "This doesn't mean anything yet, Joao! It was just a taster!"

A broad smile curved Joao's lips. "I get that, Ella! I'm happy to wait."

He shook his head in amusement and drove off.

He drove for a minute and said, "Ella, I—"

"I think sometimes you talk too much," Ella cut him off and smiled to herself. Still smiling, she looked at me over her shoulder. "Nick knows when he should talk and when he shouldn't."

I smiled at her. "Absolutely!"

She giggled. "Hi-hi! That's why a maybe for him often turns into a yes." She looked back at the road ahead.

"Point taken!" Joao said and changed the subject. "By the way, we are not far away from the desert mirage. Another five minutes or so."

"Is it really a desert?" I asked, also keen to change the subject as I started to feel too many butterflies in my stomach. And how would it have been otherwise? My wife had just told another man that she might let him fuck her, which was a huge, colossal step: letting another man fuck her for the first time in our married life!

"Yes," Joao said. "The north of Sal and Terra Boa, where we are going, is a true African desert. It's a continuation of the Sahara desert. The whole of Sal is a rocky desert. Your hotel is in the best part of the island. In fact, it is one of the best hotels, if not the best. It doesn't feel like a desert in the hotel with its gardens, flowers, and palms." He looked at Ella. "Ella, you like it there, don't you?"

Ella blushed when their eyes met. She must have felt very shy all of a sudden. Understandably so: she had promised the man looking at her that she would think about whether to let him fuck her or not.

Joao didn't show he was nervous, although he must have been. A pretty woman, married, was inches away from him, with her husband sitting right behind her, and she was considering at that moment whether to open her legs for him later on and let his cock into her pussy. He must have felt excited, if not even scared, but he wasn't showing it.

"I like it," Ella said. "It is very luxurious."

"Oh, well," Joao said, "I've been there only once, as I told you, for the gangbang."

Ella blushed again and looked at the landscape through her window. Not that there was something to look at, but just to look away from Joao and me.

Joao sighed. "It's a shame I couldn't stay longer. It's the most luxurious place I've ever been."

"You haven't been to many hotels, have you?" I asked him.

Joao shook his head. "No. I'm a poor guy, Nick. But I work hard so one day I can afford a holiday in a luxurious hotel."

"It will happen, Joao, it will," Ella said as she finally turned her gaze on him. "I'm sure one day you will be able to afford it."

Joao sighed. "I can't wait for that to happen, Ella! But for now, it's more likely a mirage, like the one we will see. But sometimes, a mirage may turn out to be real. Like, I might get lucky and have the pleasure of spending a night in your hotel soon. Like, tonight. Who knows?" He smiled.

Ella knew what he was hinting at, and her face turned red. She murmured, "You do talk too much!" and looked away.

"Yeah," Joao said, "I'm pushing it too hard, am I not?"

She nodded yes, without looking at him.

I looked outside my window. The terrain was arid, and I wondered how they maintained such luxury in the hotels, turning them into small oases.

"It's interesting how they supply the hotels with food and other goods," I said.

"They use container ships," Joao said, seizing on the opportunity to change the sensitive subject of Ella's promise to him.

He went on to explain the logistics of supplying the island while we travelled through the rough terrain until, five minutes later, he stopped the truck and said, "Here it is! This is a good spot. There are no tourists, and we are away from the gift shop." He nodded to his left.

I saw a silhouette of a building in the distance.

PHOTOS AND SOUVENIRS

Joao cut the engine, and we got out of the truck. It was very windy, and Ella held onto her dress with one hand.

He took her free hand. "Come with me!"

He led us to a spot about thirty or forty yards away from the truck and said, "Let me show you the mirage!" He stepped behind Ella and put his hands on her shoulders. "Look straight ahead!" He nodded to me. "You too, Nick. Stand next to Ella and look in the distance!"

I stood next to Ella, and indeed, it looked like there was a lake in the distance.

"Amazing!" Ella said excitedly. "I see the ocean!"

"See?" Joao smiled, lowered his mouth to her ear and whispered, "But there is no ocean, no water. It's a desert. That's the mirage." Then he kissed the side of her neck, evoking a giggle from her, and said, "If you squat, you'll see it's sand, a desert."

Ella squatted, as did I.

"Wow!" slipped through Ella's lips.

Indeed, what we were looking at was sand.

Joao offered Ella his hand to help her stand up. Then he said to me, "Nick, if you give me your phone, I'll take a photo of you and Ella with the mirage behind you. Would you like me to?"

"Yes, please," I said, rose, pulled out my phone, unlocked it and gave it to Joao.

I stood next to Ella and wrapped my arm around her shoulder. Joao stepped back a few steps—the bulge in his shorts prominent—and aimed the phone camera at Ella and me. We smiled, and he took a photo of the two of us with the mirage in the background.

Joao walked up to us and gave me back my phone.

Ella and I looked at the picture; it was good.

"Thank you! It's an excellent photo," I said.

"Thank you, Joao!" Ella chirruped too.

"You're welcome," Joao replied, and a smile curved his lips. "Would you like a photo with me, Ella?"

"Sure," Ella said.

"Nick?" Joao looked at me. "Would you take it with your phone?"

I nodded yes and walked to the spot from which Joao had taken the photo of Ella and me.

Joao stood behind Ella. He hooked his chin over her shoulder, pressing his cheek against hers, and said, "Black on white skin for your pleasure, Nick!"

I smiled and took the photo.

Joao took Ella's hand in his, and they walked up to me. I showed them the photo.

"It looks good, isn't it?" Joao said.

"Yes, I like it." Ella nodded in agreement.

"Would you like to take another one?" Joao asked me. "For your bedroom."

"For my bedroom?" I raised my eyebrows.

"Yeah. You'll like it!" He took Ella's hand. "Come, Ella! Let's have a special one for your man!"

Ella pulled her hand off his grip. "A special photo?"

"Yes. Come! You'll see." Joao took her hand again and pulled on it.

He led her to the same spot they had stood for the first photo, turned her around to face me and stepped behind her. And then he pulled on the spaghetti straps of her dress.

So far, Ella had been grasping the bottom of her dress with one hand, trying to hold it down and prevent the wind from blowing it up. Now she let go of her dress and grabbed Joao's hands. The wind blew her dress up, baring her ass and pussy.

"Joao, people will see me!" Ella shouted and, at the same time, realising her pussy and ass were completely exposed, she panicky grabbed the bottom of her dress and pulled it down.

Fortunately, no one was around to see her. Joao had chosen the place wisely.

"Relax, Ella!" he said. "There's no one to see you!"

The gust of wind subsided. Ella let go of her dress and grabbed Joao's hands again.

"Let go, Ella! Nick wants this photo. Do it for him!" Joao slid the straps over her shoulders.

Ella looked around.

The wind blew and lifted her dress up, baring her pussy and butt again. She let go of Joao's hands to hold onto her dress, and he used the moment to pull the straps further down.

Ella's breasts popped out.

"Joao!" she squeaked but did not pull her straps up. She just held the bottom of the dress, trying to cover at least her ass and pussy, prioritising them over her boobs.

Joao cupped her breasts from behind her, hooked his chin over her shoulder and shouted to me, "Now, Nick!"

He smiled a broad smile. Ella hesitated for a second but then smiled too.

I took a photo of the two of them, in an embrace, with Joao's hands cupping my wife's bare breasts.

Joao let go of Ella's boobs and playfully slapped her butt. "Was it that bad?"

Ella looked around and, having assured herself no one had seen us, she giggled. "Hi-hi! No! We got away with it!"

She pulled up the straps of her dress, covering her breasts, and, of course, as per Murphy's law, the gust of wind picked up again, baring her pussy and ass. She wasn't worried that someone would see her—having already checked and seen several times no one was around—but she still grabbed hold of the dress and covered her private parts.

I walked up to Joao and Ella and showed them the photo on my phone. "Have a look!"

Ella pushed my hand away. "Not now! Put this into your pocket, Nick!" She blushed, ashamed of the photo.

Joao tapped me on the shoulder. "You'll look at it at home. In the bedroom!" He smiled. "Maybe the three of us will look at it!"

"Stop it!" Ella squeaked and slapped him on the butt.

Joao chuckled. "Am I pushing my luck?"

Ella stared at him, and he grinned at her, asking her again, "Am I?"

"Yes, you are!" she replied and punched him playfully in the chest. "And when are you going to put a shirt on?"

"Umm. . . . Yeah, OK. It's in the glove compartment," he said. "I thought I looked sexier bare-chested."

Ella put her hand on his chest and felt his chest muscles.

"You feel sexier!" she murmured.

He smiled. "You're right, though! I can't walk into your hotel like this. I'll put my t-shirt on before that."

Ella pushed him in the chest. "Joao! You're pushing your luck again!"

"OK! OK!" Joao raised his hands in the air. "I'll put it on now!" He nodded at the building in the distance. "Shall we visit the gift shop?"

"Yes," both Ella and I said.

We went back to the pickup truck. We got in, and Joao opened the glove box.

He pulled out a t-shirt and was about to put it on when he looked at Ella and cocked his head to the side, smiling. "I guess I have charmed you enough and can put it on now."

"Hi-hi!" Ella giggled. "I guess so!"

"So, is the maybe a yes now?" he asked her.

Still giggling, she shook her finger at him. "Don't push it, Joao!"

"Ha-ha! OK! OK!" Joao laughed and put his t-shirt on.

He turned on the engine, and we left his special viewing spot.

During the one-minute drive to the gift shop, there was silence in the cab. Ella and I were thinking about what we had just let happen and, more importantly, what more we might let happen. Joao, for his part, didn't want to 'push his luck' and kept his mouth shut. The only sign of his thoughts was the faint smile on his lips.

He parked in front of a building with a sign above the door reading 'Gift shop.'

We got out of the truck and saw a jeep with tourists approaching.

"Let's go inside," Joao said, put his hand on the small of Ella's back and ushered her into the souvenir shop. I followed them in.

The shop was a large room with a counter next to the door. The owner was standing behind the counter and greeted us. He exchanged a few words with Joao in Creole.

Joao said to Ella and me, "Have a look around! Some souvenirs, like the wooden sculptures, are made in local workshops, and you'll help the local community when you buy them."

He stayed behind to chat with the shop owner while Ella and I went to look at the souvenirs lined up on shelves on the walls: small sculptures, plates, mugs, and magnets.

Ella picked up a mug and looked at it. "You want one, Nick?"

I looked at the mug. "Yeah, I like it. We'll take it."

Ella passed me the mug. "Hold it!"

I took the mug, and we wandered down to the corner with the plates.

Ella picked a plate. "What about this one?"

"Nah!" I grimaced. "Don't like it."

Ella put the plate back on the shelf.

A group of tourists entered the shop and started a conversation with the shop owner. Joao joined the discussion. Then another group of tourists joined them, and soon it became noisy.

Ella and I walked further down the shop, away from the noise.

Ella picked up another plate.

"I like it," I said.

"OK, we'll take it," she said but then changed her mind. "Um. . . , don't know. Maybe. Let's have a look at another one before we decide." She placed the plate back on the shelf.

"Let's do that. Hmm. Honey. When you said 'maybe' in the pickup truck, did you mean it?"

Ella looked at the plates on the upper shelf.

After a while, looking at a plate with a map of the island, she said, "I don't know, Nick."

"Will you let him?" I asked her quietly.

Ella stretched her hand and picked the plate that had attracted her attention.

She ran her fingers over the surface of the plate and said quietly, "I don't know whether I want to do it. What about you?"

"I don't know either," I said.

Ella put the plate back on the shelf and took another one. She ran her fingers over the rim of the plate.

"Aren't you curious?" I asked.

Ella examined the plate for a few seconds, then whispered, "I am."

"So?"

"I'm scared."

"Of what?"

Ella sighed. "Of how I'll feel afterwards." She looked at me. "And how you'll feel."

I shrugged my shoulders. "So far, I'm OK."

Ella looked at the label on the back of the plate, then flipped the plate over and rubbed the smooth surface with her fingers. "It's going to feel very different, Nick. It won't be anything like what's happened so far. You do realise that, don't you?"

"Yeah," I said, picked another plate, and showed it to her.

She shook her head. "I don't like it."

I put the plate back on the shelf. "On the other hand, Gerhard's butterflies thing is stuck in my head."

"I know, right? But I don't know, Nick. I don't know whether I want to do it." She looked at Joao, who was laughing at some joke the shop owner had made. The tourists were laughing too.

Ella bit her lips in thought, then looked at me and murmured, "I'm scared, Nick."

I sighed. "Well, in that case, maybe we should not do anything today. You'll see how you feel tomorrow. Mikkel and Johan—"

"No, I don't want to do it with them."

"You don't? Why?"

"'Cos, umm. . . I don't know. But if I were to do it, it would be with him." Ella nodded in the direction of Joao.

She put the plate she was looking at back on the shelf and took another one. She lifted the plate up against the shelf as if she had hung it on the wall and tilted her head to one side, looking at the plate.

"It's very big," she murmured and lowered the plate.

"That's why you'd do it with him? 'Cos his is big?" I asked.

Ella raised the plate and looked at it again. After a few seconds of critical assessment, she made up her mind and handed it to me. "I think we'll take this one."

I took the plate from her hand, and we walked to a board with magnets.

Ella picked a magnet off the board and examined it. "Yeah, that's part of it," she said and put the magnet back on the board. "But also, if it's going to be something new, you know"—Ella looked at me—"something different, with the risks we are taking, I'd rather it be very different. If you know what I mean."

"A black man?"

"Um-hum."

A glass sea turtle souvenir attracted her gaze. She went to it and picked it up.

I followed her.

Ella showed me the small turtle sculpture and chirruped in excitement, "Do you like it? It's so cute!"

I nodded. "Yeah! Take it! You like turtles so much; take it, hon!"

Ella's smile turned into worry. "But I'm afraid, Nick! I want to do it, but I also don't want to. Do you know what I mean? Gerhard put this idea in our heads. With his butterflies and all that!"

"I know."

"We tried to run away from it. And what are we thinking of doing now? Exactly that!"

"I know, but, hon, Gerhard's point about knowing and not knowing—"

"That's right!" Ella interrupted me. "What it could have been if!"

"I want to find out," I said.

"Well, it is tempting," Ella agreed with me. She saw a magnet in the shape of Sal and picked it up to look closer at it before saying, "I also want to find out."

"How it feels?"

"Um-hum!"

"Physically, too?"

Ella put the magnet back on the board and said, without looking at me, "What do you think?"

"It's huge!" I said.

She turned and looked at me. "It is."

"You'd like to find out how a huge one feels down there." I nodded at her crotch. "Am I right?"

She smiled shyly, almost apologetically and nodded yes.

We stared each other in the eyes. Ella was biting her lips. I was swallowing nervously while my cock was throbbing.

"Well," I said, "they say there's only one way to find out."

Ella sighed. "But there are consequences, Nick!" She looked outside the window and nibbled on her bottom lip, thinking of something, then turned to me and said briskly, "OK, let's go!"

"So, what have you decided?"

"I haven't. It's still a maybe!"

We walked up to the counter.

Joao greeted us with a smile. "What did you choose?"

Ella showed him her turtle. "A turtle!"

I showed him the plate and the mug, which Ella and I had picked out together.

The shop owner stepped forward and packed our souvenirs. I

paid, and a couple of minutes later, we were sitting in the pickup truck.

Joao looked at Ella in the passenger seat next to him. "Did you like the tour?"

"Yes," she said.

"Very much!" I chimed in from the back seat behind her.

He started the engine. "Tired?"

"A little bit, yes," Ella said.

"OK! Let's get you back to your hotel," Joao said and drove off. "It's less than a 40-minute drive. The benefit of living on a small island."

A JOURNEY OF THOUGHTS

We were tired and did not talk. But it wasn't only that we were tired. Actually, it wasn't that at all. There was simply too much tension in the air.

I couldn't stop my brain from racing. *Shall we do it? Or shall we not?* I was scared. And jealous. Oh, yes! I was very jealous. And at the same time aroused. I had a constant hard-on.

At one point, I couldn't help but glance at Joao's crotch. And yes, I had guessed right! His erection was poking through his shorts. Joao's hard-on confirmed to me where his thoughts were. He was imagining fucking my wife. He knew it wasn't certain she would let him fuck her, but it didn't stop him from hoping and imagining.

His cock is hard because it's getting itself ready to fuck, I thought. *And to fuck who? My wife. Shit!*

I felt a pang of pain in my chest, but at the same time, my cock throbbed.

I should stop thinking about it, I said to myself, *or I'll explode in my pants!*

It was easy to tell myself not to think about it, but not easy to do it. I couldn't stop thinking about it!

I looked again at the tent in Joao's shorts. I watched it for a minute or so, and I saw it! It throbbed. I saw his cock throbbing. The guy had to fight a hard-on like me in silence, unable to relieve it. Actually, it was worse for him because he had to drive. At least I could move in my seat and squeeze my legs together to restrain the urge to ejaculate, but Joao couldn't. He had to sit straight and drive.

I looked at Ella.

She had propped her elbow against the window and rested her chin in the palm of her hand. She had crossed her legs and was stubbornly looking ahead at the road, rubbing her clavicle with her other hand. She was deep in thought, asking herself questions.

I could imagine what she was asking herself: *Shall I let this black man with the huge cock sitting next to me fuck me or not? How will it feel? Good? Great? Amazing? Or will it hurt? I've never been fucked by such a large cock. What if it causes vaginal tears? I've not been with another man ever since I married Nick. What if this stranger is rough? What if he hurts me?*

But what if it feels great? So many women say it's an amazing experience to be penetrated by a big cock! How will it feel to be stretched by his massive rod and bulbous cockhead? To feel full to the brim with that penis over there, thrusting in my pussy! How will it feel to have that muscular body pressed on top of me, his hips pushing my thighs apart, his black hands massaging my boobs and his breath on my mouth as he pants and grunts, ejaculating his load into my pussy? How will it feel?

And how will I feel afterwards? What if I start blaming myself?

And what about Nick? How will he take it? He says he's fine. But he says this now. Now, he wants me to do it. Sure! But what about after it is done? I can't be unfucked. Once I am fucked, that's it! Will Nick not change his mind? What if he starts blaming me and leaves me? With two kids? Is the pleasure worth the risk? Is finding out how it feels to be fucked by a large cock worth it? Damn Gerhard and his ideas! Why did I listen to him?!?

I wished I could say something to her but couldn't. Anything I would have said could have freaked her out. I knew my wife. I knew how she looked when she was agonising over something. And right there, she was agonising over something important, probably the most important thing after getting married. She was asking herself whether she should break her matrimonial vows and let another man fuck her or back off while she could.

Joao glanced at me in the rearview mirror. It was just for a second, but I saw his expression. He was also agonising. Like me, he wanted but didn't dare to talk to Ella. He wished he could ask her what she had decided, but he knew he shouldn't. He must have been watching her out of the corner of his eye and must have noticed the internal struggle written all over her face. And he knew that the wrong question, word, or even look could tip the balance against him. And he kept driving, not taking his eyes off the road.

We were driving through Espargos when Joao finally broke the silence. "This is my house!"

He pointed at a house with only its first floor finished. The second was still under construction.

"Is it still under construction?" I asked.

Joao nodded. "Yes."

"So, where do you live?" Ella asked.

He looked at her and smiled. "On the first floor. The second level is not finished yet."

She raised her eyebrows.

Joao smiled again. "Everyone does it this way here. Builds the first floor, moves in and keeps doing the rest of the house when he can."

"Mmm, interesting," Ella said.

Joao pulled over. "Would you like me to show you inside?"

"No," Ella said abruptly, sounding almost spooked.

I guess she did get spooked by his invitation. Spooked by what accepting that invitation could lead to. She was afraid of what she might be tempted to do if she walked with Joao into his house.

"OK!" Joao shrugged his shoulders and resumed driving.

Ella realised she had been too abrupt, maybe even rude, and put her hand on his leg.

He looked at her.

"Sorry! Maybe some other time, Joao," she said and rubbed his thigh, smiling apologetically.

"Will this time ever come?" he asked and looked back at the road.

Ella replied quietly, "Maybe."

Joao glanced at her. "So it's still a maybe?"

Ella smiled. "Yes, it's still a maybe."

She turned to look at the houses as we drove through the capital of Sal. We left Espargos, and this time Joao chose the main road.

It was so quiet in the cab that it felt almost ominous. Travelling in silence, alone with each other's thoughts, was too nerve-racking. The anguish of trying to decide whether Ella should do it or not, if I should let it happen or not, was too much to bear.

And apparently, Ella felt the same way because she said, "Joao, would you mind playing some music?"

"Sure," he said and turned on the player. A few seconds later, he asked, "You like it?"

"Um-hum," she murmured. A moment later, she added, "Thank you. I like it."

Joao and Ella had not looked at each other even for a moment throughout their short conversation. Ella had been staring through the windscreen, and he had been keeping his eyes on the road. Clearly, they avoided eye contact, but that didn't mean they were not thinking about each other. It was exactly the opposite. They avoided eye contact because all they were thinking about was each other.

A couple of minutes passed, and Joao put his hand on her thigh and pushed her dress up. He gently squeezed her thigh. It was his way of telling my wife: *I'm here, Ella! And I want you!*

Ella placed her hand on top of his and rubbed his knuckles. She whispered, "I know, Joao, I know," and pushed his hand away.

Well, she knows, of course, I said to myself. *She knows he wants to fuck her. We know she knows. But we don't know what she's decided.*

Joao smiled and grabbed the steering wheel with two hands, focusing his attention on the road. He was not told "No". He was told he had to be patient. He had to wait a little longer before finding out whether he'd be given a chance to spread my wife's legs apart and stick his cock into her pussy. He was happy to wait. And why not? At the end of the day, it didn't cost him anything. It was all about a free fuck.

Ella lifted her feet on the seat and hugged her knees to her chest. She rested her chin on her knee and shut her eyes, immersing herself in her thoughts.

Five minutes passed before she opened her eyes and looked at Joao. He pretended he did not notice her gaze and kept driving, looking at the road. Ella held her gaze on his face for a while. Then her eyes moved from his face to his chest, trailed down to his stomach until they settled on his crotch. The tent in his shorts had not disappeared. It was there—prominent and apparent—eager as ever. Ella stared at his cock for a while, then shifted her gaze to his face. Now Joao looked at her and smiled.

She smiled back but then turned her face away and watched the scenery through her window.

He looked back at the road. He still had to wait for her answer.

Ella kept thinking, looking outside, biting her bottom lip, and occasionally glancing at Joao for a brief moment, only to look away through the window. My wife was struggling to decide.

We saw our hotel in the distance, and I rubbed her shoulder.

She turned and looked at me.

I read the question on her face: *What shall I do, Nick?*

I smiled my answer: *Whatever you decide, hon! I'm with you!*

A minute later, Joao stopped the pickup in front of the main entrance.

"Right!" he said and turned off the engine. "Here we are!"

He looked at Ella, then at me. We weren't saying anything. Ten, fifteen, twenty seconds passed, a minute, and it was becoming uncomfortable.

"OK!" Joao said finally. "I hope you enjoyed the day out!"

He got out of the truck, went around the front, and opened the passenger door for Ella. He gave her his hand to help her get out and closed the door behind her. I took our beach bag and got out without his help, of course.

The three of us stood in silence.

Ella was rubbing her collarbone and looking at Joao's face. He was alternating his gaze between her and me.

After fifteen or twenty seconds of impasse, he took a deep breath, exhaled, and said, "I guess I'd better go!" He stretched his hand to Ella. "Goodbye, Ella! It was a pleasure meeting you!"

Ella took his hand and held it. She wasn't saying anything; she just stared him in the eyes. He wasn't letting go of her hand either.

I swallowed nervously. My cock was killing me, throbbing and twitching. It was too much for me, and I said, "Joao, why don't you come for a drink with us?"

Still holding Ella's hand, he looked at me and smiled. "It would have been a pleasure, but I must drive this thing home." He nodded towards the pickup truck.

"Why. . . why don't you park over there?" Ella said and nodded to the nearby hotel car park. "And maybe you can. . . . Can you? I mean, maybe you can stay. . . ." She looked at me.

"Maybe you can stay in the hotel overnight," I said. "Although I guess we have to ask if they have free rooms. Or, hm, maybe we can squeeze into our room. Don't know how that would work. . . I mean, since we are all-inclusive." I raised my hand to show the hotel bracelet. "If the hotel found out—"

"Oh, I've got a solution for that!" Joao said, and a broad smile spread across his face.

He let go of Ella's hand, opened the passenger door, opened the glove box, and took out a hotel bracelet. I noticed he had a couple more in the glove box.

He put the bracelet around his wrist, took scissors from the glove box, cut the bracelet to size, put back the scissors, closed the glove box, and shut the passenger door.

He grinned at us. "Now I'm an all-inclusive hotel guest."

"How? How did you get the bracelets?" I asked.

He smiled again. "Umm. . . , a lady from the hotel gave them to me. You know . . . that night. From the photo?"

"He-he! I see!" I chuckled. "I guess it's good to know the hotel staff."

"Umm, technically, she is not hotel staff," he said.

"Well, I mean someone local." I smiled. "I guess you locals help each other."

"Hi-hi!" Joao giggled. "She's not local either. I mean. . . you saw her in the photo. Well, some of her."

He noticed that Ella was blushing profusely, so he quickly apologised, "Sorry! I should stop talking about my adventure, shouldn't I?"

Ella smiled and nodded yes.

Joao clasped his hands together. "I guess I'd better park the truck then!"

"Yes, go do that," I said.

He got into the truck quickly and drove to the car park. Ella and I stood and waited for him. He parked and ran back to us.

"To the bar. Right?" I asked.

"Yes," Ella said. "But I've got to pee first!"

Joao smiled shyly. "Me too, actually."

"OK," I said. "We'll pop in the lobby toilets first."

We entered the hotel.

6. MUSIC NIGHT

AT THE LOBBY BAR

We walked past the reception, a little apprehensive that someone might spot our deceit of smuggling in an impostor. However, no one stopped us or showed any interest in us.

We visited the toilets in the lobby, and a few minutes later, we lined up in the queue at the lobby bar.

"What would you like, hon?" I asked Ella.

"Gin Martini," she replied promptly.

"He-he!" I chuckled. "It seems Gin Martini is your new favourite cocktail!" I turned to Joao. "Joao?"

He said, "I'll have a cocktail too, but I'd like Sex on the Beach." He smiled and put his hand on the small of Ella's back. "I like this cocktail very much but always feel awkward saying its name."

Ella trembled as she felt Joao's hand on her back. I could tell she was still nervous by the look on her face and how she smiled back at him.

"I know what you mean," she said. "I like it too, by the way." She turned to me. "You know what, Nick? Get me Sex on the Beach instead, will you?"

I smiled. "You changed your mind?"

"Yeah, I did," she replied.

I giggled. "Hi-hi! When someone else wanted to have Sex—"

"Times change, OK?!" she cut me off. Then she felt she might have been a bit abrupt with me, so she smiled. "It's down to whom you're doing it with, honey."

Joao didn't know about Ella and Johan's earlier discussion about Sex on The Beach cocktails. Still, our comments provided enough context to enable him to say, "Yeah, doing it with the right person is key to the pleasure."

Ella blushed.

A table got freed, and I pointed at it. "Go grab that table, Joao!" I gave him the beach bag. "I'll bring the drinks."

Joao and Ella went and took the table while I stayed behind in the queue.

The queue was long. It was the busiest time of the day for the lobby bar when people came for coffee and late afternoon drinks before dinner. Thus, I was stuck in the queue for a while and watched Ella and Joao sitting and talking at the table. Judging by Ella's body language and how she smiled at him, it was clear she was still not at ease. Gone was the flirtatious smile on her face. She wasn't giggling either. She talked to Joao a lot, but it was more like a conversation between colleagues rather than people considering having sex together.

It looks like she got scared and is backing off from doing it, I thought to myself. *It might be for the better; it will save us so many headaches. I'll stay out of it. Let her decide!*

I finally got the drinks—I got myself whisky with ice—and joined Ella and Joao at the table.

Joao pulled the chair for me to sit down and helped me put the drinks on the table.

"Nick," he said, "Ella and I were talking about our hobbies, and it turns out that you guys like hiking and nature walking like me."

"Oh, yeah," I said. "We try to do a nature walk once a month. It's good for the kids. They develop a love for nature from a young age."

Joao nodded in agreement with me. "I totally agree. If I have kids one day, I'll also make sure they develop a relationship with nature! Ella told me about your kids and how much they like pets. I also love pets. I have two cats. You guys have a cat too."

"We do," I said. "We love cats. We are both cat lovers. I mean, we like dogs too but prefer cats."

"Same here!" Joao pointed at himself, smiling. "The three of us have so much in common. Like. I love baking, and Ella told me you both are good at baking. You went on a baking competition together, didn't you?"

I chuckled. "He-he! We did, but we came forth only! We were experimenting back then. We've got so much better recipes now."

Joao smiled. "Ella told me you guys are thinking about publishing your own baking book."

"Oh, we just fantasise." I waved my hand off. "We've put our recipes down only for sharing them with others online. It helps us socialise, you know, get to know other bakers. You learn so much more about people by talking about common interests."

"Absolutely!" Joao agreed with me. "Ella and I learnt so much about each other by talking about our hobbies."

"That's good." I nodded in approval. "The two of you need to get to know each other better."

The moment I said it, I regretted it, but it was too late. Ella blushed big time. I had reminded her why we had Joao at our table. Basically, I was telling her that if they were going to fuck, it was a good idea for them to get to know each other better.

Joao got me out of trouble by raising his glass. "Cheers!"

Ella and I raised our glasses.

Since Joao seemed better than me at having a conversation without making Ella uncomfortable with tongue slips, I let him lead the talk.

Initially, he talked about some neutral topics like work and politics. Then he moved on to talk about his family and their livelihood. He asked Ella and me about our wider families, and we talked about them. After that, he brought about the subject of friends, which led him to tell us a few funny stories involving his friends. Ella's nervousness slowly gave way to curiosity and amusement. And after I brought another round of drinks, she started to laugh and giggle again, amused by Joao's jokes and stories, tapping him on the shoulder and not minding him holding her hand in his.

We talked and joked, and an hour passed, then an hour and a half. We had a third round of drinks, and sitting at the table, still dressed in the same clothes after a long day out, was becoming a little uncomfortable, especially for Ella, who had to sit with her legs crossed or closed together, having no underwear under her dress. Yet, for some reason, my wife was not indicating she wanted us to go to our room. Probably she feared that going to our room would mean letting Joao fuck her, and she had not decided yet. She was buying time by staying at the table and drinking in Joao's company, laughing and flirting. Perhaps she wanted to get to know him better before taking a final decision. Or just getting comfortable and drunk before letting him fuck her. Whatever her reasoning, it was clear we would stay at the bar until dinner.

Joao didn't mind it. It was clear that drinking with Ella and me worked well for his aspirations because, with each passing minute, Ella's mood got better and better. She slapped him on the shoulder whenever his jokes were directed at her, or he made her a brazen compliment. She didn't object when he stroked her thigh under the table or jokingly pulled on her dress to look into her cleavage.

At about six o'clock, Ella announced she had to pee and went to the loo while I went to fetch a fourth round of drinks, leaving Joao at the table to keep it. They had opened the restaurant for dinner, so the queue at the bar was only two deep, and I didn't have to wait too long. I brought the drinks just as Ella returned, and now Joao and I went to the loo.

It was awkward when we stood next to each other to pee in adjacent urinals. We tried not to look at each other's cocks, which I think is the case with most men peeing in a public toilet.

We were not keen to talk either.

However, while washing our hands, Joao said, "I think it's still a maybe, don't you think?"

I nodded. "Yeah, I think it is."

"I'm working on it becoming a yes."

I didn't say anything and went to the dryer, but before I put my hands under it, I looked at Joao and said, "I can see what you're doing, Joao. I am not blind. You don't need to inform me, OK?" I was slightly annoyed to receive progress updates on how he was trying to bed my wife.

"Sorry, didn't mean it in a bad way," he said and joined me at the adjacent dryer.

We dried our hands and were about to get out of the toilet when he put his hand on my shoulder.

I looked at him. "What?"

He smiled. "Nick, are you sure you want me to do it?"

I pushed his hand off my shoulder and looked under the doors of the three single-toilet rooms. There was no one there. Only the two of us were in the gents' toilet.

Then I said, "Joao, one can never be sure whether they want someone else to fuck their wife."

"Mmm." Joao nodded. "I can imagine. You must feel torn apart."

"Um-hum."

"If it's any consolation, I fuck really well."

"You'd better! I'm risking my marriage."

"I know. And I appreciate it!"

I was a little frustrated and maybe feeling slightly humiliated by Joao talking to me like that, but I wasn't going to let my pride and hubris stand in the way of my chance to watch my wife fucked by another man. So, I mumbled, "OK," and we left the toilet.

Ella smiled at us when we sat back at the table.

Joao resumed the conversation with a funny story about taking tourists on a turtle-watching tour and getting lost in the night. Ella and I laughed. He built on the success of the story and started throwing jokes about misunderstandings between tourists and locals.

Joao's duty was to keep Ella entertained. Ella's was to laugh and let him feel her legs and hands and, on a few occasions, brush her breasts through her dress. My job was to be Joao's wingman: to laugh along with him and Ella, throw in a comment here and there, and, of course, bring rounds of drinks from the bar.

Thus, after almost three hours of drinking and enjoying ourselves in the lobby, Ella was in full swing flirting when I brought the sixth round of drinks. She was giggling and laughing. Joao had squatted behind her chair, and with his lips brushing her ear, he whispered jokes about the guests passing through the lobby.

"Stop it, Joao!" Ella squealed and covered her mouth with her hands, suppressing a laugh. "You'll make me pee myself laughing!"

Joao moved to her side, still squatting, and said quietly, "Go for it, Ella! You don't have panties on!"

Ella slapped him playfully on the hand. "Stop it! I'll wet myself!"

"Hi-hi!" He giggled. "Have you not already?"

"No! But will!" she squeaked.

I winked at Joao. "I think she's already wet!"

I leaned across the table towards Ella, smiled at her and took her hands in mine. We stared at each other. There was so much mischief and lust in her eyes.

She giggled. "Hi-hi! Stop it, Nick!"

"Why?" I rubbed her knuckles. "I like it when you're wet down there."

She pulled her hands out of my grip and slapped my wrist. "I'm not talking about that type of wet, Nick! I don't mind that!"

I could see through the glass top of the table and saw Joao put his hand on her leg and push her dress up, baring her thighs. Ella grabbed his hand. She looked around to check if anyone was watching us. When she saw nobody was paying attention to our table, she let Joao's hand rest on her thigh and leaned towards me for a kiss.

Ella and I kissed across the table. The way she kissed, the amount of tongue, the warmth of her breath and her moan in my mouth told me how aroused she was. I saw from the corner of my eye how Joao's hand slid between her legs, and she parted them slightly. His fingers were inches from her pussy.

As soon as we broke the kiss, I looked up at Joao, "I think she's already wet, Joao!"

"Is she?" he asked. "May I check?"

He slid his hand further up, and the tips of his fingers touched her pussy. Ella grabbed his hand and pushed it away.

"Not here, Joao!" she whispered and looked around. "People will see us!"

"He-he!" He chuckled. "OK! Where shall we do it?"

Ella ignored his question and got up from her chair. "I've got to go to the loo!"

"Ella!" Joao called her name.

She looked at him.

A lustful grin spread across his face. "Can I come with you?"

"No!" she squeaked. "Ha-ha! Are you crazy?"

"Hi-hi!" He giggled. "But, Ella, I want to check!"

"Later!" Ella said briefly and ran for the toilet.

Joao sat back in his chair.

He took his empty glass and began playing with it. There was an uncomfortable silence between the two of us. He looked around aimlessly, as did I. We avoided each other's gaze.

Two or three minutes passed, and Joao finally said, "Nick, may I tell you something?"

I looked at him.

He stared me in the eyes for a few seconds before saying, "I think I'm gonna fuck your wife."

"Ha!" I scoffed. "As if I don't already know!"

"Tonight. It's gonna happen tonight, Nick."

"What do you want me to say?"

"Nothing. I just wanted to state it."

I shrugged my shoulders. "OK. You stated it. You said it, and I heard you. Happy?"

There was silence again.

We saw Ella coming out of the toilets.

Looking at her walking towards us, Joao leaned to me and whispered, "I think she's beyond a maybe now, but I might need your help—I mean cooperation—for my next move."

I shifted in my chair, vexed with him again. "What do you want me to do, Joao? Hold your dick as you push it into my wife's pussy?"

While I was aroused at the thought of watching Joao fuck my wife, jealousy had begun to rear its ugly head, and I had started feeling animosity towards him.

He stared at me and sighed. "No. But I'd like you to play along."

"As if I haven't so far!" I raised my voice. I took a deep breath and said, "Just stop diddling around, Joao, and fuck her, or she'll get fucked by someone else. Plenty of men in this hotel are eager to make me a cuckold."

"Oh, Nick!" He grinned at me and shook his head from side to side. "As if I don't know. I know very well that many folk want to fuck Ella! I know more than you think I know!"

Ella, who had just reached our table, stood next to Joao and asked him, "What is it that you know, Joao?"

He looked up at her. "Nothing! Only how sexy you are!" He reached his hand to her thigh.

She pushed his hand away. "I'm hungry. Let's go for dinner!"

"What if we meet our friends there, Ella?" I asked her. "What shall we tell them about him?" I nodded towards Joao.

She giggled. "Hi-hi! We'll tell them he's my younger brother!"

"Ha-ha! They'll believe you!" Joao laughed and placed his hand on her thigh, just below the hem of her dress. "We're so much alike, aren't we?"

"Hi-hi!" Ella giggled again and pushed his hand away. "You are my adopted brother, Joao!"

"No, seriously, Ella," I said. "What shall we tell them? I don't want to—"

"Nick, we owe them nothing!" Ella said abruptly, raising her voice before looking around and adding in a calmer voice, "But anyway, I don't think they're in the hotel tonight. They'd have turned up by now, don't you think?"

Ella was right. We had been sitting at the table for over three hours and hadn't seen Mikkel, Johan or Gerhard.

"Hmm. You're right. That's unusual for them," I said, then slapped my forehead as I remembered they were on a turtle-watching tour. "Oh, yeah! They've gone turtle-watching!"

"Ha-ha!" Joao laughed. "If your friends have gone turtle-watching, they've been scammed! Turtle season is between July and October. They might spend the whole night out there and see nothing. Turtles do not nest this time of the year."

"He-he!" I chuckled, realising the two Danes and Gerhard had been fucked up. "Yeah, you said so. Now is not the turtle season." I looked at my watch. "We should hurry up. If we want to go to the show after dinner. It starts at eight o'clock tonight."

"Oh, yeah!" Ella exclaimed. "It's music night tonight!"

I got up from my seat and took our beach bag. "The show tonight is a musical, and Ella wants to watch it," I clarified for Joao.

"Let's go then," he said and stood up.

We hurried to the restaurant with unsteady steps. We had drunk too much, but fortunately not so much not to know we had to stay low and not attract attention, for we had a freeloader amongst us, as Joao rightly said when entering the restaurant.

We grabbed food from the hot food bar and ate quietly at the table. Ella and Joao didn't talk a lot but still flirted. They kept exchanging cheeky smiles and funny faces. From time to time, Joao would slip his foot from his sandal. He would stretch his leg under the table and put his foot on Ella's knee, staring at her with a playful spark in his eyes and making her suppress a giggle. His foot would slide between her legs, touching her pussy under her dress, only for her to slap his knee. Joao would pull his leg back, make a funny face, and Ella would stick her tongue out at him, giggle quietly and look around to make sure we had not attracted unwanted attention.

With Joao and Ella fooling around quietly and me taking part with smiles and saucy remarks, it took us longer to finish dinner.

When we were finally done eating and playing around, I said to Ella, "Honey, shall we go to our room and get changed for the show?"

She asked me, "What time is it?"

I looked at my watch. "Ten to eight!"

"Ooh!" Ella made a grimace of disappointment. "The show's

about to start! We won't have time!"

I picked up the beach bag and stood up. "OK! Let's go to the show!"

Ella's gaze fell on the bag in my hand. "Not with the bag, Nick!"

"Well." I looked at my watch again. "Do we have time to run to the room and leave it there?"

Ella sighed. "We'll be late! There won't be any seats left!"

We heard music coming from the auditorium, where the band was getting ready for the show.

Ella nibbled on her bottom lip a few times, hesitating, staring at the bag in my hand, then looked at me and, making a pleading face, said, "Honey, may I ask you for a favour?"

"Yes, hon." I smiled, anticipating what she would ask me.

"Would you mind running to the room and leaving the bag there?" She gave me one of the softest smiles she had. "I'll try. . . ." She looked at Joao. "Joao and I will try to find seats for the three of us!"

"OK!" I said. "I'll find you there!"

"Thank you!" she chirped, reached into the bag and took her phone out. "Text me if you can't find us!"

"Sure!" I replied, turned around and rushed for our hotel block.

I almost ran—not that I was in a rush to watch the show. No! I didn't care about it. Ella was the one who wanted to attend all shows and concerts at such places. She always had to drag me to go with her. So, I wasn't rushing to go back to watch the show. I had a different reason for wanting to return as soon as possible. I wanted to watch what Joao and Ella would be doing in the semi-darkness of the auditorium. I was anxious, very anxious because I was torn apart between cuckold desire and jealousy, between excitement and fear, between anticipation and trepidation.

Will she let him fuck her, or will she bail out at the last moment? I asked myself as I adjusted the erection in my shorts. *Does she realise it's time for the dessert? Will she stay at the table for it or not?*

I turned around the corner, out of Ella's and Joao's sight, and ran. I literally ran!

Unfortunately, when I got to our room, I needed badly to take a shit. We'd been out and about all day, and while Ella and Joao had probably dealt with that bodily need in the hotel toilets after we had come back from the island tour—judging by how long I had been waiting for them before going to the lobby bar—I hadn't had success there.

The next few minutes I spent sitting on the toilet seat in our bathroom were one of the longest minutes of my life. Jealousy, at that point, was killing me.

What if I don't find them when I go to the auditorium? What if they have decided to go to the beach or to the pool? No one is there! He could be fucking her on a sunbed at the pool right now!

That's what I wanted, didn't I? Idiot! I'm a total idiot! What if she gets to like him more than me? Fuck! She already likes him more than me! Of course, she does! What a stupid question! That's why she's with him right now! She'll love him fucking her. How would it be otherwise? Of course, she will like it! His cock is so big! And he is handsome, manly, and so powerful. Pure masculine power. He has a body of an athlete! And he is so kind at the same time. He's funny and charming. He is a handsome black man. He's so new and exotic to her. The newness factor is huge! But most of all, he's got such a big cock. Of course, she will like him fucking her, and, of course, will like him way more than me! I know this. That's why we are doing it, after all! For her to enjoy a good fuck! To experience fucking by a large cock. To have sex with a black man! Ella and I know why we are doing it. For the great experience. To experience great sex!

So? Why am I bothered if I know this? What's the big deal? It's not really, is it? If you think about it, it's not. My wife will have a great experience, that's all! It's not love or anything. It's just sex. It's like a good massage. A pussy massage. That's all that it is. A thorough pussy massage! That she will thoroughly enjoy! I should be happy for her! Happy for her for being happy!

Happy for her for being happy. It's not a bad thing. For her being happy.

But what if she is too happy, ah? Then what? What if he fucks her so much better than me? Like, not better, but way, way better? What if she's so blown away by his performance that she decides to stay with him? He's a bachelor, as far as we know. He is, right? He's never mentioned a girlfriend or a wife. He talked about an ex-girlfriend but no wife. No, he hasn't mentioned a girlfriend or wife. He's free, yeah, free to steal other men's wives. Ella might simply leave me for him. What stops her? Nothing. She might even marry him! Why not? An exotic black guy with an amazing cock. She's had her children with me. Fulfilled her goals in life. After ten years of marriage, she's achieved everything a wife could want. She's gone full circle. What she needs now are adventure and amazing sex! And he's offering exactly that!

Oh, fuck me! Why did I do this to myself? For what? To satisfy a fetish. I did it just because I get a hard-on watching my wife with another man! Fuck me!

I took a deep breath and looked at my cock. My cock was hard as a rock! It was twitching so much that it was hitting the rim of the toilet seat.

Oh! Fuck it! Now I have to wash it!

As soon as I finished my number 2 business, I got up from the toilet seat, wiped my ass and tiptoed to the sink with my shorts down. I started to wash my cock with soap but pressed the soap dispenser too hard and squirted soap onto my shorts!

"Oh, fuck!" slipped through my lips as I looked in frustration at the thick soap liquid splashed all over my thighs and shorts.

I decided to take a quick shower and took my shorts and t-shirt off. I showered hastily, dried myself and changed into fresh shorts and a t-shirt.

I didn't bother putting on briefs. *Joao doesn't wear underwear. Why would I?*

I left the room and looked at my watch. I had lost twenty minutes in bathroom activities! I ran and got into the auditorium. I looked at my watch again. It was eight twenty.

INDECISION

The rows of seats were packed, and quite a few people were standing in the corners of the massive hall and in the nooks along the walls. There was little chance that Ella and Joao could have found seats considering they had been late. These shows were extremely popular, and unless you were at least twenty minutes earlier, chances to find seats were minuscule.

I sighed a deep sigh, concluding that, rather than desperately trying to find seats, Ella and Joao had most probably gone to fuck on the loungers by the swimming pool or in one of the service rooms, which were usually kept unlocked as Ella and I had found out on a few occasions.

My heart murmured at the thought that Joao might be fucking my wife while I was standing at the stairs of the auditorium in the middle of some stupid show. Nonetheless, I decided to give it a final try and scanned the hall once again. It was loud and packed with people. Some parts of the hall were illuminated by ceiling lighting and light coming from the stage, and I had no problem seeing individual faces. Other parts of the auditorium were much darker, and I struggled with the silhouettes. Despite the difficulties, I checked every row but couldn't find Ella and Joao.

I took my phone out to text Ella and ask her where they were.

And then I saw her message, sent ten minutes earlier: "We're behind the broken furniture. Couldn't find seats."

Behind the broken furniture, hm. Where's that? I tried to remember where I had seen broken furniture and looked at a place in the back of the hall next to the wall on my right, which was cordoned off for repairs. Some tall cabinets, a cupboard and wooden boxes had been thrown away there, perhaps parts of obsolete décor or something.

I saw Ella's and Joao's heads peeking over one of the cabinets. They were watching the show from there.

I sighed in relief. *At least they are not fucking!* I even smiled to myself: *worried for nothing!* And that was when my anxiety and jealousy suddenly gave way to excitement and arousal. My cock was hard again.

I watched Ella and Joao for a while. It looked like my wife was giggling. *What are they talking about?*

I decided to sneak on them and walked out of the auditorium. I walked around the whole building, past the large columns at the back, and re-entered the hall from the side entrance just behind Ella and Joao.

The broken furniture formed a small nook—or rather a small castle—and the only way to get inside was by squeezing through a narrow opening between the wall and two of the larger cabinets.

I walked into the entrance of the barricade and stood still four or five feet behind Ella's and Joao's backs.

Scattered light from the auditorium illuminated them, but I was in almost complete darkness, squeezed between the larger cabinet and the wall. This way, I was able to see them reasonably well, while they couldn't unless they turned around and specifically looked in my direction.

Ella was standing on one of the boxes and peeking her head above the cabinet in front of her to watch the show. Joao was standing behind her, with his arms wrapped around her waist, whispering in her ear. Actually, Joao wasn't whispering. The music was too loud, so he was speaking with a normal voice.

I heard him say, "May I?"

He pulled her closer to him and kissed the side of her neck.

"Joao!" Ella squeaked, giggling, and squirmed out of his grip. "Let me watch!"

He wrapped his arms around her waist from behind again and hooked his chin over her shoulder.

I was behind them but also to their right, so I had enough line of sight to see what Joao's hands were doing in front of Ella's body. His hands were not idle.

He was trying to feel her breasts over her dress, but she was resisting by pushing his hands down. He settled on a compromise: placing his palms on her stomach. However, that was not for too long. His left hand slipped down from her stomach to her crotch and tried to find its way between her legs, but Ella closed them tightly together.

He pressed his cheek against hers. "Say it's not a maybe anymore, Ella, and I'll let you watch!"

She giggled. "Hi-hi! OK. Maybe it's not a maybe anymore. Now let me watch!"

Joao moved his left hand to her buttock and squeezed her butt. He kissed her cheek, then pulled his head back a little, nudged her hair aside with his chin, and gently nibbled her earlobe.

He pressed his pelvis tight against her ass.

"Hi-hi, Joao!" Ella giggled again. "Stop it!"

"Why?" Joao asked and pulled his crotch away from her ass.

There was a massive bulge in his shorts.

He slid his hand down to the hem of her dress, grabbed it and hiked her dress up, baring her ass.

"Joao!" Ella squeaked and looked around to check if anyone could be watching them, even though they were pretty well hidden in the improvised nook.

I quickly stepped back out of the entrance to their hiding place so she could not see me.

"You're so very, very wet, Ella!" I heard Joao say.

"Fuck!" I heard Ella moan. "Don't! Please!"

I sneaked back into the opening between the wall and the tall cabinets to watch what Ella and Joao were doing. Ella was looking at the stage ahead, trying to watch the show. She had perked her ass up and slightly spread her legs.

Joao didn't care about watching the show. He had slid his hand between Ella's thighs from behind and was rubbing her exposed pussy.

"You want me, Ella!" he said.

Ella's body shook as Joao ran his hand along the length of her slit, spreading her pussy lips apart with his fingers.

He kissed the exposed skin between her shoulder blades. "Why not let me, Ella?"

"Because I'm a married woman!" Ella said quietly.

She reached behind her, took Joao's hand, and pushed it away from her pussy. She pulled her dress down to cover her ass and pressed herself against the cabinet in front of her.

Joao squeezed his left hand between the cabinet and her stomach, wrapping both arms around her waist from behind her.

He pressed his chest against her back. "So what do we do then?"

"I don't know, Joao! I don't know what to do!" Ella said with an almost pleading voice, without looking at him, keeping her eyes on the stage.

Joao put his hand on her hip. "I'd say let's do it, Ella! It will feel good. You'll finally find out what it feels like. You'll like it. You'll love the complete surrender. Ripples of pleasure travelling through your body." He kissed her shoulder.

Ella's breathing became deeper and faster. She began biting her bottom lip.

Joao moved his hand from her hip down to the back of her thigh.

It became quiet in the hall since the actors on the stage began talking quietly as part of a scene, so Joao switched to whispering, "Ella, it will feel amazing." He stroked her thigh, pushing her dress up. "We can do it here or go somewhere quieter."

Joao kept stroking the back of her thigh with his fingers crawling up, over the curve of her ass cheek and then down back over her thigh, gently scratching her skin with his fingernails— slowly, gently, teasingly—whispering in her ear, "You'll feel stretched, full... down there... like never before. The most amazing feeling of warmth and fullness. You'll—"

"Joao, please," Ella pleaded with a shaky voice, crackling as if she was about to start crying. "I can't go that far, I can't." Her breathing had become heavy and urgent, and she gasped before murmuring, "I am a married woman, Joao!"

"So?"

"I love Nick!"

"But you want to feel it, Ella!"

"I am scared. I don't have the courage to do it!"

"I'll be gentle," Joao assured her.

Ella shook her head from side to side. "It's not only that, Joao! It's the afterwards. How I'll handle it. How Nick will handle it."

"You don't need to tell him."

"No! I won't cheat on him! If we do it, I'll tell him."

"OK! Let's do it now, and you'll tell him later. It's easier to ask for forgiveness than permission."

Ella went quiet. She was biting her lips. Her chest was moving fast up and down.

Joao let go of her thigh and pressed his crotch against her butt, pushing his pelvis upwards. He was taller than Ella, but because she was standing on the small box, the bulge in his shorts pressed right between her thighs.

"Can you feel how big it is?" he asked her seductively and caressed her cheek with one hand while he pulled her closer to him with the other. "You want it inside you, don't you? Let's do it here, and we'll tell Nick when he joins us!"

"OK," Ella whispered.

Joao let go of her and took a step back. He pulled down his shorts to his knees, and his massive cock sprang free.

He pulled Ella's dress up, bunching it at her waist and completely uncovering her backside.

Ella pushed her butt back and spread her legs slightly, grabbing the edge of the cabinet. I was able to see her pussy between her legs from behind.

My wife is offering her pussy to get fucked! I felt like my heart would burst out of my ribcage. Both from anxiety and excitement. *Fuck! She will get fucked! Right now! Right here!*

My cock was throbbing, and my head was spinning.

Joao grabbed Ella's hips. He spread his legs slightly and pushed his pelvis forward, pointing his cock at Ella's pussy.

A pang of jealousy suddenly ripped through me. But my cock was twitching! I was on the brink of ejaculation and, at the same time, on the verge of jumping at Joao and peeling him off my wife.

And then, Ella reached her hands behind her and grabbed Joao's wrists. "No!" she shouted and pushed his hands off her, then lowered her voice. "Sorry, Joao! I'd rather do it in front of him." She pressed her crotch at the cabinet in front of her, putting some distance between Joao's cock and her pussy.

"Ella?!" Joao whispered.

"I said no!" Ella said firmly and pulled her dress down, covering her private parts.

Joao moved his pelvis back and pulled his shorts up. "OK, Ella, text him again! I can't wait to—"

"Don't know, Joao! Sorry!"

"But, Ella? What's going on? I thought you said it was not a maybe anymore."

Ella sighed. "I said maybe it's not a maybe."

Joao shook his head in disappointment. "Maybe it's not a maybe. I see. You're so indecisive."

He was desperate to fuck my wife. He probably felt she was playing him for a fool. Cockteasing him to the extreme. But nevertheless, he was a gentleman and backed off.

He wrapped his arms around her waist from behind and stayed still for a few seconds before saying, "Ella, you so much want us to do it!"

"Yes, I want us to do it. I want you to fuck me! OK?" Ella said with a frustrated, almost angry voice. "But I'm afraid, Joao! I don't know how Nick and I will feel afterwards. Get it?" She sighed a deep sigh. "Where's Nick?"

She began scanning the hall in front of her, looking for me, then turned her head to her left as she continued to search for me. There was a risk she would look behind her.

I couldn't let her find out I was eavesdropping, so I quickly took two steps back, and it worked.

When she looked over her shoulder and saw me, it appeared I was just entering the nook.

"Nick!" she squealed.

"Sorry, hon!" I said. "I looked row by row for you but couldn't find you. Then I went to check on the terrace and saw your message." I waved my phone before I put it into my pocket.

Ella grabbed onto the edge of the cabinet with one hand and reached her other hand to me. "Come, Nick! I've been waiting for you."

I took her hand and smiled. She smiled a soft smile.

Joao turned his head to look at me, briefly smiled, then pulled Ella tight to him and hooked his chin over her shoulder. He pushed his crotch against her butt. "Ella, Nick is here now. You want it. He wants it. I want it. Let me fuck you!"

He was going full-on. He wasn't bothered that I was there and listened to him talking my wife into letting him fuck her.

Ella squeezed my hand. "Nick, come stand next to me, please!"

She pulled me to stand next to her, and I got on the box. There was barely enough space for the two of us to stand next to each other on it, but Ella was determined that I stood beside her—both in literal and metaphoric terms. Thus I was squashed between the cabinet in front of us, the cabinet on my left and her on my right, with my right hip pressed against Joao's muscular left arm curved around her left hip.

"Nick," Ella said, "I want to do it, but I don't know how we'll feel afterwards. I don't know if I'm ready."

The scene where the actors were talking was over, and the music went loud again, so we had to speak louder to hear each other.

I said, raising my voice, "If you are not ready, don't do it!"

"She is ready!" Joao said. "Ella, you are ready!"

He pulled his pelvis away from her and, leaving his right arm wrapped around her waist, moved his left hand to the back of her thigh. He found the hem of her dress and pushed it up, baring her bum. He slid his hand between her thighs from behind, and Ella trembled. Joao had touched her pussy. Her chest was rising up and down rapidly. She was staring at me with eyes full of lust and desire, fear and concern, but also love and trust.

She was looking for my support, and I loved her for that. I kissed her on the cheek. "It's up to you, honey. I'll be happy with whatever you decide. I love you!"

"Love you too," she murmured and stayed still for a few seconds before adding, "Nick, if we do, we may not be able to live with it, you know."

I smiled. "I think we will live with it, honey. Whether we'll regret it? Maybe. But it can't be that bad. So many couples do it. You heard Gerhard."

"But—" Ella gasped. She squeezed my hand real tight. Now her breathing got super-fast.

"What is it, hon?" I asked.

Joao said, "You are so, so ready, Ella!"

"Shit!" slipped through Ella's lips, and she dug her fingernails into my palm.

"What is it, hon?" I asked again, worried about her.

"Ugh!" she moaned and frowned in discomfort. "He—"

"I shoved my fingers into her pussy, Nick," Joao announced. "Look!" He pulled his hand from between her legs and showed me his fingers. "She's ready!"

Joao's middle and index fingers glistened with pussy juices.

Ella bit her bottom lip nervously.

"Is it still a maybe, Ella?" Joao asked her.

"OK. Let's do it!" she said quietly, so quietly I barely heard her with the music going loud.

Joao heard her well, though, and grinned a happy grin. "Let the good times roll!"

He reached his hand to his shorts to pull them down, but Ella let go of my hand and grabbed his wrist.

"Not here! In our room!" she said and pushed his hand away.

Joao put his hand on her shoulder. "OK, let's go to your room!"

"No. I can't!" Ella said briskly. "I can't! Sorry!"

Joao rolled his eyes, shaking his head. Then he looked at me and raised his eyebrows.

I shrugged my shoulders. "Whatever Ella decides!"

I couldn't help him and didn't want to. I was undecided myself. With jealousy and lust raging a battle in my head and heart? No! I knew I was too confused to be taking rational decisions. It had to be Ella to decide. Not me.

THE TEST

Joao stared at me helplessly for a few seconds before saying, "Ella, you know what? Let's do a short test!"

Now Ella was the one to raise her eyebrows. "A test?" She looked at him over her shoulder.

"Yeah." He nodded. "A test."

Ella swallowed nervously. "What do you mean by a test?"

"Let me enter you once, just once!" he said.

Ella shook her head from side to side. "No!" She turned to look at the stage.

Joao continued to speak. "It won't be like fucking you, Ella. Just a few thrusts. It will be just enough to know how it feels, and then you'll decide if you want to take me to your room."

He glanced over his shoulder to make sure no one had sneaked in to watch what we were doing and, still holding her by the waist with one hand, he lowered his shorts down with the other hand, just in front, enough for his erect cock to pop out without him baring his ass. Then he said, "Ella, give me your hand!" He grabbed her hand and guided it to his cock.

Ella trembled when her fingers touched the massive cockhead but did not pull her hand away. Instead, she wrapped her fingers around his cock.

Joao lowered his face to her ear. "Let's do it here! Just a few thrusts! Then you and Nick will know how you feel, and you'll take me to your room or let me go. I'll sleep in my truck if you don't want me. A few thrusts won't count for anything, Ella! It's really to get a sense of what a large black cock feels like. It's not fucking."

Ella looked at me. "Nick, what shall I do?"

I smiled cautiously. "Why don't you give it a go? Just to have a feel. It's not like doing it completely or something."

Having heard my advice to my wife, Joao instructed her, "Just squat a little, Ella, push your bum out and stand still! "

Ella let go of Joao's cock and grabbed my hand. We interlocked fingers. She grasped the edge of the cabinet with her other hand and pressed her chest against it. She looked ahead at the stage, where the action had picked up. The performers were dancing wildly to loud music; the audience was clapping and shouting enthusiastically.

Ella pushed her bum back and parted her legs.

Joao did not waste any time.

He hiked her dress up to her waist, making sure he had unobstructed access to her pussy from behind. Then he looked around once again to assure himself that no one could see us in the shelter formed by the thrown-out cabinets and crates and pushed his shorts down to his knees. Holding Ella around the waist with one hand, he squatted a little, grabbed his cock with the other hand and guided it into her pussy from behind.

Ella trembled and squeezed my hand when she felt his cockhead spread her labia.

"I'm quite large, Ella," Joao said close to her ear. "It will feel overwhelming for a few moments until I get in and you have stretched a little wider, but after that, it will be fun. You're ready?"

Ella dug her fingernails into my palm and, panting heavily in anticipation, said, "Ready!"

Joao pushed his pelvis up, and Ella whimpered. I felt a sharp pain in my hand. She had really dug her nails into my flesh. Joao thrust again; Ella whimpered again. Her whole body began shaking out of nerves but also sensations in her pussy. She bit her bottom lip to suppress moans and whimpers.

Joao thrust again; her face flinched; Joao thrust yet again and again.

"Fuck!" slipped through Ella's lips.

Joao made a powerful thrust, almost knocking her off her feet.

"Urgh!" Ella groaned. "Gentle, please!"

Joao rubbed her back between her shoulder blades. "Spread your legs a little wider, Ella! I need you to open up your pussy just a bit wider to get it all in." He gently pushed her to bend over further.

Ella bent forward and spread her legs further apart.

He thrust again.

She winced.

"That's it!" Joao praised her. "You're so wet that it slides in really well. Just get the nerves out of your system, and your vagina will open up. Don't overthink it. Just relax and take it in. Here we go!"

He made another powerful stroke. Ella groaned, and her fingernails went deeper into my skin.

My hand was hurting, probably bleeding, but I didn't care. I looked down at her butt.

What a sight were her soft white ass cheeks squashed by the muscular black thighs and stomach of her new lover!

Ella's hips were shaking. Her thigh muscles were shaking. Her entire body was shaking.

"One final push, Ella. Take a deep breath in!" Joao said and rubbed her back. "Here we go!"

He thrust real hard.

Ella moaned, "Ahh!"

"That's it! I'm in!" Joao rubbed her back again. "You OK?"

Ella nodded yes.

He leaned forward and kissed the side of her neck. "You hurt?"

She murmured, "No. I'm fine!"

"How's it, hon?" I asked her.

Ella finally released her grip on my hand and looked at me. She puffed air out. "Stretched out. Very stretched out!"

My heart was racing. *My wife is impaled on a huge black cock. She's not mine anymore!*

My chest hurt, and my head began to spin. At the same time, my cock was throbbing and twitching.

I repeated as if in a trance, "You're very stretched out. . . ."

Ella's voice croaked. "Yes. A lot."

Joao stroked her back. "Relax, Ella, relax!"

"But you expected it, hon, didn't you?" I said. "To be stretched out a lot."

Ella blew a strand of hair that had fallen across her face. "Not like this! Not this much. It's huge, Nick! Really huge! It stretches me out." She bit her bottom lip. "Fuck! Real wide!"

Her cheeks were red. I guess out of pleasure, discomfort, and shame at the same time.

I rubbed her shoulder. "But it feels good, isn't it?"

"Oh, yeah!" she rasped. "Full. It feels full!"

Joao caressed her cheek and whispered in her ear, "Feel it, Ella, feel it, darling! That's how a big cock feels. Relax and feel its girth! I feel you really well. You've got a wonderful pussy! Tight and slick! I feel it pulsing around my cock. I love the feeling! Cosy warmth and velvety grip. Relax now and let your pussy take over. It knows what it wants. Just let it do what it knows best to do. Relax!"

Ella looked ahead and blew air out of her mouth.

He smiled and caressed the back of her head. "You cute, little blonde beauty! Finally, let me in!" He kissed her shoulder next to the strap of her dress. "It doesn't hurt, does it?"

Ella shook her head. "No. I'm just stretched out. And it feels like you're poking into my stomach."

"OK. Let's stay still for a little longer!" Joao said. "You'll adjust to my size. Just keep breathing in and out, slow, deep breaths."

Ella heeded Joao's advice and began breathing deep breaths in and out.

"That's it!" Joao praised her and caressed her cheek. "You're doing really well, Ella!"

Ella looked at me and smiled for the first time after Joao had penetrated her. "Now I know how it feels," she murmured.

Joao chuckled. "He-he! Not yet, Ella! You don't know yet. The fun hasn't started yet." He leaned forward, wrapped both arms around her, pressed his chest against her back, and kissed the side of her neck, whispering in her ear, "You've stretched now."

Joao let go of her waist and stood straight, keeping his cock inside Ella's pussy.

He grabbed her ass cheeks, spread them apart and looked down at his crotch and her butt as if to inspect how well his cock had impaled her pussy from behind. Then he withdrew his cock a little and thrust in.

Ella moaned, "Ugh!"

"Yeah, you're good to go!" He squeezed her butt cheeks. "Here we go!"

Ella looked at him over his shoulder, her face red with excitement and nerves. "Only a few thrusts, Joao!"

He smiled. "Of course, Ella!"

Ella nibbled on her lip, trying to slow down her breathing before saying, "Go slow, please! And don't you dare finish inside me! Pull out if you can't hold it! I'm not on the pill!"

"Of course, Ella!" Joao assured her again and thrust in.

"Urgh!" Ella groaned. "A few thrusts, Joao! You won't be fucking me! Just a couple of thrusts, and you pull it out! Clear?"

Joao grinned at her. "Yes, Ella. Understood!"

Ella puffed air through her nose. "Fuck! It's deep!"

She turned her head and looked ahead. She grabbed the edge of the cabinet with two hands and steadied herself as she prepared for his thrusts.

Joao looked at me and flicked his eyebrows up and down. I knew what he was telling me: *I don't know how your wife defines fucking, but I am already fucking her, mate.* He shrugged his shoulders, smiling, and I knew again what he was telling me: *We'll go along with her and take our pleasure! Shall we?*

I nodded yes.

Joao looked down at Ella's butt and began thrusting with long deep strokes, slowly and gently sliding his cock in and out of her pussy, holding her steady by the hips.

I grabbed my throbbing cock and squeezed the tip to withhold imminent ejaculation. So excited I was watching my wife being fucked by another man that I was in danger of blowing it in my shorts.

Joao accelerated the speed of his thrusts. Ella held tight to the cupboard, trying not to sway too much. Despite her efforts, her breasts were bouncing in rhythm with Joao's thrusts. She pressed her chest against the cupboard to stop her boobs from swaying, concerned that an onlooker might figure out what was going on behind the old crates and cabinets. It was loud in the music hall, with a lot of action going on the stage, so no one cared what was happening in our small corner, but Ella did not want to take any chance.

Her lover was fucking her for no longer than a minute, and she began moaning quietly, "Ohh... ugh... ahh."

Joao also was grunting quietly, "Urgh... mmm... argh."

He kept increasing the pace of his thrusts until, after another minute, he reached full speed and was fucking her real hard. Ella started to pant and moan louder as an orgasm began building up in her groin, and, at one point, she turned her head abruptly and looked at Joao over her shoulder.

She shouted, "Joao, slow down! I don't want to cum!"

Joao only grinned at her and continued to thrust.

"Joao!" she squeaked.

He grunted, "Urgh! You like it, don't you?"

"I like it, yes!" she cried. "Ugh! But I don't want to. . . ugh. . . like it!"

Joao grabbed her hips tighter and started to drive his cock in and out of her pussy, faster and deeper. He looked down at his cock and watched it with glee slide in and out of my wife's vagina.

Ella's arms began shaking.

"Oh, God!" slipped through her lips as the pleasure in her pussy reached the threshold of orgasm. She shouted, "Joao! Stay still! Please!"

"Urgh!" Joao groaned, not taking his eyes off his cock, ploughing her pussy. "Why? Doesn't it feel good?"

"Urgh! Fuck! Yes!" Ella whined, feeling the first orgasmic wave ripple from her pussy through her stomach and her spine and spread throughout her entire body. She whimpered, "You promised only a test, Joao! Not to fuck me! You promised just a few thrusts!"

"Yes, only a few thrusts, Ella," Joao said and grunted, "Urgh. That's what I am doing. A few thrusts."

"Ugh!" Ella failed to suppress a moan. "OK, a few more!" A second later, she moaned again, "Ugh! Can't hold it, can't—"

"Let go, Ella, let go! Enjoy! Cum, Ella! Cum!" Joao shouted, relentlessly slamming his cock in her pussy.

"I don't want to cum!" she squealed. "Oh! Oh! Oh!" she moaned. "I can't! I shouldn't! It's just a test!"

Joao was thrusting harder and harder. His powerful thrusts were shaking Ella's body. Ella turned to look ahead, grabbed firmly onto the edge of the cabinet and bit her bottom lip to suppress her moans.

Her orgasm was gaining on her.

She shut her eyes. "Ugh! Ugh! God! I don't want to orgasm! I won't let it!"

She didn't want to let herself have an orgasm, but she couldn't stop it, and a second later, she shuddered in a powerful climax.

I looked around, concerned that Joao and Ella were making too much noise and might attract attention. Fortunately, the show had reached some culmination, and the music was thunderous, so no one could hear us unless they were a meter away from us. No one was looking in our direction either. All eyes were on the stage.

Joao fucked Ella with passion. He gripped her ass cheeks and watched her pussy as he pounded it mercilessly: pulling his cock out of her vagina up to the glans, his thick black shaft glistening in white foam of pussy juices, then ploughing his cock back deep into her love hole and stretching her pink vaginal orifice wide open around his cock base.

Ella moaned quietly but continuously, having surrendered to the pleasure given to her pussy by the massive cock of her black lover.

A minute passed before her orgasm subsided, but now Joao was coming to the point of no return and was thrusting frantically.

Ella looked over her shoulder and shouted at him, "Joao, pull it out before you cum!"

Joao wasn't listening to her. He was looking at his cock, slamming in and out of her pussy, and enjoying the pleasurable tingling sensation building up in his balls.

"Joao, pull it out before you cum!" Ella shouted again.

Thank God the music went in a crescendo, and the audience began singing along with the performers for the show's finale, so no one could hear Ella shouting.

Joao looked up at her. "Yes, Ella! Just a few more thrusts!"

"OK! But then you pull it out!" she rasped before a moan slipped through her lips, "Oh," followed by another one, "Ugh!"

She pressed her lips together to suppress her moans and waited for him to stop thrusting, but instead, he started to grunt again. His face grimaced in pleasure. He kept thrusting, and there was no sign of him pulling his cock out of her pussy or even slowing down his thrusts.

Ella let go of the cupboard, turned halfway and put her hands on his chest. "Joao, I'm not on the pill! You've got to pull out before you start to cum! Do you understand me?"

Joao nodded yes. A second later, he moaned, "Ugh!"

Ella shut her eyes and pressed her lips together again, suppressing a moan of her own. Her body was rocking under Joao's thrusts.

She opened her eyes and looked at Joao's face.

"Urgh!" he groaned. "This pussy! Love it!"

Ella shouted, "Joao! I'm not on the pill! Joao, pull out before you cum!"

He grunted loudly, "Urgh! Feels so good! Yes, Ella, I'll pull out!"

She watched his face contorting in growing pleasure and started to release that he was promising to pull his cock out before cumming but lacked the willpower to do it. He was not going to pull away from her. He simply didn't want to. He liked fucking her too much. After a whole day of waiting and teasing, he wanted to fuck her properly and take his pleasure.

Ella murmured, "You are not listening to me, are you?" She let go of his chest. "And I like it too much to stop you."

She turned to face the stage and grabbed the edge of the cabinet.

A quiet moan escaped her lips. "Ohh!" She bit her lips to suppress another one.

Joao let go of her buttocks and wrapped his arms around her waist. Her dress dropped down, covering her ass, but it was not a problem for him. His cock was in her pussy. He pulled her tight to him and pushed his crotch against her ass.

Ella looked at me. "Nick, he's gonna empty himself inside me!"

I looked at Joao. He had closed his eyes and tilted his head back. He was grunting, with his cock buried deep into her pussy and his butt and thigh muscles convulsing. He was ejaculating.

"He's already emptying himself, hon," I said and caressed her cheek.

"Fuck!" slipped through her lips. She looked ahead, and I heard her say, "He's gonna knock me up!"

Joao thrust two times really deep, one after the other, and again stayed still, with his cock deep inside Ella's pussy.

He rested his head on her shoulder and groaned something in Creole, which sounded like: "Urgh! Feels so good!"

Ella stood still, having resigned to the thought that Joao was unloading his sperm inside her womb, and neither he nor she had the willpower to stop it. Logic was telling her not to like it, but her pussy was telling her otherwise. Pleasure was building up in her body again. She was trying to contain it, but the feeling of Joao's throbbing cock inside her vagina felt good, too good to be contained.

And then suddenly, she gasped. "Agh! Joao! Oh, God!" She was on the verge of another orgasm. Without looking at him, staring ahead, she asked him, "Have you finished already?" Her words were breaking up; her muscles were shaking. "Have you?"

"Almost," he rasped. "Just a little bit left."

He thrust again and groaned. Ella whimpered and lowered her head, her forehead almost touching the surface of the cabinet. Saliva began drooling out of her mouth.

She moaned a low-pitched "Ohh!" and shook in a second orgasm.

"Urgh! Almost there!" Joao grunted, pulled his cock out to the glans and made a powerful thrust into her pussy.

They remained still until their orgasms subsided.

Ella puffed air out and looked at him over her shoulder. "Have you finished, Joao?"

"Yeah!" Joao smiled at her. "Just the last few drops! Sorry!"

Ella turned to look ahead at the stage.

Joao trusted three, four, five times in quick succession, pushed his cock deep inside her pussy and groaned a loud "urgh".

He took a half-step back from Ella and stroked her back. "Finished! Stay still while I'm pulling it out, Ella! I'm still hard." He rubbed her shoulder. "Don't want to chafe you if you clench your vagina. Here we go!"

Ella's face flinched as Joao started to withdraw his cock from her pussy.

He did it slowly, pausing at every inch, careful not to hurt her or himself.

He rubbed her back again. "I'm about to pull out my cockhead. Breathe out!"

Ella took a deep breath and exhaled slowly while Joao slowly pulled his pelvis back, looking down between his legs. I looked closer at her pussy.

The rim of her vagina, tightly wrapped around his thick shaft, stretched out further. She whimpered briefly, and his cockhead popped out of her pussy.

"There we go! It's out!" he announced triumphantly and pulled his fully erect cock out from between Ella's legs.

Only now, he remembered to look around.

After assuring himself that no one had seen him and Ella fuck he sighed in relief. "Phew! We got away!" Then he caressed Ella's ass. "Thank you, Ella!"

REMORSE AND FORGIVENESS

Ella pulled down her dress to make sure her private parts were covered. She turned around and looked daggers at Joao.

She shook her finger at him. "You were not supposed to fuck me, Joao!"

"I'm sorry," he said and pulled up his shorts.

"Sorry? Really?" Ella raised her voice.

He smiled with a guilty face. "I know, Ella. I know. But you're so sexy, and it felt so good. I just couldn't stop myself. Yours is the tightest married pussy I've ever fucked!"

The words "married pussy" startled Ella. Suddenly, anger was replaced by sadness. Staring at Joao, she bit her lower lip, and her eyes filled up with moisture.

"You. . . ," she whimpered, and her voice cracked. "You. . ." She shook her head, fighting back tears. "You said we'd just try it. Just a few thrusts, Joao!" A tear rolled down her cheek. "Joao! You fucked me! You fucking fucked me!"

I took her hand and squeezed it. "It's OK, hon, it's OK."

Ella shook her head without looking at me, staring at Joao.

The audience rose to their feet in a standing ovation, and the performers bowed down. The show had just finished.

"Sorry, Ella!" Joao smiled softly at her. He reached his hand to her cheek and caught another tear. "But Ella, it felt good, didn't it?"

"You emptied yourself inside me, Joao! I'm not on the pill!" Ella sobbed. "I told you! I'm not on the pill! Do you understand what that means?"

"Ella, I'll buy you the morning-after pill," he said and reached his thumb to brush another tear away from her face, but she slapped his hand away.

"You fucked me!" Ella continued to sob, and tears flowed down her cheeks. "How could you?!"

Joao sighed. "Sorry, Ella. Please, stop crying! You're breaking my heart now. I promise you! First thing tomorrow morning, I'll drive to Santa Maria and buy you a pill!"

Ella was shaking her head, sobbing and repeating, "You fucked me! You fucked me! You fucked me!"

Joao wrapped his arms around her waist. "Ella!" He pulled her closer to him and looked her in the eyes. "Ella, I got carried away. I know. And I apologise for that! But tell me! Honestly! Didn't you like it?"

"I liked it, Joao! OK? I liked it!" Ella cried. "And that's the problem! I liked you fucking me like a ragdoll!" She looked at me and cried again, "Nick, I liked it! Very much."

I rubbed her shoulder comfortingly. "I know, honey, I know. "

She wailed, "I cummed! I cummed on his cock! Twice! He actually fucked me, Nick! He tricked me!" She now looked at Joao and pushed him in the chest. "Let go!"

Joao let go of her and stepped back.

Ella opened her arms to me, and we hugged.

"I liked it, Nick!" she sobbed in my arms.

I rubbed her shoulder. "It's OK, hon. It's OK."

The performers came back on stage to bow since the audience kept clapping. A guy in a suit—perhaps the hotel entertainment director—was on stage too and was shouting praises on a microphone as if we had just watched a performance of the Milan Scala.

"He fucked me, Nick!" Ella continued to sob. "He thoroughly fucked me, and I liked it!"

"I know. I saw you." I kissed her cheek. "But I liked it too, hon!"

Ella looked up at me.

I smiled as softly as I could. "Yes, honey, I did!"

"You did! But. . . ." She paused. Her lower lip began trembling, and her face contorted into tears again. She buried her face in my chest and sobbed again. "But I was the one who did it! I was the one who was supposed not to like it! I am a whore, Nick! I'm such a whore!"

"Shh!" I rubbed her shoulder again, trying to comfort her.

"Nick! I had his cock in my pussy!" she cried out. "Fucking me!"

"It's OK, Ella. It's OK," I continued to whisper, although no one could hear me. The noise the crowd was making was deafening.

I nudged Ella to step back from the cupboard.

Still hugging each other, we stepped down from the box.

Keeping one arm curved around her waist, I slightly pulled away from her and clasped her chin with my free hand. I tilted her head up, forcing her to look at me.

Tears were rolling down her cheeks, and she was sobbing uncontrollably.

I brushed her tears away. "Ella, we wanted the butterflies to fly out, remember? We made them fly, hon! We did it! I feel OK. I feel great! Hon! Cheer up!"

Joao stepped behind Ella, and I felt his hands slip between Ella's stomach and mine. He hugged her from behind. Ella was sandwiched between the two of us.

She was so sexy! So vulnerable and so sexy at the same time. I pressed my erect cock against her stomach. Maybe some of my dick was pressing against Joao's knuckles. I didn't care. I lowered my face to hers and tilted my head to the side. Ella tilted her head to the other side, and we kissed. A deep, passionate, long French kiss.

When we broke the kiss, Ella looked me in the eyes.

She whispered, "We let him eat the dessert, Nick! He's fucked my pussy!"

Her eyes began filling with tears again.

I started to run out of ideas of what to say or do to console her when Joao intervened. He kissed the side of her neck. Ella trembled. Joao's strong hands pressed against her stomach, pulling her closer to him. He kissed her neck again. Ella wasn't moving, staring at me. Joao pulled his head back and kissed her behind the ear. A tear rolled down her cheek and dropped onto her chest. Joao gently brushed his nose and lips against the side of her neck and took a deep breath in, taking in the scent of her skin. Another tear raced down Ella's face but stopped on her cheek. Her black lover planted his lips on the delicate skin of the base of her neck. Her eyes stopped filling up with tears. Ella wasn't crying anymore. Joao's mouth found her clavicle and kissed it. Ella's breathing picked up pace. Joao leaned his face further and kissed her neck below her chin, then again, near her larynx. Ella swallowed. She was not taking her eyes off me, unable to move, unable to speak, unable to cry. She was like in a trance.

"I love you, Ella!" I said. "I stand by what we did. We did it together! Remember that! And I love you!"

Joao was standing behind her, but he was tall, and his lips could easily reach her chest by just hovering above her. His kisses now focused on the exposed skin of her chest, tracing the strap of her dress.

"I love you!" I said again.

"I love you too," Ella whispered.

Joao's mouth reached her cleavage.

Her pupils began dilating, and her breathing became deeper. Joao kissed her further down, into her cleavage. I felt Ella's body trembling. I saw goosebumps rising on the skin of her neck.

Joao used his nose to push the front panel of her dress aside, and he kissed her breast, not the nipple, but his lips touched her areola.

Ella gasped and tilted her head back, pushing her chest up. I felt her hands tighten their grip on my hips.

Joao moved to kiss her neck under her chin, and at the same time, he slid one hand up from her stomach to her chest. He found her cleavage and slipped his hand inside her dress. Ella let a soft sigh out as Joao cupped her breast.

I felt her body being pulled away from me and realised he was pulling on her. He wanted her to turn around.

Ella let go of my waist; I let go of her too. Joao pulled his hand out of her dress, turned her around and wrapped both arms around her waist. They looked each other in the eyes and slowly, very slowly moved their heads closer and closer until their lips touched. Joao's tongue parted Ella's lips, and they kissed. A deep long French kiss.

They pulled away from each other.

It had gone quiet in the hall as the public began leaving. The show was over.

A soft smile spread across Joao's face, and he said, not taking his eyes off Ella's, "Where's your room?"

He let go of her waist, and his hand found hers. They interlocked fingers. Joao took a step towards the entrance of the nook, pulling on Ella's hand. He took a second step. She appeared to follow him, but when he took a third step, she stopped, hesitating.

Joao turned and smiled at her. "What is it?"

"I'm not sure," Ella murmured.

He smiled again. "Ella, we've already fucked. It's done. We might as well fuck more."

She still hesitated.

"It will feel great," Joao said and rubbed her knuckles with the pad of his thumb. "Sex will feel great. Now that you've opened up down there, all will go in smoothly. Come on, Ella! Let's do it again while you're still loose and slick. It will be the most amazing sex you've ever had. I promise."

Ella was looking at his face and not saying anything.

Joao sighed. "It will be comfier in your room. Nick will join us. Right, Nick?" He looked at me.

Ella looked at me.

I smiled a bitter-sweet smile. "He's right, honey!"

She reached her free hand to me, and I grabbed it.

I headed towards the exit, having decided to take the lead, but took three steps and had to stop because Ella was not moving.

I turned and looked at her. "What is it, hon? Don't you want Joao to come with us?"

"It's not that," she said quietly.

"What is it?" I asked.

"Someone might notice." Ella nodded down at her crotch. "I am leaking."

"Oh!" slipped through my mouth. "Is it that bad?"

She did not answer my question but pulled her hands out of Joao's and my grip. She looked around to make sure no one was watching—although we were still well hidden behind the old furniture—grabbed the bottom of her dress and pulled it up. She parted her legs. Streaks of cum were trickling down her inner thighs.

Joao took a napkin out of his pocket. "Here, Ella. Use it! It's clean."

Ella took the napkin and, slowly, without looking down, cleaned his spunk from between her legs.

She folded the napkin with the soiled side inside and passed it back to him.

Joao tucked it into his pocket. "Is it still a maybe, Ella?"

Ella looked at him. "How could it be a maybe, Joao, if you already fucked me?"

He smiled. "So it's a yes."

Ella smiled for the first time after he had fucked her. "Yes. It is a yes."

"So I don't have to sleep in my truck?" Joao asked with a stupid face.

I wasn't sure why he was asking these questions. Perhaps he was enjoying his triumph, and it was his way of bragging about it. Or maybe he still couldn't believe his luck that he was going to spend a night in the hotel he had so much dreamt about. Whatever the reason, he was standing and waiting for my wife's answer. And she gave it to him.

"No, you won't sleep in your truck," she said simply and grabbed his hand. "Let's go! You'll fuck me in our room." She reached her other hand to me, and I took it.

We left the nook, exited the auditorium and headed to our room. I was leading, holding Ella's hand while Joao held her other hand. My cock couldn't stop twitching in excitement. There was a weird feeling of euphoria to be holding the hand of the woman who was my wife but whose pussy had been just fucked by another man. I was highly turned on by the feeling of pain and pleasure mixed together. I found it extremely arousing that Joao's sperm was still in her vagina, that her pussy walls were still stretched around the shape of his cock. And I wanted to see her pussy stretched out even more. I wanted to walk fast. I was eager to watch Joao fuck Ella on our bed. I was keen, but Ella was dragging her feet.

I slowed down and looked at her.

She was taking smaller steps than usual.

"Am I walking too fast?" I asked.

She shook her head. "No, Nick."

I let go of her hand and observed her walk for a few steps. She was walking strangely—as if she was squeezing her thighs together.

"What is it, hon?" I asked her. "Leaking again?"

She smiled a shy smile. "A bit."

Joao took the napkin out of his pocket.

"No, thanks!" Ella made a sign to Joao with her hand that she didn't need a napkin. "It's not that."

"What is it then?" I asked her, starting to worry.

"Umm. . . ." Ella hesitated to answer my question. She looked around to make sure no one was around to hear her, then said, "I feel open. Down there. Very open."

"Oh!" slipped through my mouth, and I frowned. *They say vaginas elongate during sex, but could Joao's massive cock have torn her pussy? She was standing. Not the best sex position for being penetrated by a thick penis for the first time.*

"How? Like how open?" I murmured.

"Like, wide open," Ella said. "Feeling the air flowing into my insides."

Now she looked at Joao.

He grinned at her.

She smiled, let go of his hand and punched him in the shoulder. "It's you! You did it!" She took a deep breath, and her smile gave way to a frown. "You stretched me open like a melon, Joao!"

Joao shrugged his shoulders and giggled. "Hi-hi! Open! That's how it feels after 'him'." He nodded to his crotch. "That's what 'he' does: stretches open! Like. . . ." He paused and took a longer look at her face. Then he raised his eyebrows with concern. "But, seriously, it feels good open, right? Not bad open, or painful or anything?"

"Yeah, it's not bad. But it's strange," Ella said.

She looked around to check again that no one was looking at us, then reached between her legs, lifted her dress, and slid her hand between her thighs. She rubbed her pussy for a few seconds, then pulled her hand out.

"Pass me the tissue!" she said to Joao.

He gave her the tissue. Ella cleaned the cum from her hand and returned the tissue.

"Yep!" she said. "I'm loose down there. That's why I'm leaking cum so much."

I shook my finger at Joao. "I hope you haven't damaged my wife, Joao!"

Ella looked at Joao with concern in her eyes. "Could've you, Joao?"

"No! It's a temporary feeling. What you feel is normal, Ella," he assured her. "It will pass. In fact, it will help if I fuck you a few more times. It's muscle memory, and your pussy will learn to widen and bounce back to normal. The more it contracts around my thicker penis, the more it learns. Your vagina muscles will get used much quicker to stretching and tightening if I fucked you more. It's like Kegel exercises." He offered his hand to Ella. "Let me help you get back to normal!"

"Ha!" Ella scoffed. "By fucking me?"

Joao nodded yes.

Ella cocked her head to the side. "Really? You'll help me tighten up down there by fucking me more?"

He grabbed her hand. "You'll see! Where's your room?"

Ella giggled quietly. "Hi-hi! You'd better be right! Otherwise, I'm filing that complaint and will sue you!"

Joao laughed. "Ha-ha! Trust me, Ella! I'm like a vagina doctor. I'm sure you'll be writing commendations!" He pulled on her hand to follow him.

Smiling and shaking her head, she followed him. "You're lucky I am so horny," she murmured. "Otherwise, I would not have tolerated such language!"

I smiled to myself as we walked: *Well, it seems the crisis is over. Smiles and jokes! Everyone's mood is up again!*

We didn't talk; we didn't look at each other. There was nothing to talk about and nothing to look at. We were going to our room to fuck my wife all night long!

ABOUT THE AUTHOR

Alex Lee

Whether reading erotic fiction is a way to fulfil an erotic fantasy in the safe realm of imagination or to get inspired to pursue a fetish in real life, I believe that, foremost, it should be about having fun.

I like to take my readers on a journey that is exciting and arousing, where they can follow the emotions, internal struggles and the fun that my characters experience, from the build-up of desire and aspiration, through the moment of fulfilment and resolution, to the final reckoning in the aftermath of their actions.

Whether a story is about a hotwife fantasy, a voyeur fetish, a cuckold kink, a naughty wife, or a cheating husband, it should be believable and, most importantly, enjoyable to read. The storylines in this genre are as diverse and nuanced as in any other, and sometimes a reader may not like what the characters do or the views they express; however, the storytelling should still be a source of enjoyment.

I value the reader's feedback. When readers tell me that they like my stories, it inspires me to write more. Please vote and leave reviews on Amazon or Goodreads.

I believe that listening to my readers is the best way to keep improving. If you would like to provide me with constructive feedback or share other stories you would like me to write, please contact me at lee.alex1604 @ gmail.com.

You can also find me online on Twitter @AlexLee1604 and on GoodReads at goodreads.com/AlexLee.

BOOKS IN THIS SERIES

Wife Tries Something New

Wife Tries Something New series consists of two books:

Book 1. Wife Tries Something New: A Hotwife Adventure

Book 2. Wife Goes For More: A Hotwife Adventure

Wife Tries Something New: A Hotwife Adventure

This story is about a couple on holiday tempted into the hotwife lifestyle.

Nick and Ella arrive in Cape Verde to celebrate their 10th honeymoon anniversary. Gerhard, an old German guy, befriends them at the swimming pool and shares his ideas about how they can best do that. His ideas are incompatible with Ella and Nick's views, but unexpectedly, just thinking about what the old man has told them makes them hornier than ever, raising questions about their secret desires. Meeting young Agnete only adds to their questions. However, when they are introduced to Mikkel and Johan, two attractive Danish men, Gerhard's ideas not only raise questions but begin taking root.
Things between Ella and the two Danes heat up, and temptation grows stronger when she meets Paulo, a handsome black barman, and discovers more about her hidden desires.
Ella and Nick are going down a slippery slope to a place they are not sure they want to go. They must escape temptation! But will swapping the pool for the beach help them? Will an island

tour with Joao, another charming black man, help them resist temptation, or will it make it harder?

Wife Goes For More: A Hotwife Adventure

This book is the sequel to Wife Tries Something New. In this second part of the story, Ella goes on a quest to find out if bigger is better and if many is more fun.

Ella and Nick come to a pact with Joao, an agreement that will help them enjoy their adventure. But things get complicated when an old rivalry between Joao and the Danes gets reignited. How will Ella and Nick manage it? And how far are they prepared to go in their quest for new experiences? Will Ella take up Joao, Mikkel and Johan's proposition to try something she'd never heard about but which sounds super-hot?
When Nick's cuckold experience is taken to a new level, his confidence falters. How will he manage his feelings? While dealing with his emotions, he sees something that takes him by surprise. Will Agnete shed light on it and beyond?
Ella and Nick discover that Gerhard's peculiar condition may not be a bad thing since he knows how to repay favours, especially when Paulo is at his disposal. Ella finally finds an answer to the question of whether bigger is better.

BOOKS BY THIS AUTHOR

A Night With Tigers: A Hotwife Story

This short story is about becoming a hotwife in a rather unusual place.

David and Dana may have divergent views on open relationships, but their views converge when it comes to wildlife and nature. So when Paul invites them to spend a night with him in a lodge surrounded by tigers, they agree.
Initially, it is an awkward proposition because they have met Paul on a hotwife dating site, but he assures them that he is interested in nothing else but watching tigers, and that seems all right. Intentions are clear, and boundaries are set.
However, exotic animals, a cosy cabin, fine wine, and the company of a handsome man like Paul can change perspective. And when Paul harnesses his extensive lifestyle experience to get what he wants, will boundaries be held?

Wife Takes One For The Team: A Hotwife Story

This is a short story about a wife's unusual first-time hotwife experience.

Adam accepts a two-day contract job on a remote island. Jess joins her husband on his business trip, hoping to have a short break in the sun. Little does she know that she will be asked to play a central role in an experiment on which so much depends. Should Jess take one for the team or not? And if she does, how will she and her hubby manage through their feelings? Will things get complicated by the clandestine actions of some of the people involved? Will Jess and Adam end up winning or losing?

Wife Takes Another One For The Team: A Hotwife Story

This book is the sequel to Wife Takes One For The Team.

Adam and Jess have returned home from the island. They have been dealing with some consequences of Jess's unusual first-time hotwife experience when an unexpected turn of events brings back temptation, stronger than ever. And the stakes are higher.
Will Adam and Jess resist temptation? And do they want to resist it? Will Jess take another one for the team? And if she does, will it be for the team or herself?

Three In An Rv: A Hotwife Story

A couple's RV trip turns into a first-time hotwife experience in some very unusual circumstances.

Mila and Peter are stuck in their RV during a thunderstorm when a stranger knocks on the door. Letting Jack in starts a 48-hour adventure that will not only change their holiday plans but will redefine their marriage.

Mila is unprepared for an encounter with a man like Jack, whose masculine appeal and charisma tempt her to cross lines she never dreamt of crossing. Jack is caught totally off guard when confronted by Mila, a wife so pretty, sexy and captivating that her spell makes him take risks he never thought he could. And Peter is surprised by how much witnessing the game of cat and mouse between Mila and Jack reignites his dormant hotwife fantasy.

Will Mila resist the urges and feelings the enigmatic stranger stirs in her? Will Jack be able to get what he wants from Mila without jeopardising his plans? Will Peter's hotwife fantasy make him surrender his wife to Jack without a fight? What about the consequences of their actions?

An Affair In The Desert

When Dan and Abby go dune riding, little do they know that it is only the beginning of their adventure. Dan has always been proud of his virtuous wife, but will that change when they meet Khalid, a local young man who is not only handsome and charming but also enigmatic and provocative? How far will a sisters' rivalry drive Abby to push her boundaries? Will a camel ride, followed by a romantic night under the stars, be enough to spark something between Abby and Khalid that will change Dan and Abby's relationship forever?
When Khalid and his equally exotic and enigmatic friend, Omar, invite Dan and Abby to celebrate their business deal, Dan senses that there is a lot more to it than meets the eye, but what is it?
Abby and Dan blame the hot desert sun and the emotions of escaping death twice for clouding their judgment, but is it not their secret fantasies that ultimately drive their actions?

A Webcam Hotwife

Jen is not happy when her husband, Andy, invites his senior business partner to stay in their house in London for a few days. Both Jen and Andy know that Larry is eccentric, even weird, but nothing can prepare them for the bombshell that Larry drops on them when he arrives.
Larry's unusual request throws Jen and Andy into a whirlpool of emotions. They are faced with a tough dilemma to choose between financial prosperity and keeping their marital vows.

And when temptation and lingering fetish come into play, husband and wife find themselves in uncharted territory.

Will Andy and Jen be able to outmanoeuvre the masterful manipulator that Larry proves to be and navigate their way through lust, temptation, jealousy, and greed? Will they be able to fix their finances without sacrificing their marriage?

A Hotwife In Lockdown

Working from home for months during the health crisis is boring and depressing for Elle. Her sons are stuck in university lockdowns, and her husband, Josh, is exhausted from long hours in the hospital. The stress has taken its toll on the couple's sex life despite their unfaltering love for each other.

When Adnan, a friend of their elder son, turns up at their doorstep, he becomes a welcome distraction, livening up the dull days with his witty jokes and thoughtful compliments. Their guest is unusual in many ways, though, not least because he is from a different culture, and he has a delicate issue that Josh and Elle want to help him resolve. But how far their help can go before a line is crossed?

Intelligent, handsome, exotic in a way, and certainly provocative, will Adnan be too much for Elle to handle? Will he be a temptation that she won't be able to resist? Will Josh be able to protect his wife from the younger man, and does the hubby want to?

Cheating On My Hotwife In The South Of France

When my wife's colleague invited us to visit her villa, the words "South of France" evoked in my mind nothing more than images of sunny beaches, swimming pools, wine, and Mediterranean cuisine.

That was until we met Pierre and his sister Julie. Their lifestyle took us by surprise, even shocked us, especially my prudent wife. And yet, instead of indignation, it engendered something very different in Emily and me. Curiosity and sexual attraction fused into a powerful force that took us on a journey of exploration of our most intimate fantasies and hidden emotions. But how far was this force going to take us?

Would my wife's little crush on Pierre make her break certain taboos?

The inner struggle between jealousy and excitement of watching the wife you love in the arms of another man is a powerful drug. Would I be able to quit the addiction, if my faithful wife succumbed to the charms of the young man?

Would I understand the enigma that Julie was? And what if there was something more sinister behind her provocative behaviour? I had less than 72 hours to find the answers.

I Cheated While Hugging My Husband

When Antony and I decided to celebrate the milestone of our 10th wedding anniversary with a tour in Peru, little did we know that it could turn into a hugely different landmark in our relationship.

Following our first meeting with Paul and his wife Jessica, my husband and I thought of them as another friendly couple to have chit-chats with. It turned out that they were to play a much more significant role than that. Paul's physical attractiveness, combined with his bravado, and sometimes unorthodox behaviour, made for an intriguing persona that provoked my curiosity like never before. The inner struggle between desire and prudence stirred hidden emotions and interests, which I did not know existed inside me neither I knew how far they could take me.

As a faithful wife to a loving husband, I believed that I could resist the excitement of newness, but could I? Would I be able to draw the line before things got out of control?

The Christmas Party: A Hotwife Story

Jane and Chris love each other and have great sex; however, when business opportunity meets sexual desire, will they go beyond the point of no return?

When they get invited to the Christmas party, little do they know that Jane will be taking up the role of Semyan's sexy Santa Claus assistant. She will be helping to give away gifts, and by the end of the party, she will have to decide whether she can give the most precious gift that she has that evening.

Semyan may be an unorthodox CEO, but he knows how to take Jane's breath away, literally. Taking a prudent couple like Jane and Chris on a journey that they have never been before, requires skills and means which Semyan certainly possess.

Made in the USA
Coppell, TX
20 September 2023